P9-BIE-130

Dracula held the woman over his head, at the end of his arms. Dracula—cape flaring from his flexed shoulders, his head thrown back, eyes like eggs of onyx—lowered the woman to his opening mouth. I glimpsed fangs unsheathing from their hiding places in his jaws, four-inch fangs extending to penetrate her small, shivering breasts. Almost cradling her over the altar, he dragged his head in a quick sweep from her breasts to her throat, cutting deeply; the red gush of her blood was explosive. Explosive too, were the howls of appreciation from the mob beneath the altar.

Dracula tilted the limp woman, her legs and arms flailing in the air, and drank from her. I guessed that he was drinking her life-force as well as her blood.

Dracula glowed with St. Anthony's fire, and swelled with stolen blood.

"My father!" wailed a voice, that of a child. It must have been *my* voice. I fell to my knees before him.

THRILLERS BY WILLIAM W. JOHNSTONE

THE DEVIL'S CAT   (2091, $3.95)

The town was alive with all kinds of cats. Black, white, fat, scrawny. They lived in the streets, in backyards, in the swamps of Becancour. Sam, Nydia, and Little Sam had never seen so many cats. The cats' eyes were glowing slits as they watched the newcomers. The town was ripe with evil. It seemed to waft in from the swamps with the hot, fetid breeze and breed in the minds of Becancour's citizens. Soon Sam, Nydia, and Little Sam would battle the forces of darkness. Standing alone against the ultimate predator — The Devil's Cat.

THE DEVIL'S HEART   (2110, $3.95)

Now it was summer again in Whitfield. The town was peaceful, quiet, and unprepared for the atrocities to come. Eternal life, everlasting youth, an orgy that would span time — that was what the Lord of Darkness was promising the coven members in return for their pledge of love. The few who had fought against his hideous powers before, believed it could never happen again. Then the hot wind began to blow — as black as evil as The Devil's Heart.

THE DEVIL'S TOUCH   (2111, $3.95)

Once the carnage begins, there's no time for anything but terror. Hollow-eyed, hungry corpses rise from unearthly tombs to gorge themselves on living flesh and spawn a new generation of restless Undead. The demons of Hell cavort with Satan's unholy disciples in blood-soaked rituals and fevered orgies. The Balons have faced the red, glowing eyes of the Master before, and they know what must be done. But there can be no salvation for those marked by The Devil's Touch.

Available wherever paperbacks are sold, or order direct from the Publisher. Send cover price plus 50¢ per copy for mailing and handling to Zebra Books, Dept. 3001, 475 Park Avenue South, New York, N.Y. 10016. Residents of New York, New Jersey and Pennsylvania must include sales tax. DO NOT SEND CASH.

DRACULA IN LOVE

BY JOHN SHIRLEY

ZEBRA BOOKS

KENSINGTON PUBLISHING CORP

ZEBRA BOOKS

are published by

Kensington Publishing Corp.
475 Park Avenue South
New York, NY 10016

Copyright © 1979 by Kensington Publishing Corp.

All rights reserved. No part of this book may be reproduced in any form or by any means without the prior written consent of the Publisher, excepting brief quotes used in reviews.

Second printing: May, 1990

Printed in the United States of America

ONE
.1.

There are times when ordinary objects seem to take on ominous significance. Suspense-film directors linger lovingly on a telephone book, a candleholder, a knife—just to make you wonder about it. Hold the camera on a kitchen sink long enough, play the note-stretching suspenseful music, the high-pitched violins, and show nothing but that single kitchen tap with its innocuous drip—and somehow the sink takes on ominous dimensions. The implication of this baleful attention transforms an ordinary kitchen tap into an object of terror.

It happens to me, without the influence of cinematic technique. When I'm afraid, I see intimations of threat in the most harmless artifacts. The coffeepot seems to be conspiring with the sugar bowl and the lightbulb's glare seems harsh: a warning glare. I don't experience that sort of sensation often—my analyst saw to that. Usually, it's not there. But sometimes. Sometimes, as with the moment I saw the letter.

Three months ago. December first. The letter on my desk.

A lot can happen in three months.

My life had been busy but banal for eight years, a plateau, eventless except for the stormy separation from my wife, Lollie. Even my weekly aggression sessions with my therapist had become a dull routine. I had no mistress.

And then the letter and snap-snap-snap—one thing after another.

Outwardly there was nothing really extraordinary about the letter's envelope. I had been an antiquarian, I knew the characteristic ink-script of a quill pen. Yes, it was fairly unusual to receive a letter addressed with a quill pen. Unusual but not extraordinary. There are a few people who still use them for amusement or a touch of class. And surely the old-fashioned spidery handwriting, crabbed and florid, was an indication that the letter was written by an aged person, *very* old, to be sure. Nothing really extraordinary in that. Though I couldn't imagine why such a person would write to the general manager of the IBEX Corporation West. A complaint? There was no return address.

It was addressed to me: *Vladimir Horescu, General Manager, IBEX Corporation West, 2311 California Street, City of San Francisco, State of California.*

Quaint way to put it, I thought: "City of" San Francisco, "State of" California. And no zip code.

The envelope was linen paper. A stuff hard to find nowadays.

Who?

Perhaps one of my associates from the old days, before I'd reformed. The old days, before my doctor had forbidden involvement with antiquarians and occultists. Someone from the Society for the Study of Ancient Arts, perhaps. If so, I would not reply. I had disassociated myself from that hoary lot.

But surely it must be from the SSAA. Nothing extraordinary.

So . . . why did I hesitate to open it?

Why did I hold the letter in both hands, at arm's length, discoloring the envelope with the sudden perspiration of my fingers? Why did I stare at the red wax signet on the back of the envelope? The red wax seal stamped with the signet *V*.

The envelope was, at that moment, the embodiment of all mischief and unpleasantry. That's how I phrased it mentally: *mischief and unpleasantry*. What I felt more accurately, gazing at the letter, was a premonition of *vengeance and violence*. To be specific. But I couldn't admit that to myself. My doctor, a dedicated behaviorist, had trained me to screen out such terms. All negative extremes were scoured from my mind, by reflex.

But still I stared at the envelope, and could not open it.

It was postmarked New Orleans. I knew no one in New Orleans.

I opened the envelope gingerly, with my fingers. Normally I use a letter opener, but I had an inexplicable fear that the harmless white paper rectangle would cry out if I touched it with metal. Perhaps it would ble—

Click. My mental screen caught the word and suppressed it. That word represented something I wasn't allowed to think about then.

But I can say it now: *Bleed*. Bleeding. Blood.

I opened the envelope, fumbled the linen-paper sheet free, spread it onto the desk, smoothed it out, swallowed hard, and read:

My Son! Know me: I am your Father.

I have found you! I am humiliated to resort to this impersonal means of making contact. I attempted to reach you through the "telephone" and was told by some imbecile that you were not accepting calls except by special arrangement. I informed the woman that I am your father, and she replied something to the effect that my "humor" was "not appreciated" and that she understood that "Mr. Horescu's father is

7

dead." This impudence infuriated me but before I could bestow upon the offender (a female!) the revelation of her insolent conduct, she severed the connection. I trust that you will have her destroyed.

I decided, then, against obtaining your home "telephone" number; it is best there be some sort of prelude to our actually conversing. So that you are less likely to doubt my identity.

I am writing this in New Orleans, will arrive in your area in two weeks. I have already sent my servants to prepare the house. One of these servants I sent to your home with a written message—

The prowler the police chased off? They'd said it was a "slow-moving, very pale, sickly fellow" who disappeared into the woods back of my house. They'd fired a shot—

—who was dispatched before he could make his mission known, apparently. Another of my servants found him in the forest, a bullet had broken his spine so that he was unable to walk. My associates decided against trying to contact you in that manner; I must congratulate you on the alacrity of your subordinates. Though it has not been easy to gain an interview with you, perhaps it is I who should be contrite, overall, since 'twas I who departed you, more than thirty years ago—

I was no longer breathing; I realized this and forced a breath. I determined, then, to press suit against whoever had written the letter. I would humiliate them publicly. I had never known my father, but I was fierce in his defense in my own mind. I did not believe the story my foster parents had told me, their claim that he was a casual acquaintance of my mother who one night raped her, raped her so brutally she went mad. She had gone insane, yes, but I didn't

8

believe that one incident could be responsible for it. I wanted to believe in my father. I believed him dead, and someone was using his memory for an elaborate joke. Scowling, I read on.

—and left but little provision for your upbringing. I regret this, in retrospect; there are matters in which you would have been useful, and there are Truths I would like to have imparted to you. Perhaps, for some learnings, it is not too late.

I am looking forward to a long stay in the San Francisco City area. The nights there are warm and languorous, filled with life. I spent almost a year just north of your city, remaining there till four months ago, when prudence forced me to sequester myself in the City of New Orleans.

I plan to occupy the Chutney house, which I purchased for them in 1953 as partial recompense for unavoidable but accidental damage done their niece, your mother. In addition, I provided a trust fund, anticipating expenditures for your care. I still retain an option on the house, should residents pass away, as they did the year last, and in keeping with this right I have made alterations in the house, and have had the utilities awakened; I am aware, nevertheless, that you are the house's chief owner. . . . I await your attendance, the evening of the twenty-second of December, this year 1977, promptly at eleven.

As calmly as I could, I pushed away from the desk, walked to the bar at the left of my office, and poured a glass of mineral water. I tried not to think as I downed a Valium. I stood trembling for several minutes. *Burn the letter,* said my analyst's disembodied voice. Good advice. But I was curious— someone had done a lot of research.

Curiosity won.

I returned to the desk, sighed, and sank into the swivel chair. I glanced at the letter, away, then back at the letter. I felt a quiver of excitement. It was no joke. It was him.

My father.

He had provided the house, the mysterious deed to the land, the equally mysterious trust fund. Chutney had refused to tell me where they came from. Only my father would know.

I glanced half-guiltily at the broad picture window to the right, then at the door opposite me, behind which (I imagined) my nosy secretary crouched, spying.

I got up and locked the door and (irrationally— since I was twenty stories up) drew the curtains over the window. I padded across the deep white carpet to my glass-topped desk. I read:

I have no doubt that our meeting will profit both of us, and I am anxious to inspect you at close range, my agents having provided little insight despite their efforts.

I shuddered. What "efforts"? What did they know? Did his "agents" know about Lollie's morphine habit?

You live a private life and you hold a position of some influence, despite your privacy. You are carefully insulated, yet you are capable of striking out, as in the instance of a certain B., the lady of the Blue Gem Club—

I had to get a second Valium then. No one knew about that woman. No one. Even the thug I'd paid to frighten B. out of blackmailing my boss was silenced. B.'s boyfriend, finding the thug beating her, shot him. B. died from a concussion received during the beat-

10

ing. Her boyfriend was killed by the thug's associates, who'd been waiting outside.

No one knew. But *he* knew.

I hadn't intended for her to die—I only wanted the man to push her around a bit, frighten her. But I covered up her death meticulously. Yet—he knew.

—and in these attributes you demonstrate your linkage to the High Lineage of our Family. You are truly Grandson of the Dragon.

Do not inform your drug-besotted wife of this appointment. Inform no one.

It occurs to me that you may be proud, unwilling to make my acquaintance. If this be the case, perhaps you will recall that my knowledge of the facts regarding B. would prove discomfitting to you if made available to these uniformed vermin who strut under the banner: "Authorities."

I will expect you punctually.

Blessings,

Vladislav Draco II, Son of the Dragon

My father?

Mr. Chutney had divulged only two bits of information regarding my father (he claimed he had met the man but once, the night before the attack on my mother): One, he was European. Two, he was of noble lineage, or so he maintained.

The letter's prose was competent, but showed strain, as if the writer was slightly uncomfortable with the English language. And he had signed himself with a name I recognized, a name which, qualified by the roman numeral II for "the second" and the flourish "Son of the Dragon," was associated with a certain Middle European king of the sixteenth century. A king best known as Vlad the Impaler. Known by some as Dracula, root of the legends on

11

which Bram Stoker based a trend-setting novel.

As one of the Society for the Study of Ancient Arts I'd done research, very exacting research, into the history of Vlad the Impaler. It had been my central obsession for three years. I'd examined hundreds of ancient documents, I knew his signature well. And—that was his signature on the letter. And it was his wax-seal, I realized, examining the envelope.

It could be a forgery. But Carlton had insisted that Dracula was alive, and he'd pronounced evidence supporting his assertion. Insufficient evidence, to be sure. But enough to make one suspect. . . .

My father?

I would have been more suspicious if the writer had been affectionate, more traditionally paternal. I knew little of my father, but somehow, by some irrefutable instinct, I was certain that conventional affection was not his way. And this correspondent was just short of callous. A man claiming to be my father, whom I had believed dead, who had abandoned me thirty-three years before—and he is only superficially apologetic! Indeed, he threatens me, implies he will deliver my dirty laundry to the "Authorities" if I do not comply with his demands.

Yes. My father.

December 22? Three weeks away.

I went to the round wall safe and spun the combination, spoke my name into the voice-analyzer, and stood back while the safe door unscrewed. I replaced the letter in its envelope and stowed this in a metal box at the rear of the safe, behind the diamonds and below the stock certificates. I closed the safe, and went to the door, unlocked it, flung it wide, hoping to catch Miss Horowitz listening at the door. (To what? The rustling of pages?) Sitting smug and petite behind her U-shaped blue desk, she glanced incuriously over her shoulder, smiled woodenly. "Sir?"

"Uhh—"

"Coffee?"

"No, no. You—you remember that folder that came from Doctor Frawley? I never opened it, told you to file it in my safe deposit box—"

"Yes, sir?"

"Bring it to me. Unopened. When you've done that, go home. For the next three days, I'll authorize a paid vacation, understand?"

"Ye-ess. Yes, sir!" Trying to conceal her delight, she went to the closet and, climbing hastily into her coat, headed for the elevator. I spotted something that made me twitch. "Miss Horowitz!"

Her spurious falls of blonde hair flounced as she turned her long, shiny nose toward me, this time trying to conceal her irritation. "*Yes,* sir?"

"The ashtray. Not only does it need emptying, a *butt* has fallen from it *onto the rug.*" She went hurriedly to clean up the mess, and I could see the muscles at the corners of her jaws tighten as she did so. "Have the rug vacuumed, tell the janitor on your way out. And I want the windows in here washed, tell him that too."

"They were washed just yesterday, Mr. Horescu—"

"*Miss* Horowitz—"

"I'll *tell* him, sir," she put in crisply, adding a shrug that said: *I should be used to this kook by now, I guess.*

She left. I looked away from the gray spot on the white rug where the ash smudged it (gray smudge like the stain of fungus-tainted fingers, fingers of bone) and returned to my office. And took a third Valium. The Valiums made me feel composed of cloud-stuff, "Valiums, Vladiums, Vladiums, Valium, higamus, pigamus—" I sang abstractedly. I was made of clouds, but the clouds were shot with lightning, and a thunderous name:

Vlad Vlad Vlad

King Vlad

Son of—

I paced (the dragon!), glancing uneasily at the curtained windows, frowning (Son of the Dragon!) at a thumb print on my glass desk. Yes, Miss Horowitz should be used to me by now. I knew what my staff thought of me. There was respect, I'd worked hard for my post. And there was contempt. I had heard one of them murmur it from a closing elevator when I'd stepped off: *That anal-retentive sonuvabitch! I brushed him and he checked his coat for a stain!*

Okay, okay, I thought, so I like things really *clean.* Ought to be more people like me, then I wouldn't have to live so far from the city. It would be clean enough for decent habitation—

But I knew I was dissembling.

Cleanliness was an obsession. It had driven three houseboys to resign. I had lost a chauffeur by criticizing his uniform excessively. It *was* excessive. But the shrink refused to treat me for it, insisting it was a healthy, if extreme outlet, and if not for that obsession, I might give way to—the *other* obsessions. I was policing myself with this furious cleanliness (as I thought this I examined my nails critically). It was the only way to be sure.

"Like all paranoid compulsions, fascination with the dead is not in need of a rationale, reason does not affect it. It must be dealt with severely or it will force capitulation. And you will find yourself purchasing corpses. Vlad. . . ."

So doctor had said.

I took my coat from the closet, carrying it gingerly

14

between two fingers to a better light where I could examine it. It was clean, no spiders or other vermin had crawled into it. I'd known it would be clean. But I had to check, all the same.

I slipped into the coat, and Miss Horowitz returned with the envelope. I scrutinized my white gloves, drew them on, accepted the envelope (after examining it for foulness), and dismissed her.

On my way out I nearly collided with Ross Pullman. He had a self-satisfied smirk on his wide, athletic face, the smirk he always wore after a successful interview with the Old Man.

"Hello, Ross," I said, as politely as I could manage. We hated each other. He wanted my job, and considered me tight-assed. Simple as that. His icy blue eyes laughed and he slapped me on the shoulder in mock comradeship; he did this deliberately, knowing I'd recoil from his touch.

"Hello, *Vlad*."

"Been talking to the Old Man?"

"Yeah, he—"

On an impulse: "You talk him into giving you my job yet?"

Taken off-guard, he sputtered, then forced laughter. "Hey, Vlad, you should know I don't—"

"Yeah. Well, up-and-coming-young-man, you may have your opportunity. I decided just a moment ago to take a three-month leave of absence. You will assuredly be appointed to take my place in my absence, and it will be your big chance to show him your competence exceeds my own."

His face was an amusing combination of distress and elation. The elevator hissed open, I stepped within. Pullman's face was, I fancied, compressed between the closing elevator doors, crushed— I could not continue to daydream then. Now, as I write this,

I can. I can picture Pullman's face crushed between the elevator doors as if they were clamping, squeezing him like a hunk of fruit, pulping him to a red ooze, a crushed corpse oozing blood instead of overconfidence. ... So I picture it now. But back then, mentally well-trained, I changed the subject.

I decided to drop by the library, on the way home. There was a certain book, *A History of Central European Dynasties,* which contained a photo of a painting: Vlad the Impaler.

.2.

I sat pensively in my Mercedes, outside my house. I gazed at its lighted, curtained windows, examining the sprawl of its three levels down the hillside. All seemed to be in order, the balustrades swept of leaves, the lights glowing from Jolson's basement quarters where he probably sat in rapt meditation. What was I looking for? I had parked across the street—normally I pull right into the driveway, trigger the garage door to open, and slide the car inside.

But still I sat in the dark, headlights out, engine clicking as it cooled, all the windows rolled up. It was absurd. There was nothing to fear ... perhaps I'd been rattled by my visit to old Doc Hoagin. He hadn't been glad to see me, he was hermitlike in his retirement. I'd shown him the photocopy I'd taken from the library book. *This man look familiar?* I'd asked. Hoagin had bragged that his memory was infallible, though he was eighty-one. He put on his spectacles, frowned, squinted at the picture in various lights. *Be damned,* he'd said. *If that don't look like that fellah that did your Mom that nasty trick, thirty years or more gone. They never did catch him—I saw him just once myself, I was visitin' Mrs. Chutney for her*

16

*asthma, th' night before it happened, and by God I
remember it still! Is that a hell of a memory, Horescu,
I ask you now—*

I'd made a hasty excuse and left when he asked me
if it was true that the man had fathered me.

Maybe that was why I was rattled. Partly. But the
house frightened me, subtly, in the same way the
envelope had, that afternoon. Unreasonable
ominousness.

I swallowed hard, shook myself, and started the
engine. I rolled the car into the driveway, pressed the
signal switch for the garage door; the metal gate
rolled up, I drove within.

With the garage door shut behind me I sat in the
car for several minutes, examining the shadowy
corners of the conrete garage. No place for anyone to
hide. I got out of the car, locked it and, clutching the
brown manila envelope, went into the house. I made
a deliberate effort to keep from glancing over my
shoulder as I went through the door.

I didn't feel much relieved on getting inside, even
when I had switched on the lights in the kitchen. The
tension was still there.

I started when Jolson appeared at the basement
door. Jolson was half-Korean, his father had been a
French colonel who'd departed for good after
inseminating Jolson's mother; so Jolson and I shared
a common bond. He took after his mother, looked
more Korean than otherwise, but his eyes were green,
and he was taller than most Orientals. He was somewhere between sixty and seventy, his shaved head
beginning to wrinkle. He'd worked for me five
months and had borne my overeager house inspections with unruffled patience. There was never a
flicker of resentment on his gaunt face when I asked
him to clean something that was already clean; this

wasn't obsequiousness, it was understanding. There were no hard feelings between us. He spoke rarely, usually only when replying; he had a way of replying with great depth as well as brevity. He was a scholar of Taoism, and I had come to treasure his advice.

But it nearly cracked his calm when I said, "Who has been here?"

He raised an eyebrow, for him, an expression of great emphasis. He nodded. "A man was here, he was inside without permission. Yet he did not break in."

"You mean nothing was broken, he had a key?"

"Apparently he had a key. Or some subtler means of entry. He left no scar on the house, no molested latches or locks. But when I said that he didn't break in, I meant that he was not an *intruder*. There was a sense that where he goes, there he belongs."

"Yes? I *knew* there was something strange about the house. Well, no man belongs in my home unless invited. So—you spoke with him? Who was he, what was he about?"

"You yourself must know, sir. You knew someone had been here, surely you were expecting—"

"No! I—had a *feeling* there was an intruder. I didn't know for sure. Is he quite gone?"

"Corporeally, yes. But I can feel his presence, also. I did not speak with him, but I looked into his eyes, and it seemed natural to bow. I bowed, and he bowed. When I straightened, he was gone." He had stated the impossible quite prosaically. "This encounter took place in the study. He was examining one of your books. He seemed amused by it—"

"But that study is locked and I have the only key!"

"It is now unlocked. The door was open, I looked within to investigate. There he stood, examining one of your books."

18

"Did he look anything like this?" I showed him the photocopy of Dracula's portrait.

"Not at all."

"Do you think—do you think the man in this picture resembles me?"

He raised an eyebrow, glanced again at the picture, shook his head. "No. This man is stocky, his eyebrows are thick, his face is squat. I have never seen so arrogant an expression! You are tall and slender, your hair is darker, your eyes lighter."

"And—well, what did the burglar look like?"

"I suspect that the term 'burglar' is malapropos. He was a lofty-browed man with a snowy beard, a canary-yellow doublebreasted suit with whalebone buttons, a yellow silk kerchief in his pocket, and no shoes."

"*What?* A fine suit and no shoes?"

Jolson made a faint shrug. "He wore no shoes. Shoes do not normally accompany cloven hooves."

"Hooves."

"So it looked, though . . . ah, no, I cannot pretend it was a deformity of human feet. They were hooves, sir. And golden eyes without whites: a slate of gold, as if the eyeball itself were fashioned of gold."

"Cloven hooves, golden eyes, white beard—"

"Yes. I have seen his like before. On a visit to Tibet, as a young man. One such, entirely unclothed, was conversing with a lama. At that time, I believed I was seeing a mental projection, but now—"

"Jolson, I respect your forays into meditation, but perhaps you went too far on your inward journey this time. The senses are irresolute. Perhaps you hallucinated him."

Jolson looked hurt. His eyes narrowed, ever so slightly. "Sorry, Jolson, I didn't mean it. I know you must have seen something extraordinary. Ah, the study—"

I went to the spiral stairs, down two flights, found the study. The door was opened. Jolson was just behind me. "Did you go inside, Jolson?"

"No. I stood in the doorway."

"I see." I looked nervously at the books on the wall. The key to my study was locked in my safety deposit box. I glanced down at the rug. In the thick pile rug was a trail of hoofprints.

I sighed, and sagged against the doorframe. I passed my hand over my eyes. Too many Valiums? I looked again. The hoofprints were there; I could not tell if they were cloven.

"Bring me dinner here, Jolson. I will remain in the study."

"Very good," he said crisply, taking my coat. "And when is the house inspection, sir?"

"Not tonight."

"No, sir? Tomorrow morning?"

"No, not until I say. Perhaps—" I looked around. I was noticing less disorder than I normally noticed. I spied a match jammed between the hall rug and the wall—it scarcely annoyed me. "Perhaps it is time to dispense with these ludicrous house inspections altogether."

"Very good." His tone betrayed, faintly, his surprise.

"Oh, Jolson. The—the person who was here? You said you saw his like in Tibet? What—what was *that* person? Did anyone explain to you?"

"I told a lama what I had seen. He explained that I'd seen an elemental. An intelligent, specialized spirit, representing an element of the spiritual hierarchy—one physical manifestation. The thing I saw in Tibet had no beard, no clothes, and it was hermaphroditic. Hooves, and golden eyes."

"Jolson, would you—" I hesitated, embarrassed. "Would you consider giving up this job and becoming my adviser, instead? I can get a maid to do housework."

"I am your adviser now, when you require my advice, sir. And the work is karma yoga." He went to make dinner.

Toting the envelope, I entered the study. I shuddered, breathing hard, my heart pounding. The musty smell of old books excited me. I had forbidden this room to myself for seven years.

Walking uneasily around the hoofprints in the rug, I went to the desk. The book my visitor had been examining was still on the desk, open.

The book that made Bram Stoker's reputation.

.3.

Changes were taking place in me. Who was the author of these changes?

When Jolson had come to take my tray, I told him he could have access to the books in my study whenever I was away. He was jubilant: he nearly smiled.

Now, sipping coffee, I began to read the document in the manila envelope. It was a transcription of a dialogue between myself and my analyst, eight years ago. I sensed it was time to reread it.

VH: Why the tape recorder, Doctor? I am protective of my privacy.

Dr: I have the recorder out in the open, Mr. Horescu. May I call you Vlad? You know I am concealing nothing from you. It is for more particularized investigation into your case. Homework. No one will see it but me. I'll have my

21

transcription machine make an extra copy, if you'd like to review—

VH: Yes, for the first two or three sessions, anyway. I'd like to have a transcription.

Dr: Very well. Now tell me—what led you to come to me? What event was decisive in your life that led you here?

VH: This is absolutely confidential?

Dr: Yes.

VH: Even if there is a crime involved?

Dr: Yes, unless I come to believe that you're potentially dangerous to some living—

VH: No, this was in the past. An accident. I couldn't kill again.

Dr: Then it is strictly in confidence. What or whom did you, uh—

VH: A young lady. I had her killed, but I didn't mean to have her killed. I meant to frighten her. She was blackmailing, ah, a friend of mine. An employer, frankly. He came to me, promised me—well, I found someone who said he'd frighten her out of it. But he killed her. Against my express orders! I covered the whole affair well. Oh, I am to blame as much as the killer. The guilt is mine, it has never relinquished me. It has coupled with my—my morbid, ah, *interests* and together it's just driven me— Oh, shit. God, I hate to—

Dr: You feel guilt? Because of your complicity in the death of the girl?

VH: A guilt complex. I suppose that's what you'd call it. It's certainly complex. It—it made me look at the other things in my life. My, ah, hobbies. The books! They became objects of loathing. But still I go to them, again and again, and— Do you see? I have to begin somewhere. Start a change. It was as if my obsession with death somehow brought about the girl's death. And I'm afraid it will happen again. Things have to change in me, I have to—to sponge it out of me. Am I making a fool of myself? I must sound melodramatic. But you can't imagine how—

Dr: No, you're not making a fool of yourself, Vlad. Relax, my friend. Speak freely, relax. Let it slide off your shoulders. Tell me about your hobbies.

VH: I can't, not yet—not—

Dr: Please, Vlad. Allow me to follow the course of inquiry I think best. Let's talk about your hobbies.

VH: They're more than hobbies, really. Okay. I'm a member of the Society for the Study of Ancient Arts, a group of mystics, some cabalists, some Satanists, Crowleyists, Rosicrucians, spiritualists; Carlton and I formed it together and—

A shadow fell over the desk. Startled, I looked up, reflexively putting my hand over the transcription sheet. It was Jolson. "Yes?"

"A phone call."

"From whom, dammit?"

"Your wife. She wishes to come here. For the night. Because a prowler has frightened her. She wants to talk to you—"

"Yes, yes. Tell her to come over. But I can't talk to her right this moment." Jolson left me. I returned to the transcription. I skipped several pages ahead.

Dr: So you trace this fascination with occult books to your time spent in the hospital as a child, and your upbringing in your foster parents' rare books store and—well, that doesn't explain why you chose *occult* books.

VH: Oh, I suppose it's a syndrome you've run across before, doctor. I was a classic case. I communicated poorly with other kids. A chronic lack of confidence on my part, and also I had been moved up two grades. A precocious kid. And I felt alienated from the older kids at school. So I began to feel inferior. To compensate for feeling inferior, I told myself *the other kids dislike me because they know I'm somehow different and that difference is a sign of my superiority to them.* It was a crock of shit, but it helped me to insulate myself from the others by reveling in my difference—mysticism seemed to exalt a different viewpoint. So it attracted me. Also, the occult books often made reference to hidden sources of *power.* I—I wanted to be powerful. And there was the influence of my only friends—Carlton and Luther and Ruby. Luther and Carlton are still with the SSAA and—well, it's obsessive—

Dr: Excuse me, Vlad, but I could hardly call a hobby with the occult *obsessive.* Many people enjoy astrology, dally with palmistry without damaging—

VH: That's just the tip of the iceberg. I—we—developed a morbid fixation. With the dead. With revenants of all kinds, vampires, even the cadavers themselves, mechanics of embalming. There was—a touch of necrophilia in all this. And when Mrs. Chutney died, I, um, I went alone into the room where she was laid out and I reached into the coffin and I felt her breasts and . . . She—she wasn't even an attractive woman. It was her death that made her attractive—

Dr: But she was mother to you—since your real mother was inaccessible—and affection does not require prettiness. Your touching the corpse might

24

indicate a frustrated need for maternal love finding an outlet in the only touching she would permit: when she could no longer reject you. You said she was not an affectionate woman, never embraced you, though she raised you from infancy, so she was emotionally corpselike—

I put the transcription aside and closed my eyes. My stomach was quaking. The Valiums had worn off. And to read about *that*—after all, he had trained me to avoid thinking of it. I clutched the edge of the desk, gritted my teeth and hung on. At last I was sure I would not vomit. I relaxed.

Another change had come about in me. I felt relaxed, even fortified.

I returned to the manuscript, and flipped through the pages. Analysis, four months later:

Dr: I see, so your fascination with the vampire legends was reinforced by your friends. Luther and Carlton especially. Carl was a well-to-do young man, was he? Were you jealous of this?

VH: No. Not at all. We had a good relationship: we traded books, wrote essays, criticized each other's work, analyzed what we conceived to be the central themes of the books. I leaned toward the poetic side—saying it was all just metaphor. Carlton believed that vampires really existed. The revenant kind.

Dr: Oh, last week you said you'd bring a relevant poem you had written back then—

VH: Yes, here it is—silly thing. Shall I read it? Okay, then. It's called:

AFRAID OF THE DARK
IN THE DAY, AFRAID
OF THE DAY IN THE DARK

A morbid child with hair gone wild and teeth like snaggled fences became obsessed and snowy tressed and sought distorted senses; with cloak of black and cloven track he slinks through brightest day out searching shadows, lairs of widows, places light won't stay. He likes such places, cobweb traces, caves where none should be; he looks for niches, nooks all rich with shadows 'neath the trees. Would he be right to walk at night and never day-embark? But night in day's the only way for one who fears the dark.

Dr: Well! Nicely put! And it sheds some "light." Tell me more about you and Carlton.

VH: We must have gone over *Varney the Vampire*, Stoker's *Dracula*, Byron's *Giaour*, a hundred times apiece. And Crowley, and certain volumes of Eliphas Levi, and Frazer's *Golden Bough*. Dozens of more obscure works. Luther could translate from Latin and Greek.

Dr: And are you still in contact with these people?

VH: No. Oh, I am, yes. Yes. Less often, though. Every time I see Luther he is more charnel-minded. Worse than I. And he is completely under the shadow of Carlton. Carlton is a megalomaniac. He reminds me of what I've read of Vlad the Second's personality—the original Dracula—and, well, he's a madman for power. He formed a cult around himself a few years back. They got scared and deserted him when he started digging up bodies for necromancy. He's always been obsessed with the Dracula image, the image more than the vampire himself.

Dr: You collected paraphernalia from vampire pictures. You claim to possess every known book on the subject. You went on an unsuccessful expedition to Rumania to find the tomb of King Vlad, and lost thousands of dollars in the venture, and yet you claim it is Carlton who is more obsessed—

VH: Yes. Far more than I. He would discuss it with such—such delight, when he talked of the taste, the anticipated taste, of human blood. Carlton identifies with the role.

Dr: There is considerable cultural fascination with vampires. I have always thought it to arise from guilt accumulating in the racial unconscious over the eating of animal flesh. Especially amongst Judaic peoples, who squeeze the blood from their meat before grinding it. We make ourselves strong by eating the flesh of things we kill. And that flesh contains blood.

VH: I think it more likely has to do with the need to dominate. At least in Carlton's case. I discussed it with him, once, and he admitted as much, and—talking about it is making me ill, Doctor. That girl—the blackmailer—I killed her, indirectly. Now she is a rotting artifact of the past. And my mother . . .

Dr: You have visited her in the institution only once in all these years—

VH: Enough!

That was enough. I put the transcriptions aside and began to weep. Tears of relief. Something had been cathartically driven from me, in reliving those sessions.

I was freer now. I could go in search of the truth about the things my analyst had taught me to conceal, these many years.

The crying spell passed, and I sat up and admired the ranks of dusty, leatherbound books. The dust coated the books like some regal mantle; the dustier the book the more significant it seemed.

I wondered about the SSAA. I had one letter from Luther, in 1973. I'd read it, though by that time my doctor had insisted I sever all ties with Luther and Carlton. In the letter, Luther said Carlton had financed another expedition to find the remains of King Vladimir, the Impaler, the tomb of the ancient monarch whose people had called him Son of the Dragon. Dracula—*drac* meaning Dragon, which locally symbolized the Devil, and *ula* meaning son: Son of the Devil. They'd found his tomb, the signs were unmistakable. It was empty. With the assistance of an archaeologist they confirmed that it had always been empty.

The local bishop shrugged when they told him. He had always known it would be empty. He'd said: "A man who can still walk the world will not willingly be entombed." That was all he would say.

.4.

"Oh, hello, Lollie," I said wearily.

She said, "Hi, Vlad," in the toneless voice that had first interested me in her. She continued to mix the drink, without looking up. "You want one?"

"No." I studied her. She hadn't degenerated much. Her coif of stiff, blue-silver hair was a little thinner, and her withered frame slightly more withered. She was pale, and would be clammy. Her skin still had a faint touch of blue, and her sunken blue eyes looked dead. I quelled a desire to seduce her.

I sat on the couch, leaned back and gazed at the stained-glass skylight. The new moon was half blue and half red, seen through the colored panes. "So you had a visitor? A prowler?" I asked.

Sipping her martini, she sat down across from me. "I don't know. Someone on the verandah. I just got scared. He went away, but—"

"Did you see him clearly? How do you know it was a *he*?"

"I don't know. But it was male. I felt that."

"Why didn't you ask Jolson to fix you that drink?"

"You know I don't like Orientals."

"I know you have a silly phobia. Ummm, how's your new apartment?"

"Very spacious, thank you. You made a nice choice. I appreciate it." She handled these amenities as mechanically as a doll with a voice-ring in its back.

"And—your source?"

"No problem there."

"No? You don't need money and you don't need morphine? So why did you come? You must have actually been frightened!"

"Don't get snotty, Vlad. I *was* frightened. I don't want to be alone."

"Okay. I'll have Jolson prepare a room for you." I watched her take birdlike sips of her drink, appreciated her profile as she turned and glanced at the wall-mounted digital clock. She could have been made of ivory, in that dim light. I wished I loved her.

She shivered, set her glass down, began to rub her bony fingers together. She would need a fix soon.

"Do you want to sleep with me tonight?" I asked.

"I don't care. Unless I'm sick, I guess. If you want. If I don't have to do much. But you don't want me to do much. The less the better, right?"

"Okay, okay. I'm sorry I made those remarks about the money and the morphine."

"Okay. Claws in! I'm going to, um, bed. If you still have the same room—"

29

"I do. I'll see you there later. Goodnight."

"Guh'night." She got up, stretched; I could see her thighs milky beneath her tunic. She had thinned some.

She bent, pecked me on the cheek—I shivered, it was a cold kiss—and left me.

I don't want to be alone, she had said. I didn't want to be alone that night, either.

"You aren't alone," someone said. A deep voice, resonant, edged with ice and touched with humor.

I turned my head. A portly old man with a white beard spilling broadly down his chest. A yellow suit, on his head a white feather swept back from a sporty yellow hat. I looked at his feet. Ordinary feet in ordinary patent leather shoes. His eyes were golden, but only in the iris, surrounded by white.

"Who the hell do you think you are?" I sputtered.

"Call me Bill."

"Are you kidding?" I got to my feet, turned to face him. He was bulky, looked strong. A saturnine Santa in a dapper suit. I looked again at his feet. "Damn it! Jolson! Get in here! Your hallucination is here and he hasn't got—"

"Your man is asleep, I've seen to it that he won't wake till morning. I don't want to be disturbed. And don't curse at your servant. What he said he saw, he saw. I have altered my feet and eyes to make you feel comfortable. I can show you the hooves, if you want. It's very arbitrary. I can show you my other aspects; my infant form, my beardless youth, my female form, my dual-sexuality form; I can manifest in scales, in fins— whatever you expect of me. So what do you want to see?"

"An explanation." I was trying not to tremble.

"Very well. I have come to you to talk about

30

your father." He clasped his hands behind his back, began to rock like a small boy waiting for his mother at the supermarket. "Your father. Vlad son of Vlad and father of Vlad. King Vladislav, the Impaler, Son of the Devil; Dracula, Lord of Vampires. Satisfied?"

I hesitated. Not out of indecision—I knew what my decision would be. I hesitated because I was considering with astonishment my attitude of acceptance. The man had appeared silently behind me, and I knew he was no hallucination, and I knew he was no burglar, con man, or hoaxer. How did I know that? Recognition. I had seen him, in a more tenuous form, as a boy, amongst the darkly laden back shelves of Chutneys' bookstore; I'd felt him there, or a spirit of his kind, and I'd believed in him as strongly as I believed in men of flesh and blood.

I'd been expecting him.

"Let's go to my study," I said.

"Splendid! Bring along that decanter. The brandy, yes . . . I need a drink."

.5.

He had been speaking for some minutes. Of worlds of shadows and shadows that hid worlds. He talked of empires in the sky and of invisible hierarchies, of changelings, of satyrs, centaurs, androgynies, and what mermaids *really* looked like. He spoke of vampires.

He spoke casually, as a man gossips to another of the doings of mutual acquaintances.

When we'd first come into the study, a fire was burning vigorously on the hearth. I hadn't ordered Jolson to make a fire. Looking closer I saw that the flames sprang from the charred brick itself; there was no log, no fuel of any kind.

We sat in the two leather armchairs, sipping brandy. His voice alternately boomed or susurrated, and his range of subjects was broad. He discoursed on as many things as did the hundreds of ancient books crowding the shelves around us; his voice seemed to come from the air itself, rather than from within his white beard, as if the dead authors of my books spoke aloud.

He talked of things animal, things vegetable, mineral, human and inhuman; all these subjects were linked by his assertion that there existed invisible systems of order consciously directing events in every level of the visible world.

"Nothing exists gratuitously. God's creation is abundant, but not actually generous. The law of conservation of energy won't allow for that. All things have a purpose, no matter how spontaneous or random they seem: Charles Manson and Torquemada. And King Vlad the Impaler, torturer of thousands. His sadistic impulses were pre-training. Vocational training."

"Bill!" I said impulsively. "Your name, your real name, what is it?" I looked upon him as an awed tourist gazes on the Swiss Alps. I sat in the shadow of greatness. There was power implied in his slightest motion, even in the casual tapping of his fingers. His fingernails were long and pointed and— silvery. They looked as if they were made of thin steel. They looked sharp.

He studied me. I could feel his eyes inside me.

"*Really*, Vlad! I would be an idiot to divulge my real name to anyone. Even human sorcerers understand the invocatory power of true names. But I'll tell you—the name by which I am most commonly known. I am the light—*Lucifer*."

I gaped.

He laughed. "No, not Satan. That's bad press, someone's mixed me up with that entity. There *is* a devil, oh, more than one, certainly, but I am not one of those. I am Satan's superior. I am the bearer of human motivation."

"I remember. The angel, the fallen angel, the giver of knowledge. The cabalistic symbol for the light of knowledge—"

"I am more than a symbol. I am more than a giver of knowledge. There are two kinds of thirsts in life. The holy and the unholy. Dracula is lord of unholy thirst, I am lord of holy thirsts—"

"Lucifer, symbol of life's urgency, patron of the desire for growth. You claim to be—an angel?"

He yawned. He looked bored. He took a draught of brandy. "An angel in the Swedenborgian sense, not in the Christian sense, Vlad. I am the earthly manifestation of a force—"

"And you know Dracula?" I couldn't keep the excitement out of my voice.

"Are you going to ask me 'What's he really like?' " he sneered. "I know Dracula, yes."

I sat up straight, suffused with the sense of destiny. Dracula was real, and I was his son. Suddenly, I resented Lucifer's presence; I wanted to test myself against him.

"You're grinning," he observed, his voice full of contempt, "like an impish child. You're a fathead, Vlad! Because you secretly *love* Dracula's image—as fatuously as a fifties bobby-soxer kissing her framed photo of Elvis!" He laughed so loudly the books trembled and clouds of dust sifted down. "You admire your father's legend and his power. And you think you are fated to become like him just because he has contacted you. Don't be an ass."

33

Somewhat deflated, I sat back.

"What do you think your father will do? Make you like him? He can't do that, and wouldn't if he could. He could make you an *ordinary* revenant, a dead and undead vampire, but you wouldn't like that—that isn't what Dracula is. He wants domination over the earth. Do you imagine for an instant that he would permit his *servant* even half as much power as *he* possesses? Yes, a servant! With Dracula one is either a servant or an enemy. What do you think your reward would be if you were to genuinely cooperate with Dracula? Eternal life? Immortality as a vampire? Yes, that is your reward! Do you think that would be glorious? It is a punishment! Dracula is lord of vampires. He is a blood-drinker, himself, but he is not one of the walking dead. The walking dead—oh, don't deceive yourself! Do you want to be one of *them*, Vlad? Oh indeed? I see your eyes shining at the thought. You bumptious oaf! Did you ever hear of the Los Angeles blood-murders? Hm? About a year ago? You must have read about it. It was a big national scandal. More than a dozen killings, girls found drained of blood. The author of those killings made certain that the newspapers were in on it. Do you know who *did* those killings? No? But you do! You knew him well! A good friend of yours! Someone who dropped from sight two years ago. Carlton Caldwell."

"Oh—that—well—I don't want—uh—"

"Don't want to *what*? Don't want to *know*? Oh, you're going to know all about it. The glory—the 'glory' of existence as an 'immortal' revenant. Here, look."

From his coat pocket he drew out an envelope, and from this he extracted about thirty sheets of grimy notebook paper. He passed these to me. A letter.

"Carlton's handwriting!"

"Very *good*, Vlad. You recognize it after all these years. Then you will not doubt the authenticity of this. He wrote it. Read it."

My hands shook. "It's probably a forgery. A lie—"

His laughter shamed me. "Read it," he said in quiet command.

"It's a letter to Luther, it seems," I murmured huskily.

"Read it!"

TWO

.1.

And I read. . . .

Dear Luther,

I recall that I looked forward to my first taste of human blood. You and Vlad will recall a similar anticipation. Occult scholars, we called ourselves— what a conceit! It was Vlad who influenced us to specialize in vampire lore . . . now—now I'm glad he's gone from all this. Remember when we first discussed with anticipation the taste of blood? It was Walpurgis Night, 1968, remember? We speculated rapturously on its taste, its feel, the heady thickness of it on the palate, the tingle of life-electricity still in it.

So I was disappointed, friend Luther, when I first tasted fresh human blood.

It tasted of corruption.

But it had not been corrupt, of course, or even tainted while it still ran through my victim's veins, just a moment before, but as every vampire discovers, it becomes tainted as it leaves the body and touches the air, even for an instant. Corrupt when it passes between alien lips. Oh, yes, you and I tasted our own blood, from small nicks, and it wasn't bad. But—it wasn't stolen.

No, I did not enjoy the taste of the girl's blood,

36

as I knelt beside the riven throat of my first victim, sucking, lapping blood freshly spilled. But I enjoyed the act. I took pleasure in the killing, in playing the role I had so long cultivated.

At last, I was a vampire.

Oh, surely, surely, I was not a bona-fide vampire. Not in the traditional sense. I had no supernatural abilities, except for the magic of my inspiration. I had no lupine servants, no fear of daylight's lethality. No superhuman strength or hypnotic power. All that sort of thing was either beyond my reach or all imagination. I'd tired of creatures of the imagination. And I was bored with the real creatures of the real world. I wanted a life of my own special making . . . oh, I'd tried to forge it by allying myself with supernatural forces. My one successful invocation ended in near disaster—the demon scorned my magic circle and struck me unconscious. I had failed to find proof of Dracula's existence; at least, proof that would convince others. I needed to convince others, I needed help to try and find him. You and the others in the SSAA Steering Committee were sympathetic, but you refused to help me find him. I forgive you, and Vlad, for that. Now grudges are meaningless. So, having failed to find Dracula, and failed as a magician, and being once too often called a "madman" by junior members of the SSAA, I decided to make myself into Dracula. A close facsimile. I would make myself into a living archetype, an apotheosis of the monstrous. Jack the Ripper was a besotted Cockney bumbler, yet he secured historical immortality; he became a symbol of rapacity, for all human memory. I lusted for that, and I yearned very sincerely for darkness. Oh, yes, there was a suicidal drive somewhere beneath it all. I admit it.

37

You know, don't you? You know, Luther.

You knew me, and you've read the papers and magazine articles, I don't doubt. You must have guessed it was I, yet you were silent. You thought you were doing me a kindness by not going to the police.

I wish to God you had turned me in.

You notice there is no date heading this later, Luther. Time means virtually nothing to me now. You and I talked, once, of how glorious it would be to be ·immortal as a vampire. How splendid to have no concern for passing years! To never grow old.

Now, I do not know what date it is, and I cannot know. I can stare at a calendar or a ticking clock— but something prevents me from comprehending it! Do you think that's glorious? Do you think it's grand to have no fix on any one time? Is it? Is a man in a rubber raft lost at sea joyful because there is no land, no fix· in all the rolling vastness, anywhere in sight?

No, he is lost.

I am lost, Luther. And I don't want you to become lost as well. You—my only true friend. That's why I write you this letter, and why I will risk myself by creeping out tonight to slip it into your mailbox. There is some tiny, distant corner of my heart which is not cold. That corner, that special place grows smaller and more distant every night. Soon it will vanish and there will be nothing in my chest but aching void. But for now, in that corner, your name lingers. And that is why, out of concern for you I have written this letter of warning. Listen, listen.

Unlike Peter Kürten, the vampire of Dusseldorf, I did not suffer from haematodipsia, the sexual thirst for blood; I did not (then) "need blood as others need alcohol," as Kürten said. Unlike Countess Elizabeth of Bathory I didn't desire the blood of virgins to keep me youthful. So I had no excuse, except, as some would claim, my madness. But my need was a natural one. It was a need that springs ever-present in the human breast, to greater and lesser degrees. The need for unfettered power, sadistic and absolute dominion over others. In me, this normally latent desire achieved superhuman proportions. And to me the most profound symbol of this domination was the vampire role, as Stoker saw it, with all its attendant horrors . . . and glories.

I had not so much money as I let on to you. (I squandered much of it on those expeditions to Europe.) I sold some land, all my stocks, turning what could have been a large fortune into a small one. And I still had the mansion, and the four acres about it.

I had the costume and accoutrements made far away, in New York. I found, in Denmark, a skilled but unscrupulous dental surgeon for the fang and suck-tube implants.

And I purchased the minicopter and hired a certain pilot, an ex-con with a suspended license—a former smuggler—to provide some of my "miraculous" escapes.

I had dabbled, as you must recollect, in prestidigitation and other forms of stage magic, and this became instrumental in creating my legend. And I planned and schemed for a year before my first vampiristic murder. I personally installed the false wall at the back of that alley where my reputation was to begin.

I acquired schedules of police beats and patrol assignments, I watched them and timed everything with an exactitude I relished. It was just as important that the police see me as it was that they not catch me.

I found the only animal trainer in the world who had succeeded in training bats. Since there was little demand for his act, he was only too glad to sell the bats to me, and to demonstrate their use. Of course, I had to kill him to assure his silence.

Doubtless you read the in-depth article on the Los Angeles police's first encounter with me, in the L.A. Times. For the first three killings I did not permit the police to see me in the flesh, nurturing an air of mystery and tenebrous intimation. The first girl was hardly more than an infant, perhaps eight years old. I was sure her youth would capture the newspapers' attention. And, too, she was the daughter of a city councilman! I found her asleep in her darling little bed, I stuffed cotton into her mouth to prevent screams, and threw myself full upon her, draining enough blood to stop her heart. Just enough. For the sake of tradition and artistic verisimilitude, I drank a pint or two through my hollow suction-tubed fangs, and drained more into the plastic sack I carried with me. This blood I later used to fertilize the mandrake plant I kept growing in the churchyard of my father's estate.

My poor dead parents—I wish I were with them now.

That girl—the first one—was too easy. She hardly struggled when I bit down, and when I drew back to operate the hand pump at her throat, filling the sack, she seemed almost friendly when her brown eyes looked gravely into mine. I took little satisfaction in it, though it was amusing to view her final spasms.

I was disappointed. I read the newspapers scrupulously, but the furor was minimal. There was mention that the girl's body had been drained of blood through two punctures in her throat. The article failed to mention that when her parents got there, the door to the room was latched from the inside, and no windows were broken or unlocked. It had cost me eighteen thousand dollars, more than half of the remaining money, to produce a magnetic device capable of locking from the outside a lock designed to close manually only from the inside.

In the second and third killings I was careful to leave traces of dirt from the graveyard on the rug of the bedrooms, as well as other telltale signs. A bedroom mirror turned to face a wall. A crucifix one of the girls had worn, broken and thrown in a corner. Blood drained as before, latches locked from the inside.

And still the newspapers callously ignored these exquisite details, remarking only that "peculiar circumstances" accompanied the killings. Without specifying what those circumstances were.

I was furious. It was obvious that the police were covering up. How sad it is that genius goes so easily ignored! I had to bring a reporter in, directly involved.

So I staged an entrancing cinematic embroglio with the police, worthy of anything Todd Browning put on film, and all timed with meticulous precision.

And, Luther, in testimony to my divine inspiration: everything went like clockwork.

I sent an anonymous note to a certain investigative reporter, one Barry Bretallmo. The note was a messy scrawl reading:

"I can bear it no longer! If you wish to find the killer of the girls Brenner, Jones and Wineburg, be at 1511 Sepulveda Boulevard at exactly ten P.M.

For your own protection, bring with you a crucifix. Conceal yourself well, my master has the cunning of a wolf! Pray God I am released from the Count's dominion. Bring two policemen with you, but only two. More and he will be warned. Look for an alley. Destroy him."

No signature, of course.

It was a lovely Southern California night. Scents of smog and citrus intermingled exotically, and the reflected glow of city lights against the horizon resembled the charnel phosphorescence overhanging a decaying swamp. The palm trees stood like huge clutching hands, stark against the bone-colored stucco buildings, and my footsteps carried a thrilling histrionic ring (I had my boots cleated for this effect) as I strode the alleyway.

As I had expected, the prostitute was just leaving through the back door of her brick apartment building, as per my instructions, expecting nothing more than an unusually furtive trick awaiting her. Instead, I awaited her. Standing in regal pose, my gaunt, aristocratic face shadowed in the dimness, my glossy black cloak drawn close about me, my old-fashioned tuxedo stiff with starch and as un-rumpled as the burial dress of a freshly laid-out corpse. And—I saw myself clearly, a striking figure in my mind's eye!—my arms slowly outspreading like the unfurling wings of a giant bat, I stepped calmly into the slanting beam of a distant streetlight so my carefully cultivated pallor would show to best effect. Below knife-edged arching brows my luminous red eyes (red contact lenses treated to be fluorescent) shone like twin windows into Hell (or so I grandiosely imagined), and my clawed fingers opened and closed in grace and spasm; my rouged lips slowly parted to expose blood-stained inch-long

42

fangs—the woman blinked, opened her mouth, chuckled in perplexity (wondering if I were just one of those tricks who prefer a kinky get-up) and took a cautious step forward. She was plump but pretty, a fairly unspoiled Chicano whore, with wise black eyes and a wry smile. "Hey, you wanna—"

"Silence!" I hissed in a compelling tone I had long practiced, and threw my caped arms about her, dragged her close. She giggled—once. And then I prodded the nerve in her back that froze her into paralysis (you recall, Luther, my martial arts training?). I lapped her neck once, compressed her in an embrace as erotic as it was threatening, and sank my artificial fangs into her neck. She shivered, and the paralysis began to wear off. She began to struggle, but I was consumed with an overpowering sense of ecstasy in utter domination of her. I felt the electric substance of her life itself fluttering between my jaws like some small, helpless animal. I held her firmly till I had swallowed just enough to make her weak. I choked down the hot, foul stuff, fighting a sudden nausea, but all the while counting off the seconds in my mind. Any second now. The tiny radio receiver clamped behind my ear whined and from it a tinny voice spoke: "They're coming, boss. A reporter and two cops. Now the cops have stopped to argue with the reporter. Now he's broken from them, he's run on ahead, coming into the alley. Get ready."

I waited till I heard the reporter's approaching clatter, then released the girl, who fell to her knees, moaning. I raised my cape to cover my face as the reporter's camera-flashcube flared, then turned to strike out with a karate thrust that sent the man sprawling. I was careful not to damage the camera, and careful not to stand in the conventional karate

43

stance, so that he would believe me invested with superhuman strength, and wouldn't associate the force of the blow with martial arts.

And hearing the shouts of the policemen, I turned and sprinted, cape trailing dramatically behind me, down the alley, bounding over trashcans as if they were pebbles. A gunshot echoed the bricked crevice and a bullet struck through my cloak, stopped by my protective vest.

I grinned and continued without pause, heard the policeman gasp. Later he would tell the reporters: I shot him clean in the back and he didn't feel it.

I turned the corner four strides ahead of the pursuing police, triggered the door, slipped through, heard it swing mutely shut. I listened to their muffled footsteps rounding the corner. I waited in the darkness of the concealed chamber and chuckled softly at the sound of their gunfire as they shot wildly at the bat that had been automatically released and spurred from its hidden cage. I hoped they'd miss the bat, and miss it they did; well-trained, it returned to its roost at my estate. After many hours, hours I crouched, hardly breathing, in the darkness of my concealment, they gave up the search.

The next day, a front-page story around the world.

I glowed with elation.

The newsphoto was vague, blurred by my motion and the sweep of my cape, but suggestive of some whirling, menacing figure.

And as I intended, the girl lived to tell her story. Vividly.

The police grudgingly released the details of my first three excursions, and the vampire scare began. Stories escalated, legends burgeoned, imitators came forth, were caught and proved to be imposters.

I had used the bat that once at some risk, since the police might have winged it, brought it down and found it to be an ordinary fruitbat. So thereafter I resolved to use the vanishing-into-mist illusion. (I recall Vlad's acid comments when he learned I was training in stage magic and martial arts. "He can't have the real thing so he surrounds himself with trappings of mystic power—more appropriate to a wrestler's publicist than a student of Ancient Arts!" Vlad was wrong. I knew even then it would all be concretely useful to me one day.) For the next instances of timed public exposure and escape, it worked grandly. I permitted myself to be pursued till I could slip just out of sight, and my pursuers caught up to find only a whirling mist issuing odorless into the air—and I was gone. This was accomplished in an ill-lit place with much shrubbery, so they would be unlikely to find the gas capsule, which remained tiny but visible till it was completely dissolved.

You must have read about it, Luther, and perhaps felt the tension in the night air. Terror arrived with dusk. The city locked its doors; sales of crucifixes rose dramatically; wolfbane was sold as commonly as lettuce. And all this in spite of police disclaimers maintaining some clever mortal madman was behind it all.

The newspaper called me "Count Question." I liked the appellation, and began to think of myself that way. As public fascination with my deeds accrued, my megalomania (I admit it! I revel in it!) grew apace. I thought: Let them tremble at my name—Count Question, Lord of Darkness!

The police tried to bait me. Harmless-seeming women, undercover policewomen, roamed the streets incognito. And certain lonely women, enamored with me in a morbid fascination, walked the street nocturnally, hoping to be my next victim. I touched none of these. I chose my victims carefully, and attacked in no explicable pattern, making it seem that the choice was random. My score rose to fifteen dead, one hospitalized.

And the mandrake in my private churchyard grew vigorously.

I used temporary tunnels to escape through the ground, in parks and overgrown lots where I made my disappearances. I carefully filled in the tunnels afterwards, but this took some time, and, in the meanwhile, they might have stumbled on one of them. But after each disappearance, the police search of the area was less thorough than the last. As if the police, too, wanted to believe I was the real thing. And after a time they made no attempt to conceal the crucifixes they carried along with guns and badges.

I suppose if the revenants had not come for me, other pitfalls would have ended my career. Overconfidence perhaps. I was coming to believe in my fabricated self-image. I slept by day in a coffin strewn with dirt, in a tomb in my family's churchyard, beside my dead parents. And this encroaching delusion would have led me to carelessness. My servants began to demand more and more money, to point out the draw of the mounting reward for information leading to the capture of the vampire. Eventually, they would have betrayed me.

Also: I began to take foolish risks. One foggy night I permitted myself to be seen by a crowd leaving a movie premier, so that I could enjoy their mixed adulation and revulsion, their deference to terror. I stood atop a broad two-story building

46

across the street from the theater—poised, pic-
turesque and straight and defiant as a statue of a
soldier. My eyes glowed, my teeth gleamed. Someone sighted me, screamed, staggered backwards,
pointing. The crowd milling beneath the neon mar-
quee looked, and erupted in shouting turmoil Some
scattered, others called for the police, still others
surged toward me. A few fell to their knees and
prayed. Utterly delighted, sweeping my cape and
displaying my jaws, I bellowed: "Down! Down,
lowly pink worms! On your knees, sheep for my
supper!" I trembled in the benighted glory of the
instant . . . the thickening fog billowed just above
me, impenetrable as the mysteries of death. Farther
up, in the well-muffled minicopter, my hireling
hovered. He was well back from the edge of the
roof, lost in the glare from the streetlights, cloaked
in dark and fog. He flew without lights, and the
chuffing of his copter blades was heard only dis-
tantly.

But the imbecile had neglected to lower the
harness as I had ordered, and I was nearly caught.

Policemen were clattering up the fire escapes, and
a heavyset bald patrolman was already on the roof.
I shouted an angry order into my collar microphone, demanding the harness, and—strangely
unafraid—I strode toward the policeman, snarling.
He cried out unintelligibly, and fired—at my head.
His hands trembled, the shot went awry. I slapped
the gun from his hand and struck him down. I
broke three of his ribs and his collarbone in doing
so, with great satisfaction.

Groaning, he lay on his face and did not see the
harness lowered beside me.

The hand of Dracula himself was on my shoulder
that night, I felt; the spirit of the Lord of Vampires

stood beside me, approving, protecting.

I slipped into the harness and was grateful that I had thought to paint its connecting-wire silver so that it was not seen in the fog as more police swarmed onto the roof, shouting and firing haphazardly at me. I ascended into the air before them—flew straight up, pulled by the copter. The copter was well above and out of sight—or almost; possibly, if one of them had looked closely, calmly, they might have glimpsed the silvery wires or the silhouette of the copter; but their eyes were riveted on me—half the trick of stage magic is distraction. . . . To the police who witnessed this escape, it was the final proof of my supernatural origins.

And it was the final satisfaction I was to have.

That night, pretending I was about to give them a generous bonus, I called my servants together. I killed them. The three of them, three quick shots. They, too, had become overconfident.

It was as I was burying them, in the little cemetery behind the chapel of my estate, that I was visited.

Luther, do not follow in my footsteps. Do not search for me. Run, leave the city. Go as far as you can afford to go. They are looking for you, too. Because they learned that you knew about me, that you had sympathy with my ambitions, and they fear you might plan to do as I did.

All the furor I had raised was nearly their undoing. Vigilantes had organized; cemeteries and sewers, subterranean hiding places were inspected. Graves were exhumed, tombs entered. Even Forest Lawn. Guards were placed at graveyards. And a vampire was caught. A woman, so they knew it was not I, but some other vampire. A genuine article. They beheaded her, stuffed her mouth with garlic

48

and left her head on a metal stake at the entrance to the cemetery as a warning to other Undead. Her body they quartered and burned. Oh, the police denounced this—they insisted there was no proof that the woman had been a vampire, since all that was left of her was her head, not enough for a decisive autopsy; they gave little credence to the mob's assertion that the woman had crawled from a sepulcher and set upon a dog, to drink its blood. But she was genuine. Merely one of many. About twelve in the Los Angeles area alone. Four of them were Spaniards who had come with the first conquistadors, then fallen prey to local vampires (two Indians, still with the group). Others were more recent recruits, a century or less behind them. They do not speak. Yet I know these things.

Unlike myself, the revenants are not the theatrical sort. They did their best to conceal their activities, and usually succeeded. They drained blood from the corpses of people others had murdered (they have a keen intuition for finding these); sometimes stole small amounts from blood banks and hospitals. They sucked dogs and cats and birds (animals are our sole diet for now, until the vampire hunts subside), or old men—derelicts no one would miss. They had a system, and I had thrown a wrench into it. I'd drawn attention to them. They faced imminent capture. So their instincts told them to take me out of circulation. Not that they would not love to be dead, truly dead, to be caught and torn apart and burned. They secretly lust for it, of course, as do I now. But their instincts, the demoniacal disease that possesses us, drives us on, makes it impossible to surrender to self-destruction.

Us. I. Me: with feral but sure instincts, they

49

found me, there in my churchyard, spade in hand. They introduced me to their world.

I looked up—and there they were, standing—more like sagging on two feet—about the grave in which I stood up to my knees in loam and carrion. They stood about me, and I knew them for what they were. I knew by the way they gazed thirstily at the still-blooded corpse half-covered in the last of three graves. I looked into their eyes, and knew I had made a mistake; their agony was visible, tenuous but visible, like a distant candle flame on a very dark night.

I tried to run, they dragged me down. They drank from me, and made me drink, and made me dead, and—after a fashion—alive again.

There is nothing glorious, nothing magnificent about them. They are gray-white, their skin resembles fungus. They are sunken, hardly more than mummies. They are strong but slow-moving, foul-smelling, and ridden with parasites. They think only vaguely (I hear their thoughts—they approach—hasten, finish this, conceal it), but they have a cunning, a cunning they used to find me, and which they will use to find you. They also have a master. I have not seen him yet, I am not sure he has to appear to us in the flesh, but I feel their—ah!—their deference to him, and one of them, once, murmured his name: Dracula.

Their eyes are lustreless, their breaths spray putrescence, their nails are incredibly long and filthy, and in each vampire's mouth only two teeth survive: two hollow, unartificial fangs. They—we—fear the day, but cannot become bats, nor command wolves, nor dissolve to mist. We wear no shiny black cloaks, haunt no stately castles. They dress in foul rags and sleep in cisterns, abandoned mines, broken-down sepulchers—anyplace free of daylight. They are dead, I am dead. I am not quite like the others yet. I am not as cold, as dispassionate, my flesh is not as desiccated and sunken. I feel, for now, a few more emotions than the two they still possess: fear and hollow yearning are all that is left them. I retain some muscle-tone, and I am not half-eaten by worms.

But the decay is coming to me. I survive on blood alone, and night by night (God, I miss the daylight now! A single ray of sunlight is like a white-hot lance to me—how I yearn for it, how it terrifies me!) I grow more listless, colder of heart, limper of flesh. I feel constantly as if I had a bad hangover; nauseous, painfully empty, enervated. I have no sexual urge, no desire for solid food, my tongue is shriveling.

And yet I can taste the stolen blood, the corruption of it, the taste of a living thing's despair still in it. God, I loathe the taste of the stuff, this stuff I endlessly desire!

And there is no end to it, Luther. I become as they (they're coming, they'll be here in moments, must hasten, conclude, extinguish the candle!) and my heart goes out like a failing ember. But my arms and legs, this withered flesh, will drag on through forever like the limbs on an insensate automaton. Cold and inexorable.

There is no glory here.

Carlton

.2.

After a time I let out a long breath, a sigh that went on and on. "Carlton wrote that," I assented, gazing into the flames of the fireplace. "His style.

51

He always had a sense of high-style. I thought he might kill someone someday, or at least commit necrophilia. I never thought he'd go to such extremes. So much trouble for his fantasy—"

"De Sade went to the trouble to orchestrate his obsessions into complex novels. He wrote plays, later, when he was put in the madhouse—I attended one of those. Amusing fellow. Oh, yes, and I knew Carlton, too. He invoked me once!" Lucifer's laugh boomed off the ceiling. "I stepped outside the circle and the poor fool said 'What! You can't do that! The laws of magic command you to stay inside the consecrated pentagram!' He was flustered. I kicked over his candles and explained that I had written his 'laws of magic' and he had better have a good reason for invoking me. He whimpered that he'd called me to request *knowledge*, and I said, 'Knowledge? You want to *know*? Then know darkness!' and I struck him unconscious. All of which *I* thought was rather funny."

"Uhh—"

"My, you certainly are articulate."

"Don't mock me."

"Light mocks the senses, since it blinds and reveals at once."

"You're deliberately cryptic. You *like* confusing me. You enjoy it. I'm having enough trouble assimilating your physical reality, without your being cryptic."

"The shoptalk of airline pilots sounds cryptic to bookkeepers; to the pilot it is mundane."

"In other words, you'll say what you please."

"Exactly."

"Should I believe in you as you are—"

"I'm not Tinkerbelle, damn it, I don't care if you believe in fairies or demons or congressmen. Behold the evidence of your senses! Do *I* amaze you? The fact of your *being* should be sufficiently astounding to you. The miracle of your being alive at all, that matter can evolve into awareness, should be so astonishing to you of itself that nothing else could stun you."

"Rhetoric. Which I've heard before. Come on—" I was becoming bolder, because Lucifer's presence was radiating ever more brightly and I interpreted that presence as a threat. "What—what do you want of me? Why this lecture?" I had got to my feet, but even standing over him, I felt smaller.

" 'What do you want of me?' he asks imperiously. Huh! I'm *only* trying to save you. No matter that saving you is an incidental side-effect to containing Dracula—even though your welfare is not my first concern, it just happens that your chances for life will be best served if you work with *me* rather than with Dracula. It is that simple. He and I will both use you, of course. But he will use you ill. He can't help it, it's his nature."

"He is my father!" It sounded hollow, even to me. "He would not destroy his own son."

"Why not? The woman whose son you are, Elizabeth Horescu, was his great granddaughter, many times removed. That is why he chose her for a conception. She did not know, of course. But he did. He raped her in such a way that she went mad, and left her."

"His—"

"Oh, stop ogling and sit down."

I sat down, feeling drained. Probably it was true. She *had* come from a family line originating in Wallachia.

"He raped others," Lucifer was saying casually, "and they were not impregnated. Why not? Abortions? Chance? No, it is a matter of his choosing. He chose to impregnate her, he wanted a son by one of his own line, and it didn't matter to him that it would destroy her. He wanted a son or a daughter because he knew the child would one day be useful."

"Still, he *is* my father. And I should feel loyalty to him."

"Is he your father?"

I looked at Lucifer sharply. "Well? Stop playing with me!"

Lucifer shrugged. "He inseminated your mother. But—"

"Then he is my father."

"You do not wish to remain loyal to him because he is your father. You wish it because he is a figure of potency and power, an image, a glittery bauble. You are no different from Carlton. You don't want your toys taken from you."

"I repeat: what do you want of me?"

"Why, I want you to contact Dracula, to pretend to befriend him, to learn his schemes, to report to me. This will expedite his annihilation. Which will be best for all, Dracula included. Originally, he worked for me. After he died, so to speak. His function—well, you know me as the giver of knowledge, but in actual fact I give motivation to seek knowledge—I do not impart the stuff itself. I am impartial. The advancement may be in warfare, medicine, torture, or spiritual enlightment. In my purest form, I motivate the sperm to wriggle his tail. Too, I led Fleming to penicillin and John Dillinger to robbery. I led the British to colonization, I led India to rebel against them. All organized human surges, those are mine. Revolutions are my children, and organized counter-revolutions are my grandchildren. There are many tools affecting these trends. Dracula, and fiends like him, I used to keep men on their toes, to keep them afraid. No man is more alert than a man who is afraid. And Dracula motivated men to seek out and overcome the mysteries of death. Dracula was a provocation. Terror provokes activity. He was on my staff. Half a century ago, he rebelled—"

"As you yourself did, Fallen Angel, resulting in your being cast out of—"

"Nonsense! Do you believe everything you read? Do you think John F. Kennedy actually laid all those women in the White House? Honestly, Vlad, you're terribly gullible. Christian institutions are as accurate about the affairs of God as communist newspapers are honest about the doings of the Soviet government. The Church has more often been Dracula's friend than his enemy. They've encouraged superstitions and the fear of him and his servants; and like Carlton, Dracula thrives on the right sort of publicity. He doesn't really fear the cross, you know. He sometimes *wears* one. But there is a force in the hearts of the Church's saints, in Aquinas and Jesus and Lafferty—the same force central to the lives of Schweitzer and William James and Allen Watts and Siddhartha—a motivation, a revelation transcending dogma—*that* is what Dracula fears. It is the heart of the man and not artifacts which defeats devils."

I felt electrically afraid, in Lucifer's presence, and electrically aware. The colors of the room presented themselves to me boldly; every shape, every geometrical structure—the rectangles of bookbindings the ovals compounding the chairs, the fibers of the rug—seemed to stand out almost angrily, to hurt the eyes when looked upon. All roads lead to Rome, and all the lines of the room converged upon Lucifer, as if the room unfolded from him like a Kirlian aura. He was gazing at the part of me which defeats devils. His eyes had gone all golden—no pupils, no whites—a slate of gold. Like the sun expanded by refraction as it sinks to the horizon, his eyes were burning orbs of gold.

With an effort I asked: "Can't you—can't *you* control Dracula? Alone? Can't you simply overwhelm him?"

"I could, but that would break him, and we need him on another plane. He refuses to evolve, though his time has come. It's time for a fresher demon to take his place. He refuses, he rebels, and I don't want to ruin him, I simply want to annihilate him. He must be insinuated, before he can be incinerated. He must go willingly to that higher place. He must be tricked into this destruction, this exaltation through death. Since he has contacted you, you can help me. I love Dracula. I love him, you see, and would not see him broken. Disintegration equals assimilation, you see. Disintegration is ectasy. It's a gift he won't accept. Because of his ego, as with all his kind; it's because he was once human."

"You have no ego? But you have—well—such a kingly glow—"

Lucifer hissed and gave me a look that would have shriveled my eyes if I had not averted them. "An ego? Idiot! I have a kingly presence because I am what I am! I am the living definition of royalty! Ego is something one dons like a mask."

"Ah, I believe you." I said, meekly changing the subject. "Dracula was a king, himself. King Vlad the Impaler. You must have known him then—fifteenth century. How much of it is true? Did he—"

"He killed thousands for his own amusement."

"I remember, uh, *if* it's true, that he would impale them, forcing a sharp ten-foot stake into the victim's anus. The victims had to sit on this until the weight of their bodies forced them down far enough on the stake to finally kill—hours of agony as the stake slowly worked its way up through the bowels and entrails. And he would have a—a small *forest* of these people, fifty of them impaled atop a hill, some dead, carrion, some alive and yowling, others being pulled apart by teams of horses or slowly roasted alive—a Disneyland of suffering. And he would sit amongst them and eat his dinner and make merry." I took a pull on my brandy to calm myself; it was a subject that had a great emotional fascination for me. "And once a servant asked, 'Lord Vlad, must we serve you here where the stink of the carrion assaults us?'"

"Yes!" Lucifer laughed and finished the anecdote for me. "And good King Vlad replied, 'So the smell of these corpses offends you? Then I shall put you where you cannot smell them, my good fellow!' And he staked the man, placed him high above the others, impaled him thirty feet in the air and shouted up to him, 'Now, isn't the air better up there?' Quite the comedian was King Vlad." Lucifer chuckled. "Once, visiting dignitaries from another land came into his court, said they brought greetings from their king, and they bowed. But they did not take off their caps. Dracula was furious. In Wallachia it was the custom to show respect by going hatless before the king. He spoke of this to them and they protested that in *their* land men did not doff their hats before the king. Dracula instantly ordered them taken, and directed that their hats be nailed to their heads. He had them, wailing, brought before him, and he said, 'Now go back to your king and show him that since I do not wish to offend him I have made sure that you will never again remove your hats, in deference to *your* country's customs!' Ah, but there was law and order in Dracula's land! Anyone caught breaking *any* law was immediately hung, burned, or impaled; such was the fear of lawbreaking that an unguarded cup of solid gold was left at the fountain in the public square day and night, and no one stole it, though poverty was rife.

"He was once captured and thrown into prison by a rival power in a neighboring state, and while jailed he worked an exchange with the guards. He consented to sew and repair their clothing in exchange for a knife, sticks to carve into little stakes, and small animals—chickens, rabbits, squirrels—which he impaled in his cell, or skinned alive, to his great glee and satisfaction.

"Yes, and he was reinstated, by some madman, on his old throne. And he warred with the Turks. And during one of those battles—ah, he was a furious warrior, legendary for his ferocity and prowess alike—he was cut off from his men and overcome, beheaded. They found a body in his clothes, decapitated. The head was nowhere about—they assumed it was he. But he was not dead; I had come for him. I was just what he needed: penance. He is a prince of vampires because I appointed him. Karma yoga, as your servant would say. And a promotion, in a way. He alone was qualified for the job, and he alone deserved it. His task, working for me, was hideous and proud. Do not envy him. You cannot be like him, Vlad. You could, at best, end like Carlton. No glory there."

"Dracula is not living-dead?"

"No. He is prince over the living dead as Pluto is lord of Hades—both crowns are notoriously heavy. Quasimodo was king of fools, Dracula is king of thirsty corpses. He has other power. Oh, I had to kill him, in a sense, to transform him to what he is now. His body was dead, for a while, and he in limbo, while I worked changes on him. Now he's preparing a haven for himself, a new kingdom, in Brazil. Soon he'll meet their negotiators, their submarine. You'll see."

"But what *exactly* do you want me to do?"

"I'll tell you later. The night before you contact him. I'll prepare you so that he doesn't make you a slave to his will."

"Lucifer, will you show yourself to me? Now? As you *are*. As you really are." I was afraid he would consent. My fears were realized.

"Very well, skeptic. But you won't see most of it, though it appears before you. The eye encompasses only fractions. I am manifold. I am legion." He shrugged, and spoke with terse sincerity: "I am amoebas and elephants! Look!"

He stood and faced me. His flesh flowed like molten stone.

The transmutation of Lucifer's clothing into lavender scales proceeded so smoothly and methodically that I wasn't startled. It was as natural as an eagle molting or a snake shedding skin. And when scales became liquid—and before me stood a being of multicolored liquids flowing in the shape of a man—it was a change as pure and unartificial as the transformation of ice into water. From liquid to protoplasmic form, to gelatinous to living stone to fish to feathers and combinations of all. A tentacled thing with feet of lion and tongue of snake.

And from that to a hermaphrodite: smooth, with

olive eyes, spilling brown hair and upturned breasts; wide shoulders, stocky legs, the genitals of man above those of woman. Then, the manly genitals shrank, absorbed into the paling flesh, the shoulders dwindled somewhat, muscles retained strength but tempered with feminine grace. The waist shrank, the legs smoothed.

A lovely, simple-bodied woman, with hair the color of clay, and eyes the same but flecked with gold. Her nipples were a fourth of her wide-set breasts, and were the color of dried blood, and her expression was as intelligent as a hawk's is intense. Gaea, earth-goddess.

There was something animalistic, feral in her movements as she reached toward me—

I wilted before her, I hid my eyes. A man who falls in love with the earth itself will go mad trying to find satisfaction.

When I looked up, Lucifer stood there as before the transformation—white beard, male radiance, golden eyes, golden suit—but now he walked on hooves.

"I will do as you ask," I said, because no other answer was possible. "But do me a favor. Dispense with the hooves and let me go back to calling you *Bill*. I don't want to think of you—as *that*—not for a while."

"Very sensible," said Bill, with a grin. I glanced at his feet: shoes again. "Call me a cab, will you? I'm tired of showing off," he said.

60

THREE

.1.

It was twelve pensive hours later that it really hit me: *Lucifer.*

And my Valium prescription had run out.

It could have been a hallucination, I told myself. Perhaps Jolson had a meditative hallucination and only visualized the man in my study. And maybe his description of the vision triggered a hysteria in me—I'd been flirting with hysteria since reading the letter from Dracula—and I'd had a waking dream, a hallucination of the thing that had come to deal with me. Perhaps someone had slipped me a drug—I had been feeling peculiar.

Perhaps I was simply going insane.

But the letter from Dracula had been real—a man dead for centuries. Why not Lucifer?

It was nearly noon. Like a lazy nurse only rarely looking in on me, sleep had come fitfully during the night.

I lay in bed beside Lollie. I wished I were a cigarette smoker. I studied Lollie's arm. She lay on her wasted belly, nude, covered to the hips by the white silk sheet. Asleep, she looked only half her forty years. My eyes traced each rib and the skeins of veins, blue under her almost transparent skin. The faint sea breeze through the open window stirred her hair and brought out goosebumps on her back. As if reading tea leaves, I tried to read the future in her tracery of veins, in her track marks and the shadows of her thin muscles.

Sunlight struck through the window, projecting shadows of clouds on the opposite wall. The sea rumbled and hissed. Cars called impatiently, honking to get onto the ferry for San Francisco.

I sat up, leaned against the leather backboard and punched the intercom button on the bedside table. "Jolson! Are you awake?"

"For some time," came his reply from the speaker. "Would you like breakfast now?"

"I'll tell you when. Did you sleep well last night, Jolson?"

"Unusually well, Mr. Horescu. Ordinarily I sleep lightly. Last night the hoof-clatter of the gods would not have—"

"Why did you put it that way? Hoof-clatter, I mean."

"I don't know. The man I saw yesterday, perhaps."

"Did you hear anything last night? Anything unusual? A strange voice?"

"No. But I slept heavily. There were voices in my dreams."

"Of what did you dream?" I asked the intercom, my eyes following the cloud-shadows sailing the wall.

"Odd dreams—nightmares—a man sitting alone in an ancient stone jail cell torturing small animals and laughing—"

"I see." My mouth was suddenly dry.

"Was there anyone—"

"No, no, Jolson."

"Will there be an inspection of the house?"

I considered. Lollie's syringe lay exposed on the

bureau, and her clothes were scattered on the floor; until the prior night this would have made me furious and repelled me. Now I scarcely noticed. Even if the visitation had been a hallucination, *something* had changed me. And someone had unlocked the study door.

At last: "No, Jolson. No inspections. You can dust the study—we'll leave it unlocked. You can read what you like while you're in there. For now."

I took my finger off the button. Something had changed me.

The phone rang. Lollie groaned and pulled a pillow over her head.

I reached for the phone. "Yes?"

"Vlad? Peckinpah here."

The Old Man! Pullman had told him I was taking a leave of absence.

"Good, um, good morning, Mr. Peckinpah."

"Yes. Enjoying your vacation? The unauthorized one?"

"Yes. I had one coming."

"I suppose so. But you should have checked with me."

"Yeah. Well, I'm nearly thirty-five, I'm old enough to know when I need a vacation. Perhaps this will do for you as an excuse to dump me for that Pullman kid. . . ."

"Horescu!"

I'd *never* spoken to the Old Man like that. "I'm sorry—"

"Look we've got four new systems coming in. Helluva time for you to take off. On top of that you're giving me this malarkey about dumping you. I'll tell you when we don't want you anymore, Vlad. I don't pussyfoot around."

"Of course. A bit of a hangover. Makes me

irrational. Sorry."

"Damn right. You can have a vacation. For *one month*." He hung up.

It was good that Peckinpah wasn't going to discard me for Pullman. But I'd made a fool of myself in finding that out.

I glanced at Lollie. She'd gone back to sleep. She moaned and scratched her leg, pouting. Why had she come to see me? Fear of the prowler? Maybe she was lonely. With Lollie, it would be startling if true. I hoped that was it, and realizing that's what I hoped, I frowned. Hoping for emotion from Lollie was, for me, unnatural. But new feelings were bursting up inside me like mountain springs after a sudden snow-melt.

Could I be falling in love with my *wife*?

Absurd.

The business with Dracula and Lucifer might be making me feel small. They were inhuman in actuality, I had only played at being inhuman. But in comparing myself with Lucifer, my blood froze. I wanted to run from it all, and lose myself in being human, in human emotions.

Perhaps that was it. I touched Lollie's back. I shivered. I smiled.

The phone rang. "Again?" I muttered irritably. It was to be a morning of phone calls. Phones, it occurred to me as I reached to answer, are strikingly inhuman aspects of the human environment. "Horescu."

"Hello, Vlad."

"Doctor! Uh, good to hear from you."

"You don't sound sincere."

"Sorry I missed the session last night. I forgot."

"After all these years?"

"Yes." Don't let him make you feel guilty. "Had

64

a lot on my mind. In fact I won't be in for the sessions for quite a while. I have an early appointment now, so goodby." I hung up with a profound sense of satisfaction.

There came a light, cold touch on my shoulder. I turned and smiled. Lollie smiled icily back.

"Get me my bag," she said.

I got up, stretched, went to the dresser. The used syringe, needle still attached, leaned against the pearl bag in which she kept her supply. The needle caught the morning light, glinted. I removed the needle, found a fresh one, fixed in onto the syringe, and brought her the bag of morphine. She took out her lighter, tied off, and prepared the solution. I looked away as she shot up. The sight of a needle sinking into skin still sickens me. Perhaps its resemblance to a fang . . .

"MMM-hmmm." she said. "Um-huh, uh-huh, uh-huh." She began to sing, "That's the way— uh-huh! uh-huh!—I *like* it, yeah *that's* the way— uh-huh, uh-huh—I *like* it—" An old Disco tune.

She put away her works, and I got into bed with her.

She nodded her pallid, sunken face, her lips quivered, I sank into her arms. She didn't lie as still, this time, as she normally did. There was feeling in her caresses.

And afterwards the ennui was not pervasive. I wanted to say: I think I'm beginning to care.

But we didn't speak. She got up, dressed, waved goodbye with a ripple of her fingers over her shoulder. And was gone.

I shivered.

The phone.

I reached for it, unthinking. "Yes? What *now*?"

"It's, uh, Bill."

"Oh." I was cold inside.

"You see, I'm no hallucination. . . . Vlad?"

"I'm here. . . . I don't like it when you read my—"
I stared at the phone: It hadn't rung. I'd simply
picked it up. "The phone?"

"Damn! I forgot to make it ring!" He laughed.
"Sorry. I meant to play it all straight, too."

I hung up.

"Anyway, Vlad—"

I could still hear him. His voice sounded in my
ear, tinny and thin as if over a phone. But no
phone. "I've decided to step up some things," he
was saying. "I'm going to send my assistant over
there to brief you on Dracula."

"I don't know, uh, Bill. I'm getting drawn into
this and I don't know why I should trust you more
than Dracula."

I looked up. Jolson was at the door. He opened
his mouth to speak. I waved him away. He looked
at me curiously, shrugged, and closed the door from
the outside.

"Is he gone?"

"Yes. Hell, *Bill*. You *know* he's gone. You can
read my goddamn mind."

"Only sometimes."

"Well, that and other admissions of limitations on
your part make me nervous about letting you tell
me what-the-world-is-all-about. You might be more
ignorant than you let on. You—you aren't God, or
even the force you represent, not in person anyway.
You aren't omniscient. You need *me*, for some
reason. If you need me, you must be—"

"I need you because I want Dracula in a special
way, a containment that will preserve him. I need
you to help me set up the situation that will make
it possible to absorb and contain him. I'm not sure

66

my plan will work. Dracula has changed somewhat since I created his role. That's why I'm sending my assistant. She will help you do research."

"Assistant? I don't need any familiars—"

"She's perfectly human. Was once a member of the SSAA, as you were, but she joined the group after you left. She co-authored a book with Suzuki. A book about Dracula's life—"

"Ah. But what is she doing involved—"

He was gone.

"Bill?" No reply. "Jolson!"

He appeared shortly at the door. "Yes, Mr. Horescu?"

I had called him impulsively, out of nervousness. Lucifer—Bill—had left me unnerved. "Oh, never mind. Just bring me breakfast. We—we may have company later, by the way. Oh, is Mrs. Horescu still . . ."

"She is gone." His anomalous green eyes flickered over me, searched my face.

"Why are you looking at me that way? You look embarrassed."

"Ah, it has to do with the fact that—Well, you've been sitting there talking to yourself, sir, as if you were speaking to someone else. But you weren't on the phone. You were shouting at the air."

"At the something *in* the air, to be precise," I muttered.

He left me. I hoped I was alone.

.2.

The doorbell rang.

Jolson was reading in the study, so I answered the door.

"Vlad Horescu? I'm Margaret Holland. Please call

me Marg."

She was not what I'd expected. I had expected someone more mysterious, perhaps wearing a sari or a black robe.

She was a tall woman, attractive in simplicity, about thirty, with short brown hair and dark eyes behind silly horn-rimmed prescription sunglasses. She wore a masculine-cut gray and black double-breasted suit, white blouse and black kerchief at her throat. Her ears were pierced but she wore no earrings. Her lower lip was slightly swollen from her nervous habit of chewing it. She had a pencil behind her right ear, a notebook under her right arm, and an air of diffidence. She stood hunched a little, as if ashamed of her height.

"That's not good for your posture," I murmured, letting her in.

"I beg your pardon?"

"I said, you couldn't be much prompter." I waved her to a couch and closed the door. "I mean, you got here an hour after he called and said you'd come."

"He? You mean Bill?"

"Yes. Bill. Drink?"

"No, no thank you, no. No. Thanks anyway. No. No, I—"

"Gin all right?"

"Fine." She sighed in relief, sat primly on the couch, knees together, spiral notebook on her lap. "Your—your stained glass skylight is—very nice."

"Thanks," I said, mixing the drink. I made hers strong; she needed to relax. Her nervousness was making me restive.

"And—that painting. Chagall?"

"Yes."

I handed her the drink. She waited till I drank,

68

before sipping her own.

I wore only shorts and a lounging robe, which might be partly why she was guarded. Good, let her be on the defensive, I might learn more that way.

"What do you know about Bill?" I asked.

Her eyes lit up. "An extraordinary man! A marvelous man! And a scholar! He speaks more than a dozen languages fluently. And with such elegance. And he seems at home in idiom as well as academic language. And he's so facile! I've only worked with him a week, steadily, but we've corresponded for several months. He provided the first real leads—"

"Perhaps you had better tell me about yourself first." It was apparent that "Bill" hadn't revealed his more fabulous attributes to her.

"Oh. Forgive me. I'm a—a free-lance journalist." She said it as if it was new to her, and she was trying it on for size.

"But you haven't been at it long."

"Is it so obvious?" She laughed nervously. Her voice was deep, throaty, like an owl's. She tapped her silver-painted nails on the glass coffee table. "Just for a month now. Oh, I worked for a magazine before that. *City* magazine, before it folded. And I spent two weeks investigating the blood-killings in L.A. I've always been fascinated with—"

"Were you ever a member of the SSAA?"

"Not very actively. Only associate membership, through the mail. You were a member, too, I understand."

"What else do you understand about me?"

"Oh, you work for a computer company, an executive position. You're an orphan, or almost. Raised by some relatives of your mother, alone in the country. You were once an antiquarian. Bill maintains that you are the son—" She stopped, looked at the painting across from us with sudden interest. "I've always liked—"

"Had you *intended* to reveal you know about my father?"

She glanced at me and bobbed her eyebrows in an endearing parody of a child admitting guilt. "Frankly, no. No, I thought you'd be reluctant to divulge certain things. You'd be protective of Dracula—if I knew your, um, alleged origins." Some of the tension went out of her, she leaned back. "Oh, forgive the sunglasses, by the way. I keep them on most of the time. I have a problem with my eyes. Light extrasensitivity."

"Do you know where Dracula is, Marg? Theories?"

"No. Bill said you'd know." She leaned forward, recognized her own eagerness, smiled sheepishly, leaned back.

"I'm not sure. I want to determine the truth about—my origins. Before I contact the man who claims to be Dracula."

"Bill said you received a letter—"

"Yes. How did Bill know that?" I watched her closely.

"He said you'd told him."

"Only after he brought it up. Well, we didn't discuss it very directly, but it was obvious he knew."

"He's a remarkable man."

"Yes he is." If she was ignorant of Bill's true nature, Lucifer must want it that way. I'd play along for now. "At any rate, the letter designated a time and a place I was to meet him. December 22, at a house in which I once lived. Just north of San Jose."

"How many times have you been to see your mother, if you don't mind my ask—"

"Three or four times a year," I lied, interrupting hastily. "That's not true. Just twice, ever. She says only one thing, repeats one thing when you try to get through to her: 'Better that than *that*!' She says, 'Better that than *that*!'" I grimaced. "She looked awful. A vegetable. There was no point in visiting her."

"You don't have to explain yourself to me, Vlad." She smiled faintly.

I examined her critically. "You're not what I expected."

She shrugged, sighed with resignation. "I rarely measure up to—"

I laughed. "That's not what I meant. How did you, uh, contact Bill?"

She looked surprised that I'd asked. "Through the SSAA!"

"Oh? Yes?"

"I wrote to them. It was he who wrote back."

"Ah. Well, that's interesting." Bill had a finger in everything, it seemed. "You still interested in the L.A. blood-killings?"

"Certainly. They were never solved."

"No? Wait here." I went to the study. Jolson scarcely glanced up from the leatherbound book he'd opened on the desk. I opened the safe, found the letter from Carlton to Luther, closed the safe, and returned to the living room. She looked up expectantly. She'd emptied her glass while I was gone—fast drinking. I handed her the grimy notebook pages and went to refill her drink.

"You want me to read this, Vlad?"

"Yes," I said, cursing because I was out of seltzer.

" 'Dear Luther—' "

I whirled. "Not *aloud*, for god's sake!"

She dropped the manuscript, looking as if I'd slapped her. "Oh, um—"

"Sorry. I didn't mean to shout. Just—just read it. To yourself." I handed her a gin and tonic, and gave her back the manuscript.

She read, I paced. I watched the dust motes whirl in the shafts of painted sun from the skylight.

At long last I heard her exclaim softly. "Oh, Christ!" She looked ill. She handed me the letter. There were tears in her eyes.

I returned the letter to the safe, and came back upstairs.

She was penning furiously in her notebook, every ten seconds taking a long pull on her drink. She looked up at me, her rhinestone sunglasses washed-out opaque in the light.

"I—that letter, Vlad. It all fits in with what I found when I was there. That's either a superb forgery—"

"I knew Carlton well. That's the real thing."

"I intend to cancel my membership in the SSAA."

"I don't blame you."

"But didn't you have a sense that—the force that Carlton described, there in the background . . . The name Dracula came up, but he wasn't sure. But it *felt* like Dracula."

"I know what you mean." I sat down. "So you co-authored a book about Dracula?"

"About Vlad the Impaler. About Dracula, assuming they're actually one and the same. Suzuki did most of it, I just re-typed it, did a little research, cleaned up the prose here and there. It hasn't been published yet. We may have to add a new chapter."

I had a feeling that she'd been waiting for the right moment to spring something on me, something she hadn't yet told me about. I was right.

"I've made an appointment at the hospital. To see your mother. If you don't mind. We have to know how it happened to her. And Bill gave me something to—to give to her. I don't think it will hurt her—"

"You don't have to explain yourself to *me*, Marg. I'll get dressed and we'll go. Let's get it over with."

.3.

"Mr. Horescu?" She was the same pasty-faced nurse with the mongoloid slant to her eyes and collapsing ankles, her hair in a net. "Some identification, please?"

Annoyed, I fished for my wallet. "Don't you remember me from when I was here before? It was only once or twice but *I* remember *you*—"

"Procedure."

"Yeah, procedure." I gave her my wallet, pointed out my driver's license. She looked at the picture, at me, then back at the picture. "Very well." She looked at Marg disdainfully. "You'll have to sign for this young lady. Sign here, visitor's responsibility form, thank you—that line, yes." She left the visitor's check window and let us in through a heavy glass and metal door to the right.

Marg was slightly drunk; she stumbled twice as we followed the nurse down the "cheerfully" painted corridors of the ward, pastels violated by handprints and smears in dust. I looked away, haunted by traces of my cleaning fetish.

Marg stumbled again, and I had to take her arm. We passed a big electric wall-clock in a protective wire cage and I imagined the resident loonies cackling: "Clock in a cage, eh? You'll never stop time by putting it behind bars!"

We stopped at a metal door, its orange paint peeling off. At eye level was a small window of wired glass. I steeled myself and looked within. She lay on her back on a padded table. She was thinner; and I was glad the sheet covered her up to her neck. Her wrists and ankles were secured in leather restraints. The nurse unlocked the door.

"She isn't likely to get violent, Mr. Horescu, she's medicated. But just in case, do *not* let her loose and stay out of reach of her hands. She may have dirtied herself, perhaps I could have an orderly bathe her before you go in?"

"No."

"As you like." She opened the door for us and was gone.

Inside the odor was barely tolerable, šour, a smell like curdled milk, the scent of starch. There was a sink in one corner.

I approached her, irrationally walking on tiptoe. Her hair was white, streaked with black. She stared into the naked overhead bulb, mouthing something silently. She was only sixty, but her face belonged to a woman of eighty, lined and crosshatched and peeling, and her sunken eyes were spotted with glaucoma. Her hands were claws, her nails broken. Her chapped lips opened. Her mouth was toothless and dry.

"Damn it why don't they take care of her here, she's half dehydrated," I muttered, filling a paper cup at the sink. I brought it to her and forced water between her lips. She sipped tentatively, then seemed to see me and snapped her head angrily, striking the cup from my hand with her chin. I must have cried out when I leapt back, because Marg said, "I feel terrible, bringing you here. We should go."

"Uh-uh. I'm long overdue for this." But I wanted to leave. My stomach was swimming. I wanted a Valium.

"Should I?" Marg held up the syringe. "Bill gave this to me for her—"

"Yes."

She licked her lips, drew the sheet back, and shot the syringe into my mother's arm.

The old woman quivered and mewed: "Better th-that than *that*!" she lisped, and her tone was that of a little girl. "Better that than *that*!"

"Is it sodium pentathol?" I asked. "You'd have thought they'd tried that."

"No. It's something similar. It's a hypnotic aid. It'll put her in a highly suggestible state. It's called TRX. It's not approved by the AMA so the hospitals don't use it."

"Nasty, nasty!" The old woman howled, struggling, spasmodic.

"What—" I began, panic welling. "What if she dies from it? She—we could be held for—"

I stopped. Her struggle had subsided. She lay still. I touched her wrist. Her pulse was strong. She closed her eyes and began to rock her head from side to side.

"It'll take another three or four minutes," Marg said.

"I must have been crazy. Bill—as if that were his name—must have—"

Marg interrupted. "Hey. I take full responsibility. Did you know your mother when you were a kid? I mean, *ever*?"

"No." I sighed. "I was given to the Chutneys

when I was an infant. Mother went mad even before I was born. I had to be delivered by Caesarian, while she was unconscious. I'm told she—" My throat contracted. I cleared it, went on with an effort, "I'm told she wanted to miscarry me. Her name is Elizabeth. She was a poet. Wordy and effusive. I've read her stuff. She was quite clever with language. Scarcely published, but she had hope. And she was an active feminist before it became fashionable. Reading De Beauvoir and Plath and Anais Nin aloud to study-groups. She could have been a great woman. Her brother told me what little I know of her. He died some years ago. She was disowned by her parents—"

"You, you, you!" shrieked the old woman, snapping her head from side to side.

"Who?" Marg asked her softly.

"No!"

"Please tell us. Please. We're friends, Elizabeth. Just relax and tell us about it. Get it all out of you. Tell us—"

"Uh-uhhh. No sir no sir no sir no. Keep it out. He ate my soul! As a child eats a gumdrop! I was *nothing*. Keep it *out*. Better that than *that*."

"Who ate your soul?" Marg persisted.

"No."

"Please?"

"No." She opened her eyes.

Marg took my photocopy of the painting of Vlad the Impaler, and held it up before the old woman. "Is this—"

She skinned her lips back and snarled, her eyes grew wide and she jerked her head back. "You, you, you!"

"You see?" Marg said softly, "We have his picture. We know all about it. We want to hear your side—"

"It began," the old woman said like a child demurely admitting she'd been bad.

"Where did it begin?" Marg asked.

Mother closed her eyes. She whispered. "He told me he'd read one of my poems. Poem. Oh, *I* was *thrilled*, oh, yes." She made a creaking sound, it — may have been laughter.

"*Who* told you this?"

"The stumpy man. The changeling with breath like iron. The man with the big teeth and hot hands and sparks between his lips. He, to me, came. Redolence of ancient pages in his hair. Oh, he was an aristocrat. An aristocrat. He was compact as a pistol. Wore a robe woven of the vicissitudes of others. He wore a crown carved of the bones of his enemies. I did not know him for what he was, but I knew him—you, you, you—I knew him for *might*! He is like a tropical place where day ends quickly and night falls like a guillotine. He comes like that, like the fall of a blade, a sudden darkness. Harken, he comes through the jungle! *The son of the devil*! Damn him, kill him, make him dead!"

Her shout echoed in the small room. I stood with my back to the cold concrete wall. My eyes were locked on her withered lips.

She went on: "They dance to him in tropical places! The juju man drinks blood, and pours it on the ground for him. They leave gifts to the stumpy man outside their huts at night, so their children will wake up with strength the next morning. He walks near and sleep is troubled; sleep is his realm. He strides there, he walks through our sleeping like a groundskeeper through a cemetery—"

"Who is he?" Marg asked.

"Many names."

"What name did you know him by."

"Vladislav."

I started. Marg looked at me in triumph. She asked, "How did he come to you, Elizabeth?"

"Who pries the lid from little Lizzie?" the old woman croaked.

"Friends. *His* enemies." Marg took a deep breath and repeated softly, patiently, "How did he come to you, Lizzie?"

"The door! Why, the front door! A stately young man, my mother said. He was not young. He was very old. And he came to me three times, and he was polite, but he frightened me, his big dark eyes were magnetic. I felt he had something planned for me. On the fourth night, my parents were not home. That was the night he told me who he was. He was very agitated, excited, his cheeks flushed. His! Whole body! Was! Standing out! With blood! As if he were about to burst with too much of it. I knew, when he smiled—he had never before shown me so many teeth, so many!—that it was not his own blood overfilling him. He was excited, and he wanted me. He flung off his cloak, and I could see his need bulging, I could see the outline of his black thing writhing like a separate animal, trying to escape his clothing! It *moved*, of its own will, snapping like an angry snake! And *he* backed me into a corner. I said, 'My parents will come home soon!' 'Good!' he said,' I will be thirsty by then! I will kill them for you, and you will be free of them,' he said. I dragged a chair between us. He brushed it aside and it broke against the far wall. Splintered. He was too strong for five men to fight. He tore my dress. It was with one swipe of his hand that he tore it; his hands had no claws and yet they were claws. And the cloth was rent and the skin of my breasts—Oh, then, then I had small breasts soft

78

as new snow. And he cut one of them with his groping nails! He saw the blood and opened his red, red mouth to laugh, and I had to look away, and there we were in the living room and the light from the chandelier caught his teeth and he moved again and in a second my dress was three torn shreds and my slip was gone and I was nude! And he was nude! And I had not seen him take his clothes off, but he was nude! He was swollen all over, the veins standing out on his corded neck and rippling arms—I was afraid to look lower. And his skin glowed red and I had to touch it, my hands went to it like iron to a magnet and they were almost burned! Almost burned! Fever-hot his flesh! Like a man dying in the tropics, where they leave lambs outside their huts that he may drink; I spat on his chest and it sizzled there! He laughed. I remember it was a laugh like a bad child makes as it pulls the legs off a cricket. He grasped both my thighs in his hands and his hands were more leather and tighter than these restraints, my friends, my friends! And his body—" She hesitated, sobbed, and shook her head.

"Please, Lizzie," Marg said softly. "We're almost done. A little more."

Mother took a great gasp and held her breath in, squeezed her eyes shut, as if about to scream. She opened her mouth, her eyes wide, and the words tumbled out almost too fast to hear: "He was hate made flesh. I recoiled as from a tarantula. But even before he fell upon me I could feel his body. Even with my eyes shut I could see him, feel him gathering his whole body up for one locomotive thrust and I thought that when that organ entered me his whole body would follow in after it, he would climb into my womb and expand me from inside like a balloon. He would tear me in half. I had no recourse but to ease it as much as possible: I threw my arms around him, smelled the stolen blood rotting on his lips, and shuddered as that thing, that monstrous thing throbbed and writhed against my belly. Oh, I tell you it *moved of itself*! His organ moved like an animal tied to his waist, struggling, nosing into me like an angry tomcat, damp, hard as iron yet it whiplashed like a moray eel, a thing apart and part of him: his familiar. His penis. He did *it*: flexed! Effortlessly, he lifted me up and spread my legs and I whimpered: 'Will you bite me?' And, laughing, he said, 'No! I would not make you dead, Elizabeth Horescu, it is your living I desire!' But I begged him, 'Bite me! Better that you bite me with those wolf-teeth than enter me with that thing! Better to die! It will eat me alive from the inside! Better that than *that*!' And he laughed shortly, and snarled, and slammed me back against the wall, and I was stunned, and he lifted me off my feet, and his eyes glazed and he went into a kind of trance and the thing thrust and I glimpsed it just as it entered, the two cold golden eyes on its snout, and it was big as a cat and like a cat trapped in my womb it ripped me inside, it was big as a strong man's arm, a monstrous thing, a tumor alive unto itself, spitting semen like venom. *It—*"

The old woman began to quake. Then she lay still, gasping.

I checked her pulse. I was saddened: she was not dead.

.4.

"Why did you want her to be dead?" Marg asked, with no flavor of accusation. We sat in the study, in

80

the two chairs by the dead fireplace.

The room was dim and cold. I said as much.

"Cold? I'm too hot, myself. I saw the thermostat in the hall set on eighty-five. You don't want to answer my question?" Marg persisted.

"I wanted her dead out of pity and shame. Simple as that."

"I understand. Forgive me, Vlad, but I can't help wondering what attributes, other than your predilection for morbidity, Dracula passed on to you."

"What?"

"Suppose he has many children. And he knows where all of them are. Suppose he has power over them. Some kind of, um, hypnotic power, because of blood-relation and because of his extraordinary nature—and he calls them and makes them—"

The idea disgusted me. I said so as acidly as possible.

"Okay, Vlad. I guess that was a bit of fantasy. Maybe the old woman's story was a fantasy, a paranoid vision to explain in her own mind the rape by some ordinary brute—"

I snorted. "After her reaction to the picture? And the concurrence of detail? No. You *know* it was no fantasy."

"I guess I do. It made me sick: I didn't want to believe it . . . but we should have recorded her story. I was drunk, sort of. It didn't occur to me."

"I'll transcribe it from memory later. I remember every word, exactly. My memory's like that."

"Am I getting on your nerves?"

I hesitated. "I *do* want to be alone. Nothing personal . . . but we shall get together again. After we've had time to think. I'm not sure we learned anything of use today."

"Bill told me to interview the woman because we'd learn Dracula's weakness that way. 'His eyes glazed and he went into a kind of trance.' Remember that?"

"Yes. You know," I said thoughtfully, "sometimes I have the feeling you're discussing all this sort of haphazardly, noncommitally, as if you're saying what I'd expect you to say, so I don't question your role in all this." I stared at her. The accusation didn't make her angry. But that didn't make me less suspicious. It should have made her at least defensive. "I mean, you claim to be a journalist, but you didn't suggest you reveal to the world Carlton's letter to Luther. Any other journalist would have."

Too reasonably, she said, "But I'm really an inexperienced journalist. And anyway, I didn't think we had enough evidence, the kind the world would accept, proving the letter wasn't a forgery or Carlton lying." She smiled, and adjusted her dark glasses.

"Huh," I grunted. "I'll accept that for now." I rose, extended my hand. Her handclasp in mine was too warm, too soft. I shook it quickly and let go. "Oh, what's Bill's phone number, by the way?" I asked nonchalantly. "I need to call him about something, and he never gave me a means to get in touch with him."

She sighed. "I'm afraid I don't have it. Just a post office box number, which you can have if you like. *He* always contacted *me*; he insisted on doing it that way."

"I see. Never mind. Why don't you and I get together next Wednesday? And, listen, till then, if you want to do some research, look through the library newspaper files for articles about unexplained violent killings. Especially in the North Bay area prior to three months ago. I have a theory."

"Good. Until then, Vlad."

She turned to go, then turned back. "One thing. There's another woman. A woman who suffered from—from a sort of similar-style rape, like your mother. Bill knows. Next Wednesday, can we go to see her?"

I shrugged. "We'll go."

She left.

I was alone with my books. One of them was open on the desk. A nineteenth-century grimoire. Jolson must have left it there.

A pen was laid horizontally underneath a paragraph, as if to emphasize it:

. . . and sucche Unholy Elementts, Ye Elements taking Manly form, the Old Priest sayeth These walk for Purpose unkenned by Manne, stille mayest Manne and His Kinde know that sucche Spirit is not bereft Purpose, and He Seest alle Menne to be His toolles to that Unknown Ende, and so it is wise for Goode Menne to make Heede and Warning. . . .

FOUR

.1.

"Doctor Sol Boem?"

"Yes?"

"This is Vladimir Horescu. I've been on this phone for two hours trying to get someone to give me a straight answer, Doctor. I was referred to you. I want to have my mother transferred to the care of my private physician, and no one seems to—"

"Your mother's name?"

"Elizabeth Horescu."

"And your father?"

"He's dead."

"Hold please." There was a click; I waited for what seemed an interminable limbo in the static-filled land of Hold, until: "Mr. Horescu? Here is the file. I see, ah . . . oh."

"Oh?"

"You haven't been told."

"Told what?"

"When did you last see your mother?"

"Last Wednesday."

"I see. I'm sorry. She died on Friday. I cannot understand why you weren't notified. The police said they would notify you."

"I've been—out of touch. The police? Why were they involved?"

"According to this file—and this is not my wing

of the hospital, so I had no direct involvement in the investigation—according to this, she was murdered. Rather, ah, grisly. Her head separated from her body. Someone got into the hospital during the night. The window had been forced and—Now how did they break down that door without alerting—"

I hung up.

.2.

"And you think Dracula did it?" Marg asked. She shifted in her seat.

"Dracula," I said heavily. "Or Bill, or someone who wants me to think it's Dracula or Bill or some unknown agency of—"

"Not *Bill*! Bill, you said? How could Mr. Lupis have any connection with—"

"He told you his name was Lupis?"

"Yes, he—"

I laughed, wildly but briefly. I glanced nervously at the front window. I'd seen something move outside it, out of the corner of my eye. I decided I'd seen the light shifting about the setting sun, the sunset bleeding all over the horizon. Two terse red-tinged clouds above the blazing, sinking sun were like crimson eyes glaring from the edge of the world. The eyes of oncoming darkness. The sun slipped over the edge. It was abruptly darker, the sea went black—but the two clouds remained, still red.

I looked back at Marg. She wore a kelly-green suit, the pantlegs flaring with a silk slit. And ludicrous sunglasses. "My mother's dead," I said as evenly as I could. "I wish I had some mourning in me. But it was hard for me to feel that she was my mother. Mrs. Chutney was my adopted mother—not that *she* gave a damn either." I stood up, went to the bar, reached for the gin—and withdrew my hand, empty. Drinking was becoming a reflex. Dangerous. The desire for drink suppressed, my body tried to order me (with a tightening in the temples and an aching ball of fuzz behind the eyes) to get a Valium.

No, I decided. No Valium, no drinks.

"What's changing me?" I wondered aloud.

"Mr. Bill Lupis," said Jolson, coming into the room, "is on the phone."

"Oh!" Marg sat up straight, pleased and agitated. "Let me talk to him when you're done."

Jolson brought me the phone, plugged it in. "Yes?" I said.

"Sorry about your mother." Bill's voice.

"Why did you bother with the phone?"

"Did I forget to make it ring again?"

"No. But why—"

"Because you need all the day-to-day normality you can get. You're about to lose most of it. Better stock up."

"Did you kill my mother?"

"You sound strangely emotionless."

"I didn't know her."

"And you don't want to feel responsible."

"You can take your analysis and stick it in your—"

"Vlad, I didn't kill your mother, but you're caught up in the game whether you like it or not. You're already on the board, you've got to play it through. So cooperate. Now listen: There is a woman I want you to interview. 3227 California Street. You got that?"

"Yeah, I guess so."

"Don't be sullen, it's infantile. The woman's name is Belle. You pay her two hundred dollars, she'll talk about anything you like. She's a hooker. Semiretired, had a nervous breakdown after the rape. Best let Marg ask most of the questions. Listen to details of her encounter with Dracula. And—"

"Why the hell don't you interview her yourself?" My voice was breaking. I cleared my throat, cleared the hysteria from my brain, and said: "Are you going to pay me for doing your legwork?"

He laughed.

I glanced at Marg. I frowned. Her head tilted back, she gazed unblinking into the final glare of the setting sun, sans sunglasses. Hadn't she told me her eyes were extrasensitive to light? And why did she look so entranced?

"Never mind *her*," Bill cut in. *Pay no attention to the little man behind the curtain, said the Wizard of Oz.* "Vlad, I've been trying to corner Dracula for decades. Every time I—my corporeal extension—comes near him, he *knows* it, and defends himself. Sometimes when I question people he's been in contact with, he shudders, and feels me near. Because, like an invisible web, some of his influence lingers over those people; a spider feels the lightest step on the farthest skein of his web. Forewarned is forearmed. So it has to be you and Marg, doing the legwork." He hung up without amenities.

Marg started, and looked as if she'd just awakened. She stretched, blinked, hastily put on her sunglasses, and looked up attentively. "Could I talk to him—Oh, you've hung up? What'd he say?"

I stared at her. "Are you sure you didn't hear what he said? Weren't you listening in, somehow? He wasn't really talking over the phone, you know."

She looked faintly annoyed, tilting her head and crooking her mouth. "You're getting more enigmatic by the hour."

"I don't think I should trust you," I said, half to myself. "Ah! Now you look *insulted*. But that's an act, I suspect. I shouldn't trust you, but I'm afraid to let you out of my sight, where I can't know what you're up to."

Marg stood, stamped a foot with restrained fury, and reached for her purse.

"You anticipated me," I said, pulling my coat on. "I was just about to suggest we go—"

"I'm going nowhere with you," she said airily, "I don't care to inflict my untrustworthy person upon you." She strode to the door.

"I'm sorry," I said, as sincerely as I could manage. Whatever Marg was, she was an ally; I was afraid to face Dracula alone. "I'm full of crap sometimes, Marg."

She stopped, facing the door, her back to me.

I put a hand on her shoulder. She shrugged it off, saying, "We've got business, then."

I smiled in relief. Marg wouldn't expect me to make love to her. I disliked the feel of most women in intimacy. Like Marg, most women were too alive and warm to interest me. I experienced a flush of nostalgia for Lollie's marble placidity. *I'll always feel that way about women*, I thought, following Marg out the door. *I'll always want Lollie as cold, as heartless as possible.*

I was wrong.

.3.

Belle counted the money twice. "Okay, man." She was slender above the waist, but her crossed legs were heavy; her small, pointed breasts pressed proudly out through her red satin blouse. Below navy-blue gaucho pants her leather knee-boots tapped impatiently. Her cheeks were high and round, her chin very pointed and her plucked eyebrows slanted upwards; she looked pixieish. A suspicious pixie as she looked from me to Marg, shrugged, and nodded toward the door of her flat's bedroom. "Both of you? At once or one at a time or is one of you going to watch?"

"We just want to talk," I said, smiling. I sat on the couch, the opposite side from Marg.

"Oh." Belle nodded, a faint smirk crossed her glossed lips. "Well, did you bring me something you want me to read or are we going to make up fantasies—"

"Neither," I said hastily. "This is just an interview. Not for publication. A private investigation of some events, um, things that have been going on locally."

"For TV?" Her wide brown eyes widened even farther. She smiled, and patted her streaked, shoulder-length brown hair into place.

"Yes," Marg lied glibly, "For television. Preliminary research for a TV show. Like *Helter-Skelter*, rather."

"Oh." She got up, went to a lace-draped table, plucked a Silva Thin from an ornate sterling box. She seemed suddenly nervous. "*Helter-Skelter*, huh? You must mean the rape. The cops put you onto me. Huh. The guy that raped me makes Charles Manson look like Billy Graham, man. Huh." She lit the cigarette, one fluid motion so practiced it needed no thought, like a bird's motion in preening its feathers. The toe of one boot idly traced the weave of the Turkish rug. It was an old apartment,

crowded with antiques and carved ivory, relics of
Chinatown. She turned her back on us, supported
one elbow with a cupped palm as she smoked, and
said, "I don't like to talk about it. Not for the
money you gave me. I'll give it back. I almost lost
my—Well, after it happened it took me a looooong
time tuh get my shit tugethuh. Y'know?"

"There may be a TV contract, later," Marg
suggested softly.

I groaned inwardly.

Belle swiveled to face us, jarring ashes from her
cigarette to drift toward the floor. "Sonuvabitch!"
She caught the ashes in a glass ashtray before they
hit the rug. She reminded me of me: it was a very
clean apartment. I wondered if she'd been so
neurotically meticulous before the rape. Smiling
vacantly, she replaced the ashtray. "TV! Okay,
then. But I ain't gonna tell it to you more than
once till there's a camera here, after I've signed a
contract. Talking about it gives me these dreams,
see. Well, I don't even smoke opium anymore
because when it gets stony I dream it and—You
understand? I mean, I'm not trying to be coy with
you."

"I understand," I said.

Marg smiled and nodded encouragingly.

Belle stubbed out her cigarette, lit another, and
went to the window, where she stood in silhouette
against the streetlight's glare. "It was on the coast,"
she began. "A resort by Big Sur. Real pretty place,
but expensive. Me an' a girlfriend, we had a deal
worked out with the night manager, you know? We
got free room and he got a percentage, and he set
us up with some tricks. I was coming home with
this trick one night, some dumbshit Navy guy on
leave, a real dumb jock this guy was, and I step

90

inside the door, and I hear a—" She hesitated, crushed the half-finished cigarette, lit another and sat down across from us. She looked from Marg to me, searching our eyes, as if seeking some kind of support. She lowered her voice to a half-whisper: "A horrible sound. In the dark, in that room. Just thinking about it, ick-*ick*. Um, I saw a shape in the darkness, the shape of a man, all darkness, a hump of a man squatting on the floor, and I could barely make out another shape on the floor, and that was—Well, it turned out to be my roommate. Dead. But this man—his eyes—I could see his eyes clearly. Big black eyes. Eyes like some animal got, all wet and the pupils too big, you know? And I couldn't see anything else about him, except some kinda outline. It was dark—"

She got up so suddenly it startled me, and made a quick circuit of the room, turning on three lamps and the overhead light. She sat down, glanced around, bit her lip, and went on, "And the guy with me—I guess the dumb jerk didn't see him, cause in he goes, turns on the lamplight, and my throat it was, like, frozen, I couldn't talk, I felt paralyzed, and the Navy trick, he switched on that light and turned around"—she smoked furiously, a gray-black cloud collected about her face, speaking through this netherworld-wreathing too rapidly, as if she wanted to get the story out and done—"and the man crouching on the floor, he jumped the Navy boy, and it happened fast, like this rapist guy is some martial arts expert or some lion-man combo, because in two seconds the guy on the floor had jumped my trick and then the trick was lying on his face, with his head half ripped off his neck—held on by just a sliver of—of skin and—and he—his arm was torn off—and the stranger he turned

91

to me, and I started yelling, alluvasudden my strength come back to me, see, and I see Lana, and her throat's ripped open—not just holes in it, but gouged open, and blood is splashed on the wall and he—" She stiffened, and stared aghast into space. She got up stiffly, went to the bathroom. There was a bubbling, coughing sound, the sound of the toilet flushing.

"Are you okay, Belle?" Marg called.

From the next room: "Yeah, yeah, just wait a goddamn minute, I just puked my guts out and just wait, I'll be back. Shit. You'll get it all. Jeez."

We heard her gargling, the clank of a bottle on porcelain, and the bathroom door opened. Belle went to the kitchen, walking so quickly she might have been pursued. She returned with a glass. "Tequila anybody?"

"No, thanks," I said. Marg shook her head.

Belle sipped, grunted, and settled into the wicker armchair. "Okay. Okay now." She closed her eyes.

"Take your time," Marg said.

"He was naked," Belle said huskily. "But I don't think he was naked a moment before. It was like, um, like his clothes just *dissolved*." She lit a cigarette, picked up her drink; there was cigarette in one shaky hand, drink in the other, and tears in her eyes. "I been raped before. I hate it. But it wasn't so bad as this. But he had some weird ability with his—his, well, if you can even call it a dick. Whatever it was. Maybe it was some kind of fancy dildo. It was like one of those hypnotic cobras, the way it moved. Black and shiny like a new tire. And too big. And I almost thought it—Oh, hell, never mind. I was half-crazy from seeing my friend dead, and that Navy guy ripped up: I mighta imagined anything.

"But I didn't imagine it when he jumped on me. I—it was like being hit by a car. Bang! I bounced against the wall and slid to the floor. My pants were gone—like that! He ripped 'em like they were tissue. And there was blood coming from his mouth—it wasn't *his* blood—and it dripped on me." She choked, and sipped the drink, and slumped. Her eyes glazed, her features froze, as if she'd gone into a state of psychic shock. She told the rest mechanically, with no emotion in her voice. "It ripped me up inside, and some part of me wanted it. I didn't enjoy it. But it was like he—I could feel him wanting me to want it, and I felt like, like if I *didn't* want it, he'd kill me. And I knew he could kill me easily. So I—did. I made myself want it. He was so hard and—his skin over his whole body felt like a hard-on, but he wasn't really muscular, though there was no fat on him. He was so—like he had a fever! But no sweat on him, just this steamy feeling to his skin, and no fat on him, but it was like he was all swollen up. And his mouth—like the poster for that movie about the killer shark, remember?—and he stunk, but breathing what he—his odor—it was like, like the kind of stink opium has, and you learn to like opium's stink, and I started feeling numb and stoned. Which was a relief because he made me feel like I was sitting on a four-inch-thick wooddrill. It was ugly as a kitten falling in a garbage disposal. I couldn't have no sex with tricks or my man for, oh, six months after that. It kinda spoiled it for me, with men anyway, for good in fact. But he was inside me, and I went black from pain and—god, what a relief it was—out like a light. And when I woke up my crotch was bloody and I was all bruised and my tits were torn and between the legs I felt like I'd just had sextuplets and the Navy guy was all bloody and Lana was all bloody and the floor was all sticky with the stuff—But you *know*, don't you, that most of Lana's blood was *missing*? The cops don't talk about *that* much; in fact they covered the whole thing up because the local resort owners bribed 'em because they didn't want a maniac-loose-scare to screw up the tourist trade. Just like that blood-killer stuff in L.A. last year. Made big headlines and then died out and some court order stopped the books that they were gonna write about it and the lid clamped on the whole thing. I mean, this guy is *still out there*. . . . I know what he is. I know what he is. I don't know who he is, but I know *what* he is. That's why I stuck that piece of broken chair through Lana's heart. Don't put that part on TV, okay? But I know what he is."

She was talking about my father.

.4.

"Okay," I said irritably, "what is it that's 'on the increase' that you think's so important, Marg?"

"Rapes have increased, that's what. I mean, astronomically: this city's got the rest of the country beat by a good five times. Dracula is responsible. But I don't think Dracula did them all personally, though in a sense it was him. That was him, in person, with Belle, but so many of the others—"

"Hey. Shut up, just for a few minutes. Please. I need to think."

A few weeks after the talk with Belle, we were sitting in my car, parked near the beach, just south of a housing project scabbing the cliffs over the sea, five miles north of Chutney House.

94

Dracula's house.

It was dusk, and the sun glowered from behind a lampshade of thin cloud and thick pollution, poised like one of Lucifer's eyes on the horizon. The sea was indigo, tinted golden-red near the impending sunset's ground zero. The sea air smelled of petroleum, garbage, and brine. I opened the window, enjoying the chill of the growing easterly breeze. The dimmer it got, the less substantial the world seemed. The beach was going from yellow to cocoa, the asphalt parking lot about us was deepening its blue to black. The cars tracing the cliff road one by one switched on their headlights. Night was coming, the corporeality that accompanied day fled before it. I reached out, felt the dashboard of my Mercedes for the comforting solidity of hardwood and glass. "Well, tell me about the rape statistics, if you feel—"

"I feel just plain—weird," Marg remarked softly. "It's been two weeks since we interviewed Belle and I keep hearing her."

"Yeah. But these rape statistics are part of that data you gave me about the ritual murders, right? We already went over that."

"No, I—"

"Good, because I don't think there's any solid reason to tie the ritual murders to Dracula. I don't think he's been in this area that long, and the central-northern coast of California's been notorious for that series of slayings for, oh, almost a decade now. Bodies washed up without their heads, with the same insignia carved into each one's chest. They never found all of Manson's family, so maybe they're behind it. Or La Vey and the Satanists. The blood missing from the bodies could have been sucked out by natural sea parasites—"

"But what about the markings? That sign. You admitted it was close to the Dracula signet."

"Maybe someone's doing it in his name. He'd be crazy to advertise it like that."

"He *is* crazy, remember? I think attracting attention is a part of his operating modus. It's like Carlton said, it's almost as important that he gets good coverage as it is that he doesn't get caught."

I reached into the back seat for the six-pack of beer. "Damn it, the beer's warm. Well, I'm going to have one—you want one?"

"Sure."

I snapped the tabs off two cans and gave her one. The beer was tepid but bracing. It reminded me of the surf, forty yards below us. I wanted to swim. "I wish the water was cleaner," I said wistfully.

"You don't want to think about all this," Marg observed.

"You're right," I admitted. "I'm playing for time, I guess. It's December twenty-second and I have to go up there. Bill said he'd contact me, tell me what to do, but he hasn't. I'm going in there blind. I guess I've been trying to think of some reason to send the cops instead."

"The cops have been there already, remember?"

"Sure. But that was because of a complaint about his house, the Parks Department complained it was revolting or something. The cops went near the house, gagged, and went back to the station to call *me* and complain. They didn't even knock on the front door. I hardly call that a police investigation. 'We've had some complaints about some property that we understand you own, Mr. Horescu,' they said. I don't think they even went up on the porch! You know, I remodeled that house last year. Completely redid it. I was going to give it to Lollie.

96

She was scared to live out here, though, all alone—and after I'd spent fifteen thousand on it, too. It was like a new house. Even the grounds were cleaned up, trimmed, and Dracula moved in and now the place is like a rotting stump. 'Gangrenous,' the cop called it."

" 'And like a mantle he carries with him despoilment, his feet char the earth over which he walks. Like the Barbarian scourging the Holy Roman Empire. Where he goes men think things that will shame them at Sabbath confession, and where he goes children lament in their sleep and flowers wither at his touch—' "

"What the hell are you quoting?"

"A nineteenth century mystical text. I thought you were an antiquarian."

"I don't recall that one."

"A very limited edition. It's about the coming of the Antichrist, 'who drinketh blood as it were wine.' "

"Do you think—"

"Dracula? The Antichrist? I doubt it. But Bill said something about Dracula's hunger sucking the life from things around him. Things rotting at his touch, unless he's had his fill. . ."

"And when he touches *me*?"

"You don't have to go there tonight, Vlad."

"I—actually, I want to. Is that perverse?"

She shrugged. "He's your father."

"Perhaps . . . yes . . . I don't know."

We sat in silence. The darkness gathered around the car like a fall of black snow.

I started the car, switched on the headlights. The headlight beams pierced the gloom, made two vague circles on the surf, the nighted water in those circles like the wet over-large pupils of his black eyes.

"I'm coming soon," I murmured.

"What?"

I started. Who had I been speaking to? I opened the car door, set the beer can on the asphalt, closed the door, shivering in the influx of wind. "Let's get on with it," I said. "What *about* the rape statistics?"

"Well, it just demonstrates that rape's been mounting steadily for years, all over the country. Psychiatrists claim it's the result of massive alienation due to unemployment, general frustration at the sterility of American life. Men feel ineffectual, they take it out on women. It's not sexual so much as a sadistic outlet for their own feelings of inadequacy."

"I'll buy that."

"Yes. But the rate in the San Francisco area grew at a steady pace till two years ago. Then it quadrupled around here. It continued to rise, then dropped, radically and unexpectedly, three months ago. When Dracula left the area. I checked—New Orleans experienced an unprecedented surge of rapes, starting about three months ago. It got so bad the city police declared a strict curfew. A few weeks back the rape-rate suddenly went back up to epidemic proportions in *this* area, and dropped in New Orleans."

"I see. Follows his pattern of movements. But he can't be doing all that alone, unless he has the power to be in many places at once."

"I don't think it's him directly. But it's his influence, Vlad. He's exerting a psychic influence to effect an outpour of rape. I don't know why. Maybe it just happens when Dracula's near, like radiation poisoning happens when fallout's near."

He's near us now, I thought. The open spaces of

98

the beach seemed to teem with lethal possibilities. What was I afraid of here? I looked around. Empty parking lot, empty beach. Horizon banded by layers of purpling clouds.

I put the car into gear, backed up, and fled that place.

.5.

It was the only house for more than a mile in either direction.

I rather expected Marg to insist that she be permitted to enter the house with me. I had the speech prepared. *No,* I would say, *you've got to remain outside. Not gallantry on my part, I need to have someone ready, at the wheel of the car, in case I have to leave in a hurry.*

But she didn't ask to go along. I felt let down.

We sat in the parked car, lights and engine cut, same distance from the house as we had been from the beach. The house was about three hundred yards below the main road, screened by a wooded hill rising to the left; a gravel road led to the house's driveway.

The house was changed.

It had been a bulky, solid house, with two wings at right angles to one another, making a V, the point of which faced the sea. The house occupied a rocky knoll eighty feet above the log-strewn strand. The grounds contained a eucalyptus tree, an elm, a stand of birches, a single ancient maple. In the courtyard between the circular driveway and the house were a large goldfish pond and what had been a rose garden. A low wooden fence, constructed less than a year before, had girded the half-acre atop the hill. The three-story house had been dilapidated and empty when I'd begun remodeling; we'd shored it up, painted it bright blue, repaneled every room, installed new appliances. I had had the roof reshingled, the chimney rebuilt, and new plumbing put in. On completion it had been a real estate broker's dream.

Now the fence was tumbled, only a few snags remained. The chimney was entirely gone. The very architecture seemed to have been altered. The house was almost pyramidal now, the outer walls (blue paint blistered away, exposing the old red paint beneath like open sores) leaning in to one another, making a wedge, roof unnaturally steep. The shuttered windows were overgrown with moss thick as asphalt—a moss that looked like a century's growth; it had somehow grown there in weeks.

The maple was gone; a blasted stump remained. The other trees were there, but they looked strange. The leaves! It was December, yet they had all their leaves. Looking closer, I wondered if it was foliage covering the trees so densely. Too thick for leaves. A fungus?

I could barely make out the tangles of thorn overgrowing the garden.

"The house shows no lights," Marg remarked huskily.

"The windows are shuttered."

"I feel so—"

"So do I. Drunk sort of, yes? Numb. Melting inside."

"Yes. Same sensation. The house is emitting something."

I opened the door, stepped outside the car, I hardly felt the brisk wind off the sea. The house filled my senses.

"Where you going?" Marg asked dreamily.

"You're early."

I laughed.

And like a somnambulant, I walked home to the house where I'd grown up.

I climbed the stone steps leading from the sunken drive to the courtyard. I swallowed hard to keep from gagging. The stench was a stomach-churning mix of ammonia, carrion, and menstruum. The steps were coated with a slick lichen. I tripped on the top step and fell to my knees, my palms striking the gray-white rug of lichen. I drew back, hastily wiping my hands on my shirt. The stuff was viscous, and the viscosity was caustic—my skin tingled and burned. The trees flanking the house were consumed with the same ruglike growth, their upper expansions like huge lumps of solidified smoke. I made my way through the choked garden, following a thin trail that was just a silver trace in the moonlight. I glanced at the sky—the blue-black clouds were ragged and moved with unnatural speed, intermittently exposing the moon. I had to tear at vines repeatedly to free myself. I looked once at the goldfish pond, and then quickly away.

The liquid in the pond was not water. It looked like crude oil. Yet something lived in it, something pale and long as a man, with shiny white eyes as big as silver dollars. It submerged as I glanced at it.

But I didn't experience fear. I was overwhelmed by an extraordinary keenness of the senses, every scent and sound divisible into infinite permutations; every film of light and darkness shifting and intermixing in a recurrent pattern as hypnotic as it was sinister. Out of the corners of my eyes I glimpsed a flurry, a black fluttering. When I turned to look, nothing moved but the coarse foliage in the wind.

As I stepped onto the slate-stone porch, I noticed

a thin effluvium leaking from cracks between segments of wooden siding in the house's peeling outer walls. The house seemed to sweat this plasm, the source of the reek.

I took a deep breath to calm myself. (The stench was not so bad now, and I almost enjoyed it, the cloying musk underlying it; it was like the redolence of cooking meat.) I knocked at the shiny wooden door. Though I struck hard, my knock sounded faint as if heard through a heavy fog. I waited. A minute passed, and another.

As I waited, I turned periodically, trying to catch off-guard the fluttering things ranging the corners of my vision. It must have been an optical illusion; there was nothing there.

Yet someone moved through the bushes bordering the siding. They were tall bushes with thick vines intricately tangled, showing fluted blue-white blooms the texture of dead skin. Through this scraggly cloud a human silhouette drifted, without disturbing the vines, as if passing through water. A gray shuffling shape, bent and ragged. It was coming toward me.

The heady atmosphere began to lose ground to common sense: Fear reasserted itself.

The door opened. Murky red light spilled onto the porch.

There stood a man, tall and gaunt, with stringy blond hair and a carefully clipped goatee. His blue eyes were deeply sunken, and his pug nose was so upturned as to resemble that of a skull. He grimaced, and looked me up and down. His sneer expressed disapproval. Surely, *this* could not be—

"Go away!" said the stranger in an impatient whine. "You're too early. He's not ready. Go away till—"

"Do not give orders to my son," came a voice from inside the house, a voice carrying unchallengeable command.

I pushed past the stranger at the door and stepped inside.

I viewed with some surprise the man at the head of the stairs.

The young man beside me (clad in dusty dungarees, loose gray sweatshirt and worn tennis shoes) shut the door behind. "Your son, Lord?" he asked. His tone was unctuous.

The man on the stairs gestured briskly to a side door. The young man in the goatee bowed and said, "Forgive me, Prince." He left the room.

The man at the head of the stairs gazed at me for a full minute. I tensed under the unblinking appraisal of his wet black eyes.

He came down the stairs, moving with youthful, carefree spring.

He approached me, and I looked at him more closely. My fear receded.

He was perhaps five foot five, his curly brown hair swept back neatly from his sloping forehead; the hair looked to be sprayed and styled, cut just above the collar. His white suit was strikingly cut for his blocky frame, and the blue tie and sporty blue shirt, with cuff links of gold dollar signs, gave him a casual, personable flair, like a talk-show host. He wore black patent-leather shoes below neatly creased white trousers. His wide face was ruddy, his lips slightly puffy, the jaw almost prognathous. His lips were firmly closed, but his smile was lighthearted. And his cheeks dimpled. "Good to see you, Son," he said, extending a warm handclasp. I shook hands with him; his skin was feverish, his grip was vise-strong. I had a brief glimpse of his teeth: they were sharp and plentiful, to be sure, but there were no fangs. In point of fact there was nothing terribly exotic or phantasmic about him. Not even an earring. His nose was blocky, his eyebrows nearly grown together—but ugliness alone is not exotic. He could have passed as any business executive. And I was six inches taller.

I was disappointed. "Father?"

He laughed. "There's incredulity in your voice, Vlad. I'm your father, yes. I'm sorry I've been out of touch. As you will discover, my duties are many. I'm afraid the house is in a terrible state. Some of my associates are not as clean as they could be. We'll see what can be done. When the shipment comes in, things will perk up and look—cleaner." His accent was audible but faint; for the most part he used English like any West Coast American. He put an arm around my shoulders and locked his eyes onto mine. The pupils of his eyes resembled the nighted pool of oil in the garden.

The numb, reckless mood returned to me. His voice changed, slightly. It became more even, modulated lower, with an edge of command to it. A hypnotist's tone. "Son, now, we're going to be friends as well as business associates. Yes? And we're going to trust one another. Yes?"

"Yes." I heard myself say.

"Well, then. Tell me. You came with someone, did you not?"

"Yes."

"It's a woman." He nodded reflectively. "Yes. A woman with an odd aura about her. Something keeps me from discovering everything she is. What name did she give you?"

"Margaret Holland."

"Why is she in the car?"

104

"I—she—we weren't sure you were at home. I came early, so I thought she should wait till I made sure, seeing as it was cold, so we wouldn't both have to go out in the cold . . ." The lie came with difficulty.

"I see. I'll take your word on that, Son. Since you wouldn't *lie* to me. We just *agreed* there'd be no lying. Now that she knows someone is home, she'll come up here to see us, won't she, Son?"

"I—I'd have to signal her."

"I believe, by the way," his tone was gently chiding, "I told you to come alone. But it has been some time. Perhaps you forgot. Well, go and signal your friend now. Tell her to *come here.*"

I didn't like the way he said, 'Come here'; it brought me out of what must have been a trance. I looked around, pretending to be interested in the house's interior. Rummaging in my mind for a dodge, I said, "As a matter of fact, it's late. She might, uh—" I murmured vaguely. The antechamber contained the first flight of stairs, a mahogany bench, a framed and yellowed Turner print of a ship in a golden fog, and two closed doors, one to either side. The door on the right had recently had a padlock bolted to it. That door led to the basement. The door to the left had swallowed the brusque young man. The room was lit by a single red light bulb in one of the chandelier's sockets.

"Tell her to come here, *Son*," said Dracula.

"Say, uh, why the red light?" I asked innocently.

"Yes, yes. The light. My eyes are delicate. That's the sort of light used in photo darkrooms. White lights hurt my eyes. But see here *Son*—" He tightened the grip on my shoulders and leaned nearer, an intimation of threat in his smile.

"I'll get her," I said, resigned.

105

He took his hard, heavy arm from my shoulders. I went to the door and opened it. I could barely see Marg's outline, in the car down the road . I waved and beckoned. She started the car, its lights lanced out, and she drove toward us. I tried to conceive of a signal that Dracula wouldn't notice, something that would warn her away. But why? Why protect her?

"Son," Dracula stood beside me in the open doorway, "What's bothering you?"

"There is—some question about our family history. How our status as father and son came about. You have much to fill me in on, Dracula." I added the *Dracula* as an experiment. He didn't react to it.

"You won't be disappointed, Son," he said, clasping my arm with his hand. An electric thrill went through me, and the moon, emerging from its veil of cloud, cast a fairy light on Dracula's features. He seemed, then, like a jolly, middle-aged wizard, perhaps a sideshow astrologer; and within me, another fortification of caution relaxed. He turned and his eyes caught mine, and images flooded my mind: I saw myself as a child; I saw him lifting me up in his strong arms and whirling me around, laughing. And I saw us together, our faces joyful, riding a black chariot drawn by winged horses over lofty mountaintops. I saw us standing together over a fallen deer, an arrow in the deer's chest, a bow in my hand, my father's hand on my shoulder, his approving smile. I glowed with satisfaction. None of it had happened. But I didn't care: Father approved of me. But I seemed to hear Belle's voice again: *I know what he is . . .*

Marg was coming up the path toward us, her face hidden in the house's shadow.

I felt giddy, exhilarated. I trembled, and clasped

my father's hand. He laughed a rich, booming laugh. He nodded, and spoke portentously: "Son, we're going to scour the earth for women lovely enough for the two of us, lovely enough for the grandest of father-and-son teams! We're going to walk the face of the sun without burning our feet! We're going to have a helluva good time."

I seemed to hear a brass band playing stirring military music.

"Son, we're going to fish for mermaids and keep the beast of Loch Ness as our pet."

I seemed to see people cheering us in a tickertape parade.

"Son, we're going to be king and prince of the Mardi Gras and we'll haunt the smoky dens of Paris."

Marg's voice snapped me out of the trance.

"Your father has learned from Madison Avenue," Marg said, stepping boldly onto the porch. She wasn't wearing her sunglasses.

The trance was gone, but I believed everything he'd said. I addressed Marg giddily: "Hey, this is my father. He—he asked to meet you, and I think we made a mistake about him, and everything's fine," I bubbled, only half-aware of what I said, "So come on in, my friends are welcome in my father's house, and, and—"

"I'd like to," said Marg somberly. "But I really can't stay. It was nice meeting you, sir, and I hope we meet again."

Their eyes met. Dracula's expression changed. A veil slipped from his face as clouds pass from the moon; the light of his personality played across his features. His red lips moved restively in their compression, the skin over his cheeks and jaws tightened. His hand clenched my biceps. I heard a ripping, and saw his fingers had penetrated the cloth of my coat. Pain raced into my shoulder. "Who are you?" Dracula hissed at Marg.

His face held fury, and he released me, took a step closer to her. They were less than a yard apart. Still she stood her ground. Her eyes did not stray from his, and her expression was casual.

Confusion replaced fury in his features. He hesitated, swaying, his hands clasping and unclasping; he cocked his head, bent toward her as if drinking in her scent. She stood unmoved.

Childlike delight replaced confusion; he beamed at her. "Gaea!" he whispered. He reached a trembling hand to her. She took his big, pawlike hand between her small ones, and put her lips to his wrist.

Dracula quivered.

Then she dropped his hand. "I *wish* I could stay," she said lightly. She turned on her heel and walked down the steps.

Dracula stared after her. I heard him say, to himself: "I can hardly believe it. The centuries melt. . ." He began to walk after her. Too late.

The car started, the headlights flared toward us, the light flooded Dracula; he swore, stopped, averting his eyes.

She backed up, turned, and drove away at great speed.

"Thanks a *lot*, Marg." I murmured.

My father returned, a peculiar smile quirking his lips. He motioned toward the interior. I preceded him. He closed the door behind us. The giddiness was gone from me. Fear returned. I turned to face him—before I was entirely turned around, he struck me.

I must have flown two yards through the air. I

hit the wall, and he came to stand over me. I was sitting, trembling, on the floor, blinking stupidly, my legs splayed. My chest felt as if it'd been slammed by a two-by-four. He'd only backhanded me, but if he'd struck me in the head, the blow would have broken my neck.

Casually, like a man retrieving a coat, he reached down and plucked me up by the collar, dragged me to my feet. I steadied myself, and he let me go.

He took a cigarette from his coat pocket, lit it, and inhaled. He stretched luxuriously, and blew the smoke in my face. "You're not going to lie to me anymore, are you son?" He asked mildly. Now that some of his pretense was gone, his accent was thicker.

"No. I won't lie," I replied, in all sincerity.

"Tell me what you know about that woman."

He smoked, blew smoke rings, and figure eights in smoke, as I replied.

Shamelessly, I spilled it all. I gave him her phone number, a description of what I knew about her activities, and her connection with Bill. I described Bill, but I stopped short of admitting to having dealt with him myself.

"Bill?" Dracula looked at me in astonishment. "*Bill?*" he laughed, showing a red tongue, and he frightened me again. But it was a fear with a thrill riding it.

In spite of what he was, and what was to happen between us, let no man say that I did not love my father.

Dracula turned and glared a silent summons at the door through which his disheveled young servant had gone.

The blond young man pushed through the door, bowing. "My King?"

"Yes, Toltin." Dracula beckoned. Toltin came nearer. Dracula ground out his cigarette on Toltin's forehead. The man hardly winced. "Toltin, our old friend is near. That One. But he won't chase us away this time. With the coming of the new shipment we will have the capacity to fight. No one defeats That One, of course. But we can stalemate him. Oh, Toltin—" Abruptly, Dracula was speaking like a suburban homemaker telling a racy anecdote to a neighbor: "That One no longer calls himself *Lucifer*. Do you know what name That One is going by *now*?" He began to laugh. "He's ha-haa!—he's going by—ah!—his new name is fashionably provincial. He calls himself *Bill*!" Dracula looked at Toltin expectantly.

Toltin dutifully laughed, shaking his head and screwing up his face in contrived mirth.

"Bill? Ho-hoo!"

"Yes." Dracula glanced at Toltin. Toltin stopped laughing. Dracula turned to me. "Tell him, Vlad, about this Margaret. As *she* calls herself."

My heart felt like a lump of lead.

But I had already taken the left-hand fork. I wanted something from Dracula, and I couldn't find it without cooperating. And anyway, I rationalized, he could find Margaret if he really wanted to, without my help. Lucifer would protect her (though he apparently had done nothing for me).

I repeated the information. Toltin took it down on a notepad.

"I want that woman, Toltin," said Dracula. "Bring her here tomorrow. Spare nothing to do so. She may be working closely with 'Bill.' His emanations are about her, so he at least has had contact with her recently. Be prepared. I want her. She is the Principle."

Toltin raised his eyebrows.

Dracula nodded. "She will be my wife. I looked at her and knew. Perhaps she will come willingly, when you explain the honor that will be hers. And make sure she understands that she will not be violated; all love-making between us will be voluntary. If, on explaining this, she insists on reticence, then bring her by force." Now he sounded like a business executive again, casually reeling off a memo. "However, the man who so much as bruises her will be fed to the revenants. A piece at a time, his senses stimulated with an alertness drug so that he misses none of the pain."

"I understand."

"Now, take my son to the third chamber outside the chapel, and give him whatever preliminary initiation you have time for. Clothe him properly: he is the son of Dracula. There will be another rite—the sight of this woman has emptied me—see: thus." He laid his hand on the wallpaper, and where he touched, it disintegrated, leaving a hand-print of crumbling concavity.

Toltin nodded. "Will one be enough, my king?"

"Yes. A female. Do not drug her. Now take my son with you, but treat him with respect, and do not punish him for slowness in assimilating the initiatory rites. Only Dracula may punish his own son."

Dracula smiled icily at me and wearily climbed the steps.

I gazed after him. I wanted to go with him. And I reviled myself. Why had Lucifer allowed me to come unprotected?

"Come on, then," grumbled Toltin. I followed him through the left-hand door.

We strode the long outer hallway, lit by the same

dull red lights. Ahead, something shambled along the narrow way. As we approached it, Toltin called out a stern monosyllable, and the thing moved to one side in deference, mewling faintly to itself. It had been a man. Now it was almost a mummy, mouth empty but for two long, uneven teeth. It had white stones for eyes. Its stench—I held my breath till we were well past it.

"A revenant, one of your father's primal servants," Toltin explained offhandedly.

We stopped at a door marked with an arcane sign, and Toltin took a ring of keys from his pocket, unlocked the door; we stepped within. On one side of the red-lit room were gray metal gym lockers, and wooden benches scarred with initials. On the other, racks of clothing.

"This was a storeroom, when I was a boy," I remarked.

Toltin grunted. He opened a locker for me. "Be kind enough to undress," he said with forced civility. "Put your clothes in here. Tell me your shirt and trouser size." I told him. "You may keep your shoes and socks."

I undressed, feeling increasingly vulnerable.

Toltin dressed me in a frogged doublet with silk trim, velvet breaches, flaring but tied at the ankle, and an ornately woven jacket, overflowing with gold braid. The clothing was ancient, but in fine shape, and smelled faintly of musk. It fit too tightly in some places, too loosely in others. Toltin donned a loose black robe, and he slung a silver cross on a chain round his neck.

He inspected me and nodded, "Now, you almost look like his son. He wore those clothes himself, almost five centuries ago."

I noticed, then, the bloodstain on my right sleeve.

As we climbed the steps to the attic, I asked, "Toltin, how many people live here?"

"A score of his congregation. His servants. Also, a half dozen revenants, and a few prisoners."

"Toltin, if things deteriorate rapidly around my father when he is hungry, then how can he climb the stairs without their crumbling beneath him, and how can he touch me without melting my skin?"

Toltin answered me as he answered all my questions—with ill-concealed contempt for my ignorance. "Why, he can *control* the hunger, of course! He is the King! It would be many days of deprivation before he lost control of the hunger, and that would mean his death."

"And, Toltin, why is it that you wear a crucifix?"

"Idiot!" Toltin snarled, stopping and turning on me so suddenly I almost ran into him from behind.

Conscious already that some hierarchy, a power-structure, regimented the inhabitants of Chutney House, I was determined to uphold as high a post as possible. I slapped Toltin soundly across his face. "Never forget, I am *his son!*" I hissed, in a fair imitation of my father's tone of command.

Toltin looked unconvinced; but rubbing his cheek ruefully, he nodded his acquiescence and mumbled, "Forgive me." His eyes glinted. Perhaps he was afraid I would take his place there; he had been, apparently, Dracula's favorite.

"I wear a cross," Toltin said, "because King Vlad commands it. He isn't afraid of the cross. Oh, damn the films! And damn their gross misinformation! What do *you* know of my Lord? He is the living avatar of all lust! He is the son of the Dragon! He *can* walk by day, but he finds light distasteful, as does any man of true power. He does not 'become a bat'—that would be demeaning! But the lower animals are indeed his servants. He is not a heroin-addicted movie actor, and he is not a walking corpse. *He is a god.*"

He turned and led the way up the stairs.

We came to the top floor, ascended the ladder to the attic. In the attic: red and black. Sheer silken curtains of red and black draped the walls (since it was a triangular room, the attic just beneath the room, the walls and ceiling were one). The alternating strips of red and black created a tunnel of concentric rings set off by the glow of oil lamps close to the wall, inside the gauze.

Seated on the bare floor to either side: a score of young men and women, bedraggled fanatics in black robes. At the far end of the long, triangular chamber, someone had recently installed glass windows and doors, looking out onto a balcony.

Stalactites of gauze folds hung like fangs making the triangular window resemble a huge maw, about to snap shut on the hooked moon and the night sky. The impression of the window as a mouth suggested that the chamber itself, with its soft red-and-black walls and crimson lights, was a monstrous throat.

At the far end of the room, against the silvery window, an altar of black wood upthrust like a tongue.

On the altar was affixed a silver crucifix, above which, on a wooden plaque, was the signet of King Vlad the Impaler.

Feeling unreal but transfixed, I walked, stooped under the low ceiling, between the incurious faces of the acolytes. Their eyes were sunken, heavy-lidded and glazed; I wondered if Dracula provided them with heroin. I joined Toltin at the altar. As he had instructed me in the locker room, I stood to the left of the altar, and he to the right.

I noticed new details. Behind the gauze, just five feet to my right, two public address speakers were mounted on the wall. On the floor beneath the speakers: an amplifier and a 24-channel mixer. There was a microphone at the throat of each acolyte.

At the base of the altar, a trap door was opening. The trap fell with a clack, exposing a narrow flight of wooden stairs leading into darkness. The back stairs to the cellar. In that rectangle of darkness a woman's face surfaced. She was climbing the stairs, someone behind her forcing her upwards. She came into sight, a young woman, Latin American. Her brown eyes were slitted with rage, her fists, hand-cuffed, clenched in defiance. She wore a black robe. She ascended cautiously, jumping occasionally as she was prodded from behind. She held her head up proudly, glaring balefully at us, trying to conceal fear. She stepped clear of the trap door. Her eyes were lovely, her hair was bountiful and shiny black, her teeth white and even, her cheeks were rough and the bridge of her nose askew, as if it had been recently broken.

I admired her pluck. But I respected her as one respects a brash heroine in a movie: one never thinks seriously of climbing up from the theater seat and attempting to succor the victim on the screen. It seemed to me that all this was a macabre entertainment. The pain of it would be histrionics, and the blood of it the blood of sheep daubed by some makeup man.

But I am not excused by my illusions: I know I

should have attempted to save her. Because later, I came to believe in it: the pain was real pain, the blood was human blood. I should have done something. I recognize my responsibility, now...

But at the time...

I didn't so much as smile reassuringly at her.

A revenant followed her from the pit, and another. These two rotting gray hulks, man-shaped, flanked her, swaying like dead trees in a winter wind.

Before me, Toltin bent to close the trapdoor; behind me, the glass door opened; a cold wind admitted my father. I didn't turn, but I knew he was there. Because the revenants stiffened like dogs hearing their master's distant call; the acolytes moaned in awe and pleasure. And cold electricity tracked my spine.

I heard the door shut. Out of the corner of my eye I saw Dracula come to stand behind the altar. "Toltin!" Dracula called.

Toltin bent and opened a panel at the base of the altar. From a cabinet he withdrew a glass bell, which he set on the altar's flat top. The bell was divided into two parts by a vertical sheet of glass which could be withdrawn through a slot, removing the barrier between the two sections. In each section of the bell, something crouched. On one side, a small brown finch, fluttering nervously. On the other side, a tarantula pawed with four of its bristly legs at the glass, snapping its mandibles at the bird.

The dark woman gazed at the bell in uneasy fascination.

I applied the same gaze to her and Dracula.

Dracula had shed his business suit for a silver cuirass intaglioed with a golden bat-winged dragon.

116

His legs were encased in chain mail and leather. On his head sat a silver crown set with three oval blood-red rubies. His lips were grimly set, his great jaw thrust forward. One hand held a fistful of his purple-silk cape. King Vlad, the Impaler; Dracula, Lord of Vampires.

His posture was peremptory, regal. There was no trace of self-doubt in his face, and no exertion to his assurance as he spoke:

"I experience all pain for you!" He paused. "What have you for me?"

His hooded tribe erupted in a frenzy of howling, writhing as if afire, faces strained, eyes squeezed shut, lips frothing. They gnawed themselves, tore hair with fingers, scratched gouges in their skins, and shrieked and shrilled. This collective howling outcry was collected into the microphones and amplified mightily through the speakers. The walls of the narrow room shuddered with the repercussions of the wailing.

I had to clap my hands over my ears; the amplification was shrill and painfully loud. They didn't let up. The sound, like the screech of metal raked on glass profoundly amplified, crackled the air in vacillations of bass and alto. The revenants swayed, and tried to moan; a dry rattle escaped their lipless mouths.

The woman looked from one face to the next, confused, tears of panic starting from her eyes.

I began to believe in the reality of the situation.

"I am," Dracula thundered, his voice carrying even over the careening grind of amplified screaming, "the Lord of Pain. Not because I inflict pain, but because my experience of it is more profound than that of all humanity." He articulated clearly, dramatically, with the full resonance of a practiced evangelist, "My senses are acute; even through your shouts of exaltation, I can hear a leaf drop outside. I hear the slap of a shark's tail breaking the surface a mile at sea! I feel every line and skein of weave in my clothing and every particle of dust that strikes my cheek; I taste, individually, every corpuscle of the blood I roll on my tongue; I scent the exhalation of a clam on the beach below us, I see the minutest details of every scene set before me. And everything that I feel, see, hear, smell, or taste *hurts*! It hurts! Because I should not be! I am what should not exist! I exist in the fabric of being like a burr under a horse's saddle! I 'don't belong!' Am I *outside the law*?" Dracula asked, his voice heavy with sarcasm.

The acolytes responded liturgically: "*Do as thou wilt shall be the whole of the law*!"

Dracula continued, his voice like the first rumbles of a coming avalanche, "The world's 'authorities' maintain that I should have died five hundred years ago! The universe maintains that I should not exist! And yet I exist and it cannot prevent me! So it seeks to take away the savor of my existence, by making my senses so acute they are painful. It *hurts* to exist. But there is one thing I look upon without pain, one thing I can smell with pleasure; I hear its dripping with pleasure—" his voice was tender "—the pleasure I experience feeling it, and . . . *tasting* it—"

"BLOOOOOOD!" cried the congregation in unison.

"Blood," said Dracula, nodding. "Blood is my reward. In defiance of the universe *I exist*! I do not shirk my senses. I exult in my pain." He raised his fists over his head, brought them down with a tremendous bang on the altar. It cracked, split, and nearly fell apart. "And I do it for *you*!"

"Dracula!"

"*For you!*"

"Dracula the martyr!"

With snake-striking speed, Dracula snapped the chain from Toltin's throat and raised the crucifix for all to see. The light limned in red a miniature figure of Jesus.

The woman cried out and looked away.

The congregation fell silent. On the crucifix the tiny figure of Jesus, small argent outline of the thorn-crowned king of Jews, began to writhe. It— He—moved, was alive, and I saw His tearful, miniature eyes open, and the blood—real blood—started from the nailed hands and the slash in His heaving side.

Dracula closed his fist and, concomitant with the sudden uproar of the assemblage, the diminutive Jesus was pulped in the Impaler's fingers; the blood of Jesus Christ ran down the vampire's wrist.

When he opened his hand, nothing was there, except a spot of blood.

And then Toltin fell to his knees before the cracked altar and intoned, according to the ritual, "Lord of Pain, we entreat you, illustrate your word! We are stupid crawling things who must *see* to understand!"

Dracula spoke: "Out of my pain arises an all-consuming hunger, and out of that hunger arises a will! See my will being done!"

He reached out and casually withdrew the pane separating the oversized spider from the bird.

The spider struck, a blur of black, the bird thrashed, the struggle was brief; the tarantula's venom took hold. The bird settled into paralysis, the spider began to drink its blood.

The acolytes came forth and clustered round the altar.

119

Dracula glanced at the revenants, silently compelling them. They put their cold fingers on the robed prisoner, and that's when (shaking, weeping, helpless) I looked away. For a minute.

When I looked back, Dracula held the woman up in both his huge hands, held her outstretched over his head, as if she weighed nothing.

He had removed her clothes, and sweat gleamed on her honeydark skin. One of his hands wrapped around her neck was clamped so tightly her nerves were pinched; she was as paralyzed as the bird in the grip of the spider.

There was a hush in the room. The hoarse sighing of the woman's breathing was the only sound.

"I give you my pain!" Dracula boomed abruptly. "What do you give me in return?"

"*We give you this woman*!" shouted Toltin and the congregation.

Dracula held the woman over his head, at the end of his arms. Dracula—cape flaring from his flexed shoulders, his head thrown back, crown aglitter, eyes like eggs of onyx—lowered the woman to his opening mouth. I glimpsed fangs unsheathing from their hiding places in his jaws, four-inch fangs extending like sudden erections to penetrate her small, shivering breasts. The woman screamed, found strength, struggled in his grasp, handcuffs flashing. He drew her close. Almost cradling her over the altar, he dragged his head in a quick left-to-right sweep from her breasts to her throat, cutting deeply, laying her open like a plowed field; the red gush of her blood was explosive. Explosive, too, were the howls of appreciation from the robed mob beneath the altar, lapping at the excess that dripped and fell.

Dracula tilted the limp woman, her legs and arms

120

flailing in the air, and drank from her, spilling blood past his lips, blood thick as syrup dribbling down his jaw and trickling onto his shining breastplate. He drank her as if she were a wine skin. I thought to see a scintillation of blue-white play about both figures, vampire and victim, and I guessed that he was drinking her life-force as well as her blood. He sucked her liquid as a man might drain an orange, in seconds squeezing her nearly dry, tossing the wrinkly husk of her corpse to his mob, who dismembered her remains, fighting over scraps.

Dracula glowed with St. Anthony's fire, and swelled with stolen blood.

His face was contorted in rabid joy, as he shook his fist and screamed: "And NOW the PAIN is GONE!" He stood poised thus, fist upraised, a harsh silhouette against the triangular glass and the blue-black night-sky beyond. The curved silver of the moon, an ivory sickle, rested just behind his crown so that its points were the scything uplift of two icy horns.

Bathed in red and the argent of the moon, head thrown back, jaws and throat outlined in blood, his extruded fangs raking his lower lip, he was, I saw, at least a kind of king. No one who saw him then, no matter their righteous revulsion, could have denied that he was kingly.

"My father!" wailed a voice, that of a child. It must have been *my* voice. I fell to my knees before him.

"Toltin! Come here!" Dracula bellowed, his voice echoing brassily above the jubilant shouts of the blackrobed revelers who had begun to copulate indiscriminately in the floor's wet record of blood. The revenants had fallen to their knees and with papery tongues they lapped stray splashes of red

121

from the bare boards around the altar.

Toltin stood, trembling, wiping his mouth, his eyes baleful. "My King?"

Dracula motioned toward his cuirass. Toltin hastened to unstrap the armor and unhook the cape around Dracula's shoulders. He peeled off the king's doublet. My father stood before me, barechested. His swollen hairless chest was flushed, evenly sprayed with a kind of steam that wasn't sweat. Muscles rippled in his pectorals as he reached out with his bare hands and grasped me by the shoulders. His hands were like bands of hot iron. I tried not to cry out as they burned me. He stood me on my feet; with his right hand he drew a dagger from his belt. "You are my son, but you are mortal. The taste of blood, of stolen human blood, is unpalatable to your kind. You cannot abide the flavor of corruption, the savor of murder. You cannot know its excellence because on some level you feel guilt in drinking it. Your men of wealth ascended through the ranks with ruthlessness, and they try to conceal this corruption with ostentatious clothes and luxurious surroundings; all such is deodorant, to hide the ugly odor of their corruption. You spice your meat to hide the taste of its blood because you cannot bear to be reminded that it was once part of a living thing. Your kind, all humanity, is forever corrupting itself, yet it hasn't the taste or the fortitude for corruption. You cannot stomach your own deeds. That is why this blood, which I shall give to you, tastes foul. Oh, these here"—he indicated the adoring, red-stained faces of his worshipers—"these drink blood eagerly. But it is the act and not the taste they adore. Secretly"—he lowered his voice to a conspiratorial whisper, and winked—" they *revile* the taste of the stuff. I am a primal force," Dracula said airily, shrugging. "I can no more regret than the tiger regrets killing the fawn. But you—you'll gag, my son."

"Must I drink this cup?"

Dracula laughed. "Don't take our little rites *too* seriously, Son." His voice was almost gentle. "But yes. You will learn. A few mouthfuls will do. I will take memories from my brain, and put these memories in my blood (her blood is now mine!) and these memories will flow from me to you, and you will experience what I experienced. What I experienced on a single night, one week ago."

Then, as indifferently as a man dipping a quill into an inkwell, Dracula dipped the point of the dagger into his chest, over his heart, and ripped a jagged wound long as a man's thumb; the wound gushed blood like an impassioned oratory for vengeance.

Afraid but obedient, mesmerized but willing, I closed my lips on the pouring wound, and drank.

It burned and choked me, it tasted like the horror that had been on the dark woman's face as Dracula bit into her.

Choking, I fell back, and felt poisoned. I was weak, I staggered against the sloping wall, sank to my knees, slumped on my side, full length on the floor. I was sure I was dying. My stomach seethed. But the fire in my gut lit up my brain and by this light I began to see pictures. Call it a vision. Call it a vivid memory transferred chemically from my father to me. Call it telepathy. But I saw—as Dracula, a week before; I experienced, as if in a dream, his life for one night.

I was vaguely aware that Dracula, engorged and thirsty for more than blood, was bending to rape one of the female acolytes, who screamed in ecstasy: *Destroy me!*

And then the vision hit me full force, and I was there.

FIVE

.1.

As if I were there, invisible, feeling dust in my throat as he breathed dust, scenting the sea as did he, wincing at overloud sounds—feeling what he felt, a part of him and detached as well: A night in the life.

Of Dracula.

.2.

The cry of a gull a mile down the beach awakened him, drew him to sit upright in the open coffin. The return of his senses brought the return of the usual initial fear. Prince Vladislav shivered and nearly cried out, but caught himself. The underlings would hear. It would be disaster to let them know he had weaknesses.

Dracula climbed free, stood nude in the semi-darkness of the basement room. Stretching, he regarded the tapestry on the far wall ruefully. It was a woven image of himself, nicely crafted four centuries before. An armored Prince Vladislav rode astride a great gray stallion, bearing down on the viewer, sword uplifted. The likeness did not impart divinity—a shortcoming—but Dracula was touched by the tapestry's homely antiquity. It had been a gift from Toltin, presented the prior night. Toltin must have invested a small fortune in the purchase (or theft?) of the tapestry from the Rumanian State Museum.

The ancient artist's likeness of Kind Vlad's features was fairly accurate, and Dracula suspected that the man must have been one of his soldiers in the war against the Turks. Simpler times, blessed times.

Toltin had obsequiously offered the tapestry, apparently expecting some show of gratitude from Dracula.

Prince Vladislav demanded obedience and the respect of his inferiors; it was natural that they should offer up gifts. Gratitude on Dracula's part would be inappropriate. There was only one thing for which Dracula was grateful: cessation. The peace of nonbeing. It escaped him in sleep; his dreams were many and lurid. He found nonbeing only in the satisfaction of utter dominion, temporary peace borne on the flood of blood and rapine. Afterwards, for a time, the endless hunger was almost abated, his senses dulled, and he could, (or very nearly could) forget himself. For *that*, he could be grateful.

When it is done, Dracula thought, and I have taken all there is to take, the peace that comes is no different than the peace of utter defeat. Except that the peace of ultimate defeat lasts forever.

Again, as with every awakening, he was tempted to destroy himself.

Again, as with every advent of this temptation, the desire for oblivion was overcome by the tide rising within him, the great hunger for dominion surging up, blinding him to everything else, making him as tormented as he was invincible.

Below the tapestry, dimly seen in the red light,

the craftsman had stitched a motto (here translated from mid-European dialect): *Lord Vladislav Veovod, Son of the Dragon, In All Things Invincible.*

"In all things," Dracula murmured to himself, hot-flush of confidence returning.

The self-doubts were the work of That One, he assured himself.

He shuddered, gritting his teeth at the sound of footsteps above, in his own ears thunderously loud. His head throbbed, and the dust settling on his bare skin seemed to swarm on him like bees. But—on this awakening—the pain was, comparably, not extreme. As always, he muffled most of it under a blanket of fury, reducing the agony to an annoying background throb, like the hiss of static behind a radio transmission. His fury mounted, and he felt the beginnings of the great hunger. "Toltin!" he roared.

Toltin, who slept outside the room on a cot, stumbled sleepily into the basement and fell to his knees by the unnecessary coffin. "Lord Vladislav. Your servant—"

"Yes, yes, enough doglike cozening. Send the women to bathe me."

"Will you want—"

"No. The hunger will wait; I'll be satisfied by an infusion at eight. I've work to do, appointments to keep this evening. I'll go hunting afterward, at ten. We'll keep the prisoners for a while, the next shipment may not be here for another month, damn those greasy worms! Oh, feed a dog to the revenants. And bring me a little wine, and some water—*pure* water this time. Go!"

He struck Toltin down, to send him on his way. Getting to his feet, swaying, bowing out backwards, Toltin went.

Striding the nighted sand as if it were a carpeted hallway in his homeland castle, Dracula glanced at the guards he had posted on the two peninsulas enclosing this mile-long stretch of beach. Except for the angry-wasp buzz of cars on the highway above the bush-tangled cliffs, he was alone. He wore surplus army fatigues and boots and a broad-brimmed black hat. The sea sounded itself, his skull rang with its belling, his ears were pierced cruelly by the high-pitched whistling, the echoes of gurgling ocean denizens, the rattle of smooth pebbles dragged by surf. The lapping shoreline glittered blue with fluorescent jellyfish, the moonless sky burned with stars, smoked with occasional strips of purple cloud.

Dracula enjoyed the heft of the submachine gun carried in the crook of his right arm. He nestled it against his side, heard the faint clinking of bullets in the magazine. He cocked the carriage, listening to the metal fittings mesh. Here was a sound not painful to him. He smiled, listening to the faintly clicking perfection of the inner workings of the machine gun, like a burglar with his ear to a safe smiling as the combination lock slides into place. Starlight glinted on the blue metal barrel. Dracula nodded to himself, admiring the gun's silhouette against the dun sand, a compressed definition of violence. Such weapons were the modern world's justification for existence, Dracula decided.

He regretted having missed out on My Lai.

A gull's cry split his skull; Dracula winced. Annoyed, but faintly smiling, he snapped the sub-machine gun to firing position; shooting from the hip, he gritted his teeth at the noise of gunfire as he sprayed steel-jacketed slugs at the white blur darting overhead. The gull's shriek cut short, the gunfire racket echoed off the cliffs like distant, throaty laughter. Feathers and gull-blood spattered the sand.

A signal light from the guard on the left-hand outcropping. Dracula froze. An intruder? No, two short flashes. They'd brought the quarry. Hitchhikers, probably.

He muttered, "Release them onto the beach, Toltin. Tell them to work along the rocks toward the water. Tell them if they reach the water they will not be harmed. I'll gamble they're stupid enough to believe that." Dracula was quite alone; Toltin was a mile distant. And Dracula spoke to the misty breeze, his voice no more than a murmur. But Toltin heard: Toltin was Dracula's right hand.

Dracula loped toward the black headland of windworn rock stretching like a gnarled finger from cliffs to sea.

His subhuman eyes pierced the darkness: three-quarters of a mile to the right two nervous figures crouched beside a twenty-foot boulder. The boulder, a gray dome pitted with black, an island in the sand a few yards from the main bulk of headland, resembled the skull of a sea-giant, petrified and half-buried. His quarry moved furtively to the nearer side of the giant "skull," their backs to him. A pair of long-haired men. Young. Late teens, one of them, early twenties, the other. Infants in men's clothing. Even here, at a distance of fifty yards, he could scent their beer-stained breaths, the cigarette smoke clinging to their ski jackets. Even here, now forty-five yards distant (he ran low, a half-crouch, fluidly closing in, no hurry, no wasted movement, the gun tucked close in his armpit, his boots crunching faintly), he heard their frightened conversings through the hiss of sea and wind. "You don't think they're, shit—they weren't *serious*?" one of the young men said.

"Didn't you see 'em slug me inna head? Didn't that look *serious* to you? Doesn't this cut on my head look like it was made by somebody serious, man? They shot bullets at our feet and *laughed*. You think *that's* 'Candid Camera?' You betcher pimply ass they're serious. Fuck, people are always disappearin' along this coast. These creeps are playin' some kinda goddamn wierdshit *game* with us, man. Hey, where'd he go? That guy standing on the big rock with the lantern? Maybe we're near enough the water. They said we could go if we—"

"Oh, Christ, do you think they gave up? Already? God, I want to get—"

Dracula was twenty yards behind them. He frowned. This was much too easy. A bore. He could cut them down from here. Perhaps he should put aside the gun and chase them barehanded. No. He hefted the gun again. No, it was so rarely he had an opportunity to put the Thompson to use.

So he raised his face to the onyx void and gave out with an animal cry, a howl like that of a wolf disemboweled.

The figures skulking under the giant skull whirled, cursing. He sprayed the rockface over their heads with two short Thompson bursts, to get them running. He grinned, savoring the eager bucking of the gun in his hands, the snicker of bullets sliding neatly, one after another into the chamber, sweet metallic uniformity, and the contrasting anarchy of explosions firing slugs through the barrel. Loping easily after his prey, he reflected that the Thompson was much like a microcosmic model of the ideal army: the ideal fighting force moved men like perfectly machined gun-parts, interacting with unthinking precision to effect chaos.

At times, Dracula admired technology.

They climbed the crevices of the small rock peninsula, sobbing in panic, one of them glancing over his shoulder. Dracula smiled and waved at him.

"Maybe," puffed one of the young men, "we could ambush the guy." He spoke in a whisper, wrongly assuming that Dracula—who was twenty yards away—couldn't hear.

"He's got a machine gun, you jerk," the other replied.

They climbed an oblong boulder, topped it, and started up a crevice between two higher out-croppings. Dracula fired over their heads, bullets fanning rockdust. He chuckled as one of them squealed and covered his eyes for fear of the bullets. This loosed the boy from the rock and he slid down to Dracula's feet. He rolled onto his back like a surrendering dog, one hand thrown up over his face innocuously blocking the gunbarrel. Dracula grinned down at him. "A five-year-old girl-child of the Wallachian peasants had more pluck than you two together," said Prince Vladislav. He bent and with one hand jerked the trembling, bearded youth to his feet, shaking him so that sand flew from his back. The man—really just a boy, no more than eighteen—flailed ineffectually at Dracula's face. Said the Prince: "Permit me to assist you." Exerting the flat of his hand against the boy's chest, he swept him into the air, flung him straight up and backwards, thirty feet into the air, so that he landed bruised but unbroken on his back, on the rounded crown of the boulder from which he'd fallen. "Now, take greater care," said Dracula.

"Hellfucking Jeezus *Christ*!" shouted the boy.

Dracula listened to the sounds of their scrabbling, the older youth helping his friend back up the escarpment. The sea breathed heavily, almost panting: a strong wind had sprung up. A semitrailer whined and lanced headlight beams from the highway half a mile above.

Casually, Dracula slung the machine gun over his shoulder, adjusted the leather strap, and began to climb.

He was just twenty feet short of the ridgetop when he paused, crouching on a flat rock. Listening. He could hear their breathing. He could hear their hearts beating. One, the older, breathed more regularly; he was controlling himself, trying to think things out and remain calm. The younger was half-sobbing, breathing in irregular rasps, rattling rocks as he searched frantically for a weapon.

"Shhh," said the older, "don't make so goddamn much noise."

"What? Whudjuh say? I couldn't hear," said the other (though Dracula had heard quite clearly).

"Quiet down. Now listen, maybe you're right. The—the only way we're gonna get outta this is to get them first. Maybe if we get above the guy and, um, we can brain him with a rock before he—"

Dracula drew a well-balanced knife from the sheath at his belt and shouted, "Here's a weapon! Don't bother with rocks! Use this!" He threw it up to them.

The knife clattered.

There was a few moments of near-silence. Only the sounds of their breathing and the sea, the eager hiss of the sea. The sea wants some, too (thought Dracula). Very well. She shall eat tonight.

"The guy is really insane," the younger boy said. "But fuck, I'm gonna use the knife." A metallic

132

scraping as he retrieved the knife.

A crunch of tennis shoes displacing small stones as they moved into position on either side of the rock outcropping, one armed with the knife, the other a sharp stone. They poised, waited.

Dracula could hear their hearts beating.

He bent low at the knees, gathered himself up—and sprang straight into the air. Twenty-five feet up, his boots connected with the top of a boulder. An easy jump. Shouts of astonishment and terror from below. He looked down at them, now. "Hello, and convivial greetings," he said dryly. "Going to 'ambush' me from down there, are you?"

His black boots, the fatigues tucked in their tops, were just a few feet over their heads. Their drained faces were turned up toward him, stricken eyes wide, lips skinned back in animal frustration. Dracula sighed. He unslung the machine gun and took aim. "Tell you *what,*" he said (using a recently-learned Americanism) in a tone of sterling sincerity. "If *one* of you takes a step back, I'll kill him—and let the other go free."

"Oh, fucking— Hey, leave us *alone!*" hissed the older youth, uncomprehension in his eyes. "Why—"

"Craig . . ." the younger said, looking at his companion pleadingly. He was crying. "He said—I mean, you're older, Craig, you've lived a couple-a years more—it's only fair, uh—"

The scraggly-bearded older youth looked at the other in disgust. "You believe him? Idiot, he'll kill us no matter what—"

"Craig, *please*—" choked the younger. His voice was raspy and uneven, and Dracula winced in irritation. He sighed, seeing urine leaking spasmodically from the younger boy's trouser leg as panic loosened his bladder. Chewing a thumb the

133

boy said, "He—he gonna—mister—hey, don't—"

Dracula *expressed*.

He expressed silently, without moving. Looking at the younger boy, Dracula laid a part of his rapacious soul, his self-image, his *will* upon the boy. Dracula silently commanded.

Something broke in the youth. Terror mixed with rage. He flung himself on his companion, squealing, "Godammit, Craig, godamgodammit!"

Craig was stabbed three times before he fell, staring at his friend in astonishment.

The younger boy knelt by the crumpled, punctured body of the older boy. He stared with astonishment, the same sort of astonishment his friend had shown on receiving the wounds, at the bloody knife in his hand. "Goddammit . . . Craig . . ." he whispered.

Dracula was pleased with himself, with the iron-hardness at his groin.

He wished that one of his prey was female.

He sighed.

The younger man stood, one spastic hand daubing blood on his cheeks. "Hey, mister, can I go—"

Prince Vladislav the Dracul-son crouched, thrust his long arm straight down, driving the barrel of the submachine gun between the teenager's teeth, down his throat. He pulled the trigger and his arm bucked with the repercussion as the slugs tore the boy's head into surprisingly neat chunks of red and gray and yellow. The corpse staggered, went limp, fell back onto the other.

Dracula took a deep breath. For a few moments there was peace, and the distant sullen hum of cars was not so painfully loud, and the whines and clatters of the sea were not so piercing.

Then a sense of ennui, drugged weariness, stole over him. The tang of brine in the air was too sharp, the roar of the sea too loud. He felt the sandstone stuff of the boulder crumble beneath his fingers, and rust appeared where he gripped the barrel of the gun. The hunger bit his world. It was time.

He leapt from the boulder down into the crevice. Kneeling by the founting corpse, he began to lap.

Long minutes later, the taste of corruption still rich on his tongue, the scent of ultimate thievery ripe in his nostrils, he stood, wiping blood from his lips, and stretched.

The older boy, the one stabbed by his friend, twitched and exhaled raggedly. He was still alive. All the better for the sacrifice to the Undine.

Slinging his submachine gun over his shoulder, he wrapped blunt fingers around one ankle of each victim, and began to drag them unceremoniously down the narrow way between the boulders.

After many twists and turns and a stretch of open sand, he reached the surfside and dropped them, bent to trace certain signs in the wet sand. He stood up and raised his arms over his head. Facing due west, he intoned: *Undine Asa Desdinova Vericus Ashtaroth Deu Dagon!*

You or I could stand at such a beach on such a night, with sacrifices at our feet and the same symbols on the sand and the same words on our lips—and nothing would come of it. But Dracula spoke the words as they were meant to be spoken, each syllable backed with the proper emotional permutation. He spoke the sacred black names with familiarity, with ease, with confidence, with assertion, and with command.

For Dracula, something came of it. Something happened.

Something rose up out of the surf and glided toward him.

It was a man-sized thing, but it was not a man. It had breasts, and female genitals, but it was not a woman. Nor was it mermaid. The cabalists had called her *Undine*.

Steaming, the sea fuming and boiling about her great legs like pillars of black marble, she stood before Dracula and shivered in the unfamiliar open atmosphere.

"Long since you tasted air," said Prince Vladislav in a language forgotten before his Wallachian castle was built.

"Long," replied the Undine in her gurgling cough.

"And long since you've tasted the wine of corruption."

"Long since man-blood," agreed the Undine, eyeing the corpses with her perfectly round, pale orbs. Eyes big as silver dollars, and twice as cold. Her lipless mouth bubbled when she spoke, the gills in place of a nose opened and closed spasmodically. Her transparent skin showed pulsings of nonhuman blood, her two sets of conical breasts bobbed. What looked like nipples on her breasts were, instead, small and hungry beaks. This had been the distressing discovery of more than one unwary, woman-hungry sailor, deliriously mistaking an Undine for a mermaid.

"This one," said Dracula, pointing to the older boy, "is still alive."

The Undine's eyes shone. Her hairless head was spangled with fluorescence.

"They are yours, so I declare by *Ashtaroth Deu Dagon*, if you pact with me, as once before. This I require of you: Let your children guard my coast. Any spies from the sea—kill them. Be at hand to kill those I designate, should I request it. But men will come in a submarine, and the prow of the submarine will bear a red 'X.' If you see this, do not destroy it, unless I bid it of you. Do these things for me, and more man-blood will be yours, some of it living and untouched."

"Yes," repled the Undine. *"Ash-Tra-Deu-Dagg*. . . Vladislav Veovod, the sea is dying, choking. Surface people poisons. My world diminishing. Son of the Devil—you bring the old world back?"

"That," said Dracula, "is precisely my long-term ambition. I wish to bring the old world back. With a few exceptions." He patted the gun at his shoulder.

Dracula turned, and walked back to the house. From behind, there came a shriek. The dying youth had awakened. He shrieked again. And then the sound of four beaked breasts feeding.

.4.

"Will we hunt tonight, Lord?" asked Toltin.

"I think so, yes." replied Dracula. "The earlier recreations were not satisfying. I had to give up most of the spoils to the Undine."

Toltin was silent. But his eyes widened.

Dracula laughed. "So, Toltin, she'll be guarding our coast. Don't venture near the water at night, unless instructed to do so. Tell the others. This month's disobedient will be fed to the Undine, for now, instead of the revenants. We'll give the revenants some animals. Understand?"

"Yes."

They stood together, Toltin a step respectfully back, on the balcony overlooking the overgrown backyard. The horizon was gray-black and ruffled

137

by a rough sea, resembling ashes; and like a luminous phoenix the moon rose from the blackened world's edge, a scythe golden-edged with copper. Dracula smiled. The twisted, fungi-choked trees flanking the grounds seemed to lean toward Dracula's balcony, supplicantly creaking in the wind, as if begging for release from his dominion. The predatory brambles grew impossibly, feverishly fast below, and as Dracula glanced down, his attention spurred them. Toltin sucked his breath in hard, seeing the vines stirring and stretching, moving out from the phosphorescent humus like an awakened nest of snakes; where Dracula's heavy gaze struck the ground, his will called forth more tokens of his entropic dominion: sumps pooled greasy-green in depressions, lilies ghastly-pale sprang up like the withered arms of deadmen thrusting restless from the ground. Skunk cabbages and mandrake; monstrous, misshapen toadstools; black, phallic plants no botanist would recognize—all spreading in fast-action like a sudden leprous malaise. Dracula chuckled, and tired of the game.

He turned and strode into the house, down the winding stairs and along a hallway, feeling his own psychic presence echo from the ectoplasm-soaked walls, resonating in the enclosed space to return to him, rebounding like a supersonic peep in the ears of a bat with a soundless, mindful whispering: Dracula, son of Draco, offspring of the Dragon, son of the devil, Vlad the Invincible, he comes, he nears—Dracula, son of Draco . . .

The blackened, waxy wood of the hallway gave up gray wisps of smoke as he passed, the red overhead lights flickered and pulsed more strongly in his wake.

At the intersection of halls, just as he reached the

corner, Dracula heard a soft whisper from the right: "*He's* coming. I can feel it. Let's go down to—"

"*Stay exactly where you are!*" Dracula shouted, smiling as he turned the corner and saw the frozen-pose into which his disciples had obediently stepped. Their eyes leaked fear. Three young women, hair shaved close to their heads; and two young men, bald except for the strip of Ares bisecting their skulls. They wore black night-robes and in trembling hands each carried a wooden bowl of stew. "Ahh," said Dracula, in his kindly grandfather mode, "are we having our supper? Very nice! I *do* worry about your health, children. It is good that you should eat. I imagine you are *very* hungry, having gone without breakfast and lunch as I decreed. Did you resent it when I punished you for the one who doubted my word—when I took away your eating privileges because of that boy?"

"No, Lord!" said the taller of the women. "There was no resentment. We understood." She was a willowy blonde with blue eyes glistening. She was, Dracula sensed, sincere. He decided not to punish her.

"No resentment whatsoever? *None?*" Dracula asked the younger man at his side—about nineteen or twenty, this boy, rather unpleasantly reminiscent of the young man whose head Dracula had blown off an hour before.

"No, no, Lord. No resentment," replied the boy too firmly. He was obviously fighting an urge to retort.

Dracula smiled.

The boy shuddered.

Dracula reminded himself that he should not destroy the young man, at least not physically. No *permanent* physical damage. He was short of agents who could walk in daylight. There was a window at the end of the hall. Dracula beckoned, and the group followed him there, though their eyes strayed to their bowls and their tongues wetted lips.

Dracula opened the window with one hand. The night wind came in, sniffed them, retreated. Dracula turned to the acolytes. "Who among you whispered, *'He is coming'*?" he asked softly.

They cast their eyes down. All except the young woman who'd spoken before. She spoke up, "It was *he*, Lord." She indicated the young man in whose bearing Dracula had discerned rebelliousness.

Dracula nodded. "I knew it, of course. I recognized his voice from his whisper. I wonder why he thinks he can hide things from me. Even now, I can hear his heartbeat. I could forever stop that heartbeat with the force of my will alone, if I chose . . ." Dracula stared at the young man, whose desperate eyes traced the rug-patterns. "Perhaps this young man is stupid. Perhaps he thinks Dracula is fallible. Perhaps he thinks I can be killed by a 'wooden stake' or 'a ray of sunlight'? Perhaps he thinks I need a coffin in which to sleep with my 'native earth'?"

"No Sir," said the boy hoarsely. "I know those things are lies. I know you are infallible. I—"

"I suspect," Dracula interjected, his voice rising sharply, "that he wanted to avoid me because he hoped to avoid my wrath. He was afraid I might capriciously order him to go without his supper. His precious *supper*." Dracula's tone dripped contempt. "His supper of cooked cow's meat and vegetables. His precious! His light of de*sire*!"

The others laughed, partly in relief that Dracula's anger had chosen another target.

The young man, swallowing, looked up. He met

Dracula's gaze for a moment, then pretended to be distracted by something outside the window.

"Well," said Dracula, gently, "I won't deprive him of his *supper*. It is entirely up to *him*. I—oh, not *I!*—would not deprive him of his burnt *cowflesh*."

Dracula looked at the young man, and with his will dragged the boy's eyes upward.

"Are you hungry?" Dracula asked tonelessly.

The acolyte hesitated. Dracula could hear his stomach growling.

The young man shook his head. "No, Lord." He turned toward the window. His hand wavering, he reached out and dumped the contents of the bowl out the window. There came an answering rustle in the grass below as one of Dracula's pets slithered to lick the discarded meat.

Dracula nodded. "Good lad. But the sad thing is, you did that to avoid punishment. Not because you wanted to sacrifice to please your Lord."

Tears came to the acolyte's eyes. His hands fisted.

"Bring me a rope," said Dracula to Toltin.

Toltin ran to the storage room, returned moments later. Dracula tied the rope to the young acolyte's neck. With a slight jerk of his hand he imparted such force to the tether that the man was snapped off his feet and flung whimpering facedown on the floor. "You others," Dracula said, "may go and finish your supper in the common room."

They hastily departed.

Dracula, alone with the remaining acolyte who remained on his belly, said, "What is your name?"

"Dwight. Dwight Cooper, Lord."

Dracula bent over Cooper and whispered. "Last

night you were present at the rite. Your voice was one of the most enthusiastic. You expressed giddy joy at the proceedings. Did you experience pleasure in the orgy? Yes?"

"Yes," said Dwight Cooper miserably.

"So you see, when you adore Dracula, you are rewarded. You have Dracula's love when you deserve it. When you are cheerfully obedient, when you are adoring to the very marrow of your bones. Dracula can give you pleasure, Dracula can give you pain. When you love Dracula, when you gladly sacrifice for him, he gives pleasure. When you resist Dracula . . ." With that, Dracula slung his end of the rope over his shoulder and began to stride carelessly down the hall, dragging the gasping acolyte behind as if he were a pet on a leash. The boy had to scramble to keep from being strangled.

"Isn't there something you want to sing to me?" Dracula suggested, doing a few capricious Wallachian dance steps, dragging Cooper along.

Dwight Cooper began to chant: "Ave Draco, Ave Draco's Son, Ave Vladislav Veovod Invincible Prince of Thirst. Hail the—" he coughed, choking, clawing at the rope reddening his neck, forcing it to give him just enough slack so he could scarcely breathe and weakly rasp: "Ave Draco—" Cough. "Ave Draco's Son, Ave Vladislav Veovod Invincible—" Cough. "Invinci—" Cough. "Invincible Prince of—of Thirst—" Choking, clawing, face contorted, sneezing at the dust from the rug raised in his face as he was dragged on his belly.

The Prince went on a short inspection of his makeshift castle, descending to the subbasement to toss rabbits into the revenant pit. And here he dangled the choking boy over the revenants, as if about to lower him to their desiccated mouths. He tired of this and reeled Cooper back in, towed him flailing and weeping thump-thump-thump up and down flights of stairs, from one room to the next, encouraging laughter from onlookers as he dragged him through the common room.

Forty-five minutes of this extinguished the flicker of rebellion in Dwight Cooper's eyes. Dracula bent over him and asked softly, compellingly, "Whom do you love above all others?"

"Lord Vladislav, the Son of the Dragon."

"Would you die for me? Would you starve if I ordered it on a whim? Would you tear out your eyes if I requested it?"

"Yes, yes, yes, yes, yes, yes . . . Yes."

"Then"—yawning, Dracula loosed the rope from Cooper's purpling throat—"go to the common room and eat."

.5.

The submarine, a renovated U-boat, was dimly visible on the casting waves. On its prow a red X. A yellow rubber raft bobbed incongruously in the surf. One of the three men in the raft got out and stood, up to his hips in sea, pulling the raft to the beach. Two luminous eyes approached them from the right. Something slick and phosphorescent reared from the water. One of the men swore and drew his gun.

"Ashtaroth Undine Dagon!" Dracula shouted. "See the red sign on the prow? Do not destroy these unless I command it."

The Undine slid back into the water.

Coming onto the beach, the three Brazilians viewed Dracula with new respect.

"The gun would not have killed her," said Dracula.

"No?" A Portuguese accent. He was a large-eyed South American, his broad lips accented with a pencil-thin mustache, his nose flattened close to his cheeks by an old accident. He wore a black and gray uniform, the sleeves excessively gold-braided. "I believe you. What was that thing. That—what?—monster-woman?"

"Do not speak the word *monster* in my presence," said Dracula icily. "Unless you employ it correctly. Literally and originally it meant *omen*. The one in the sea is simply one of my sentries. As for what she is *specifically* ... You would not wish me to pry into *your* military secrets, eh, my friend?" Dracula smiled thinly. The man grinned and looked Dracula up and down with slightly raised brows. Dracula wore the regalia of his kingly office. His cape, crown, and cuirass. The cape whipped darkly in the night wind.

The other two men were somberly dressed. One wore a black knit cap and an uninsigniaed sailor's uniform. He carefully averted his eyes from Dracula, muttering under his breath. Dracula was amused: the man was *praying*!

The third man was portly, dressed in an overcoat and rubber boots, a gray rumpled suit. His white hair stood out against his dark skin, the gray creases around his eyes were intricate as spider webs.

"Please come with me, gentlemen," said Dracula politely. The older man came first, the soldier behind, one hand on his pistol. The sailor waited nervously behind.

Toltin came with a lantern to light their way. Dracula took the long way around. Avoiding the zigzag path up the cliff, he led them to a wooden stairway a quarter-mile south along the beach. The men climbed in silence, but for occasional grunts and heavy breathing.

At the gravel road atop the stairs they got into a blue rented limosine and rode silently to a hotel in Santa Cruz. There, in a rather run-down room rented for the meeting, they sat around a chrome kitchen table, a single light bulb on a fraying black wire dangling overhead.

"Both of you speak English?" Dracula asked. He sat rigidly upright, his hands on the arms of the chair. The others leaned back, away from Dracula.

"Yes, Prince Vladislav," replied the older man, Chavez, carefully.

"Then we will converse in that language. I speak Spanish, but not your dialect of Portuguese. I think there will be less confusion this way. Now. The matter of delivery. You came without—?"

"A separate ship is bringing them," Chavez interjected hastily. "She will arrive, weather permitting, tomorrow morning. We will remain here tonight, and in the morning we'll be present at your inspection of the cargo. I think you will find that all are healthy. There are several women, as well."

"You speak English with facility," said Dracula.

"Thank you," said Chavez, nodding slightly. The emissary was tense. Dracula could hear Chavez's fingers rubbing together beneath the table. He listened to the man's heartbeat, compared it to the heartbeat of the general, who sat smoking silently at the other end of the table. The general's heartbeat was more rapid than Chavez's—Chavez's heartbeat was evenly paced. So the General was excitable, would be the more dangerous for the time being. But Chavez, tense but calculating, would be more dangerous in the long run.

"First," said Dracula, "I want to know about the land."

Chavez and the general looked nervously at one another. Chavez spoke. "What you have asked for is a very difficult thing to obtain. At this time. Money is no object. A plantation, of as much as 30,000 acres, is readily accessible to you, once your part is carried out. But your own sovereignty—these are not the old times, my friend. Life is not so simple. One cannot simply declare a war against the Turks, for example, simply because they are heathens—as you once did."

Dracula smiled faintly. "I was young and did everything to please the Church. I believed in many things, then, which now mean nothing to me. The Church. Guilt. But there is one belief I have carried with me through the centuries, Chavez. I firmly believe that enough gold will buy anything. Even a nation—"

"But," Chavez coughed politely behind his hand, "Lord Vladislav, one can no longer declare a nation on the strength of arms alone. Not even through revolution. One must have allies and the felicity of one's neighbors. Shared political sympathies, economic interests in common. Endless complications. Certain parties must be placated—"

"Your country's economy is deteriorating rapidly. You have grossly overextended your investments. Brasilia is losing its fight to stay free of the jungle. You've pinned your hopes on help from the United States. The State Department assesses the policies of each foreign power which it plans to back, utilizing a computer. That computer is about to be replaced with a larger one which will contain every known fact about your land. Since the computer is programmed by liberals to support a liberal administration—one that is playing up its support for human rights—its statistical shufflings will cast your

146

policies in a dim light. You will not get the military or financial aid you desire. You will fall to the guerillas."

"The situation is not so hopeless, surely," Chavez objected. "We—"

"You're lying, my friend. My agents are plentiful in your country. All report to *me*, through a means you might have difficulty comprehending. I *know* what condition your state is in. Without help, I give it one year. With my help—and I *can* affect the determination of the computer—you will survive, and flourish. I ask for no pitiful 30,000 acres. I *demand* 40,000 square miles!"

The general leapt to his feet, shaking with the effort at containing his anger. "Uh—*40,000—*"

"Sit *down!*" snapped Dracula. He gave the general a look, the sort of look that is a statement in itself. The look said: *You have offended me; do so again and I will crush you.*

The general fell back in his chair. He lit another cigarette.

"My Lord," Chavez began, shaking his head and chuckling, "but 40,000—"

"Is the area of land I commanded in Wallachia. Ah. South of Transylvania. It was stolen from me. The Turks took it." He said the word "Turks" as an arachnaphobe would say "spider." "And others conspired with them. My cousin Stephen betrayed me. And the Boyars—I should have expected no better from them. They arranged for the assassination of my father, and they ordered my brother buried alive. So you see, gentlemen, if there is justice, then what was taken from me will be returned. Unfortunately, Wallachia is beyond my grasp, for the time being. But I could establish a parallel sort of nation. It is, you see, my *right* to

147

rule. As befits the purity of my breed. In the name of justice I will take nothing less. But it is not so much—it is less than one hundredth of your nation's land. And I do not ask for your richest grounds. In fact, the more secluded and inaccessible, the better."

"I can see that you're resolved," said Chavez thoughtfully. "I respect your determination. Perhaps we can reach an understanding—"

"Chavez!" The general interrupted in a hiss, turning toward his compatriot, "We don't have the authority." He spoke in Portuguese.

Chavez raised his hand for silence. He glanced at Dracula, lit a Balcan Sobranie, looked out the window. "I think we can come to an agreement. I will recommend that you be given, ah, *governorship* over 40,000 square miles. You could succeed to full authority in time. In a generation you could be absolute dictator. I think that—"

"The plan would be agreeable were it not for the self-satisfied smirk on your companion's face," said Dracula dryly. "It's obvious he believes—as perhaps you do—that what is promised is not necessarily delivered. Or perhaps he assumes that I will be given the land for a time—until a convenient assassination takes place. Perhaps he supposes it can be arranged for me to die at the hands of guerillas who are not really guerillas—"

The general's eyes grew round. His cheeks reddened.

Dracula went on, "Live with your delusions. I am not a man, I am a force. To try to kill me with bullets would be like attempting to strangle a wave on the sea. I would slide through your grasp and come crashing down on you. There is only one who could destroy me, but That One is forever beyond your control. If I am given the land, I will keep it. If I am not given the land, I will destroy you. Can one man fight your armies? No. But what is an army without its generals?" Lips quirked, Dracula glanced at the bristling general. "If I am betrayed in this, I will come to your land—and not all your radar or border patrols could find me, or stop me from entering if they *did* find me. I will come and kill your president and his cabinet and *all* the chiefs of your nation. I will kill them personally. I will not make them revenants or seek to control them in that way. Their subordinates would not tolerate it, there would be a troublesome uprising. No, I will simply kill and kill and kill, one president after another. You will seek to protect each leader, president and cabinet—and generals. Perhaps you will surround them constantly with hundreds of armed men and crucifixes"—Dracula laughed—"and other absurd artifices. I will pass, and the men will not know and your president will die. What do modern 'terrorists' know of terror? They are dilletantes. *Look at me.*"

Chavez doggedly looked away. The general glanced defiantly at Dracula, and shuddered as his gaze met that of the Lord of Charnel Hosts. "Do you believe me?" Dracula asked softly. "Do you *know* that what I say is true?"

The general swallowed and nodded.

Dracula permitted him to look away.

Chavez nodded as well, letting out a deep breath. "I believe you. *Without* the force of your will to influence me, Vladislav. I hear it in your voice. You're not exaggerating. Be assured: we will do our part. But you—in order to approve your, um, position, we have to know some of your plan. Please. Just how will you get to the computer?"

149

"Why should you be told how I do it? Results are more important. I ask for no remittance until I have delivered as promised. You run no risk of being cheated. It is enough for you to know that my son is very influential in the organization responsible for the computer's construction. And he will do my bidding."

"Your son? How could you, I mean, the son of a *monst—*"

The general was silenced by the back of Dracula's hand. He got to his feet, shaking his head like a dog with mites in its ears, raising a shaky hand to his split lower lip.

And he muttered an apology, in Portuguese.

"Sit," said Dracula.

The general sank into his seat.

Dracula returned to his chair. "How are the revenants performing for you?" he asked.

Chavez shook his head. "Some work very well. The guerillas are cleaned out of the mountains east of the capital. But one group rebelled against the human leader." He shrugged. "They killed him. They're wild now."

"So, indeed?" Dracula murmured. "Were they not—as I instructed—fed fresh goat's blood?"

"Yes. Apparently the man-leader tried to make them march in the daylight."

"Idiots," Dracula muttered. "The revenants are a tool, like a rifle. Your man acts as if he would expect a rifle to shoot accurately under water. Rifles cannot be shot under water; revenants cannot march during daylight. Adhere to this simple rule and control them as I have taught you and they will serve well. I will send one of my assistants down to round up the strays for you, and they will be back at work shortly. In the meantime, what of the

150

shipment you promised me? Details."

"Five healthy women, two men," said the General hoarsely. His eyes were watery and dispirited. "When we return, Lord Vladislav. Three weeks from tonight."

"Good. At that time bring with you a written agreement confirming the land grant. It need not be legalized till I provide irrefutable evidence that my task has been properly performed."

"It will be as you say, Lord Vladislav," said Chavez, bowing slightly.

.6.

San Francisco. Chinatown. One A.M.

Dracula wore uninsigniaed army fatigues beneath his trenchcoat. His mirror sunglasses made him an anomaly in the city night. Toltin, at his side, wore a black leather jacket and black knit cap.

It was a warm Saturday night, and there were still tourists and revelers walking the neon-burnished street. The club and restaurant signs were Chinese ideograms, luminously enigmatic. In the perspective of distance the severe lineaments of the street converged in a patina of bright scales: refraction of neon lights, headlights, streetlights, and metal; glints diffused through a cloudy lens of cigarette smoke, steam from manholes, and carbon monoxide.

The warm breeze mixed odors of cooked meat and garbage. The city was unnaturally vivid in Dracula's wound-sensitive eyes. Its sounds were unnaturally vivid in his ears—boys whistling, pistons gnashing, gears clashing. Too loud, too loud, loud as the unsounded inner scream of a gagged rape victim. Dracula ground his teeth. He wanted to explode in retaliatory rage and drown the city noises with the

151

screaming of his victims. He wanted to kill the source of the cacaphony and leave the city quiet as a graveyard.

But boyish laughter echoed to them from the left. Dracula turned that way, on to a tenebrous side street, where garbage was piled on the sidewalk and against the backdoors of Chinese groceries, reeking of fish and vegetables gone bad.

"What are we hunting tonight, my Lord?" Toltin asked in a whisper.

"Shut up," Dracula commanded briskly, pausing near an alleyway. "Listen . . ."

Voices from within the alley. "I don't care, I want some action," someone said. A boy's voice.

"This izuh wrong *time*, man!" said a girl. "We go looking for the Culters tonight, we go up against the cops and a fight against them ain't fair, they got guns and cars—"

"*Fuck* the cops. They come around every two weeks. Don't mean nothin' and they won't do nothin'."

"I dunno, shit, maybe she's right," came a third voice. "Um, uh—huh!—we could uh give it maybe a couple weeks, man, till the fuckers, y'know, cool off—"

Dracula motioned for Toltin to conceal himself in a doorway on the opposite side of the street. Silently and swiftly, Toltin obeyed.

Dracula began to climb the brick cornice of the four-story apartment building edging the alley. Where there were no handholds he sunk his metal-hard fingers into the mortar, by strength of limb clawing his way up. Swiftly and liquidly as a cat climbing a tree to escape a dog, Dracula was at the roof—in forty seconds.

He pulled himself over and crept along the tar,

between necklike tin chimneys, to the far edge. He looked down, into the alley.

Six teenage Chinese boys were there, arguing in harsh whispers. A girl stood to one side. Like the others, she wore a denim jacket with a dragon insignia sewn on the back.

"I didn't join this club to go bowling, man. What the fuck's it mean to be a Dragon if we don't—"

"It means you do what *I* say," said the tallest boy. "Long as I'm prez, mothuhfuckuh."

"Hey, look, we can find something to do besides cut the Culters tonight," said the girl. "We could roll some nodders, buy some skag. We could—hey! The crowd at the movie theater down on Kearney oughta be gettin' out—shit, yeah!—um, 'bout twenny minutes. Right? We could go down there and scare th' *shit* outta em, rip off some purses in all the racket—"

"Not a bad idea—"

"Is this cunt running the club, Greg? We can't *cut* nobody an' get away with it at the theater with all those people down there—"

"Yes, you can," Dracula said loudly and distinctly. The group froze. As one, their faces turned upward. "You can kill whenever you like," said Dracula, grinning, "if you have the courage. You can kill and take and rape and take *and take*."

"Who the mothuhfuckin' Jeezis jizzum-shooting bast'ud iz—"

"Am I?" Dracula laughed. "Boys, I'm one of you. The same electricity runs through us all, the same sort of charge. For me, there's more of it. In fact, I am nothing else." He stepped off the roof into midair, and dropped like a stone.

The gang scattered, yelling. Dracula dropped four stories and landed catlike on his feet, unhurt, chuckling. He straightened. The gang stared at him, bunched up at the mouth of the alley. They began to back up. Their faces were carved by a mask-maker obsessed with fear and perplexity. They had heard the stranger chuckle as he hit the ground after falling four stories—they'd seen his eyes. They turned to run.

"Toltin!" Dracula shouted.

Toltin emerged from his hiding place, drawing his submachine gun from under his cloak. He pointed it at the gang and said, "Back into the alley and turn to face God." Toltin pulled back the bolt.

The seven teenagers turned, glancing nervously over their shoulders at the gun. One of them began to edge his hand toward his jacket pocket.

"My Lord?" Toltin inquired, nodding toward the boy reaching for a pocket.

"Let him," Dracula said, shrugging.

The boy drew the gun and, dodging into a backdoor of the alley to shield himself from Toltin, fired point-blank at Dracula's chest. Twice. Dracula staggered slightly, then stepped forward and opened his coat. Two holes smoked in the green fabric. Blood spurted, for a moment, then ceased. The wounds closed. Dracula coughed, then opened his mouth and spat two blunted slugs onto the pavement.

Seven sharply intaken breaths.

One of the boys sank to his knees and wept. The boy with the gun gaped. Dracula stepped toward him, held out his hand. Shakily, the boy (a gaunt Oriental with small brown eyes and equally brown teeth) handed over the gun. "What are you going to—" Dracula crumpled the gun in his fingers as if it were tinfoil. He tossed it aside. He beckoned casually, with one finger. Numbly, the boy stepped

154

forward.

Dracula gripped him by the throat with his right hand, with his left tore his shirt. The teenager struggled weakly. Dracula drew him near—feeling the boy's life pulse between his hands—and with a sharklike motion of his head ripped wide the soft throat with his teeth. The girl threw up. One of the boys bolted; Toltin's gun chattered briefly. Dracula, drinking deeply, hardly heard Toltin's victim hit the ground.

The blood was hot, yet it cooled him inside, made him pleasantly numb, icy-hearted, cloudy with exultation; the screeching background noises of the city quieted to a faintly abrasive murmur. Dracula drank for a full three minutes. Then he straightened. His eyes drank in the looks of horror on the faces of the teenagers. They looked as if they were all about to make a run for it. Except one, a sallow-faced boy, chubby and hyperactive, delighted by the scene. Dracula wiped blood from his lips and nodded to the boy.

"Are you *Him*?" the boy asked softly, eyes deep with wonder.

"Yes."

The boy sank to his knees.

Swaying as to some inner music, half-chanting, Dracula said: "I am that which motivated you to form this gang. I am your need. And I have good news for you! Good news. You may all go free. Go free. Once I have delved the girl, she may go free also, if she survives. You may all go. This one," he indicated the drained corpse at his feet, "is dead, but he will rise. I have need for him. His wound, yes, *his wound*," Dracula took a deep breath, shuddering with glory surfeited, "his wound will heal and he will walk with me. The rest of you may watch me now. Then go thou"—he laughed—

"and do likewise." And he reached for the girl, who shrank from him, turning desperate eyes to the other, her mouth making soundless pleas.

The boy on his knees watched hungrily.

With a single motion Dracula unzipped and that which had been waiting, coiled at his thigh, filled itself with blood, the blood Dracula had just stolen, and stiffened itself as hard and curved and dark as the horn of a water buffalo. The girl screamed at the sight of it.

The boy on his knees exclaimed, "It's got eyes. And it moved. By itself!"

The thing that inhabited—usually dormant—Dracula's crotch pulsed warmth into him, which clashed deliciously with the icy chill of stolen blood freezing his spine, and his need rose to a peak of desperation. Sobbing, the girl crumpled, fell on her back, and Dracula fell heavily upon her and the predatory spirit that lived in his organ ripped through her clothes and entered her in one cobralike strike.

Dracula shivered and arched his back and into his mind raced images—

He feasted: A high hill overlooking the stony towers of Targoviste. About him the impaled shrieked and writhed on their stakes, and blackbirds took their eyes. Dracula sucked blood from raw venison.

He entered her again and again and each time it reminded him of thrusting a white-hot branding iron into cool water—the protesting shriek of metal, the hiss of steam—

He was riding full-tilt into battle at the vanguard of his army, his sword carving a red wake in the endless sea of Turkish soldiers. They fled before his red-eyed intensity. They fled shrieking: "Kaziklu

156

Bey! Kaziklu Bey!" The Impaler! The Impaler!

He impaled her again on his organ—

He was a small boy alone with a fluffy white rabbit, in the barnyard of his father's castle. He gripped the rabbit by the throat and plunged a dagger into its anus.

The girl had gone limp. Her life-energy faded, retreated into the maze of her subconscious. Dracula could not reach it, and so the enjoyment of ravaging vanished. He withdrew, and his organ slithered back into its den. He closed his fatigues, whispering to himself: "Lucifer—warming light—break the cycle, Lucifer . . ."

"My Lord?" Toltin's voice.

Dracula looked up, shouted at Toltin because he was annoyed with himself for showing weakness. "Oaf! Speak when you're spoken to!"

Toltin winced, and lowered his eyes.

Dracula glanced down, his throat tight. The girl, bleeding from the crotch, was white-faced. She stared blankly. Drool leaked from her slack lips.

Two of the boys had vomited, were leaning against the brick wall, shaking. Two others, the plump, twitching boy and a tall, thin young man fingering a dagger, were whispering excitedly together.

"The, the crowd should be getting out of the theater, now." Dracula said. He felt a bit enervated. But he marshalled his will and looked each of the four teenagers in the eyes, one boy at a time.

They nodded, and went to Kearney Street.

Dracula followed.

He and Toltin watched, from half a block away, as the four boys ran into the crowd and threw themselves upon the first women they came to.

Blood and screams and more blood.

157

In an alley, three blocks south, a teenage girl, a few feet from a corpse that was beginning to stir, sat staring into the spaces between the bricks on the wall across from her. She was trying to remember her name.

SIX
.1.

I woke. I sat up. I remembered. I was in a bedroom at Chutney house. I remembered more. And ran to the window, opened it, bent out into the sharp morning wind, and raggedly vomited.

"Feeling better now?" said someone behind me as I shut the window.

I turned, wiping vomited blood from my lips.

A young woman stood in the doorway. One of the acolytes at the ritual of the previous night. Now she wore bluejeans and a T-shirt, and her expression was placid; she looked quite ordinary. The temples beside her small blue eyes were rayed with smile-lines and her mouth was weak but friendly. She tugged at long straight black hair, smiling. Her teeth were rather yellow, but I saw no blood on them.

"You want something to eat?" she asked.

I shook my head. Yeah, she looked harmless enough. But the sight of her brought back, more fully, the night before. And I remembered how they'd butchered the dark woman. I turned to the window again and my insides tried to crawl out into the world; I coughed up bile and a little more blood.

Voices behind. The girl tapped me on the shoulder. I turned, she offered me a glass of water. I drank gratefully, washing out my mouth, spitting, sloshing water from the glass because my hands trembled. I glanced down at myself. I was in my own clothes again, somewhat rumpled, the shirt wrongly buttoned. Someone had dressed me as I slept.

"Perhaps some coffee?" I said. She nodded.

"My name's Christie," she murmured, turning away. She left the room.

I closed my eyes and waited. The room smelled musty, and my fingers were cold.

Dragging minutes later, she returned with the coffee. My vision swam as I stared into the gauzy-steamy cup of tarry black. It was a chipped blue cup, with the initials PC on the side, peeling off. It had belonged to my stepfather. I drank. It was a caustic instant coffee. "Thank you, uh, Christie," I said, feeling better though my stomach burned.

She sat down beside me. Trying to conceal a quality of urgency, she asked, "Are you really *his* son?"

"So he tells me."

She put a hand to my brow, ran it down my cheek, let it rest on my throat. Her lips parted. Her fingers touched my lips. A caress and a suggestion both.

I shook my head. "And besides, why would you want to, really? So you could say you'd made it with *his* son." Bitter laughter slipped out. I looked at the faded wallpaper, but could not quite make out the pattern. My eyes were blurred.

She left me.

I did a few quick calisthenics, trying to awaken myself, trying to find confidence. I went to the door and looked into the hallway. It was deserted, except for a moth slapping itself silly against a naked bulb. Where were they? I heard voices, laughter, the sound of a television set from downstairs. I went cautiously to the left, along the corridor. I was wary, but hoping I looked as if I had every right to go where I pleased. I found the door I sought. Opening it, I stepped inside, onto the stairs leading to the attic room. Silently cursing the creaking of the wooden stairs, I climbed.

I emerged into the attic with a curious warning sensation rippling my chest.

No one there, the room uninhabited except by the implication of violence, a bloodstain near the glass doors. Staring at a sticky brown patch, the dream came back to me—the remembering, reliving a night in Dracula's life. Nausea welled up in me. The face of the teenage boy he'd killed on the headlands was superimposed on the window. The boy pleaded with me. I blinked, he vanished. I had to sit down. I remembered it all, then, in greater detail than I have related in this text. In perversely meticulous detail. I shook my head violently and the vision began to fade.

But I remembered. The Brazilians. The girl had been a political prisoner bartered to Dracula for revenants. Why did the Brazilians want the revenants? I recalled more. Because the Brazilian hills were increasingly thronged with guerillas. The revenants terrified the rebels. Fascist terror tactics.

I searched the room.

I found a trap door hidden under a rug. It wouldn't budge. On the floor behind the altar I found an ancient pitted saber; on the blade was etched *DRAKULYA Anno Domini 1461*. The saber tingled in my hand. I used it to prise the trap door. Steps descended into darkness. The steps were of new wood, recently installed. I had grown up in this house—there should have been a fireplace chimney here. Instead, the narrow stairs wound down to—the basement? Or someplace lower?

From below, a muffled sob.

I didn't want to go down there.

But I put aside the brittle sword and drew out a book of matches. I lit the matches one by one, to light my way as I descended. The way was narrow and steep. I singed my finger when I let a match burn down too far, and I stumbled, cursing, dropping the matchbook. I steadied myself on the wall and peered into the darkness. My eyes adjusted. A patch of light showed below and to the left. The air was damper. Above, it had smelled like dust and woodshavings, here it smelled of earth and something else . . . human sweat and excrement.

I groped, my hands to the walls, feeling my way gingerly with my feet. Down. My fingers met dirt and what felt like an eight-by-eight post. So I had descended to a newly-dug chamber, *below* basement level . . . Below the basement chamber wherein my father slept, theatrically reposing in his unnecessary coffin.

The light from the left showed a heavy wooden door constructed of recently cut two-by-fours. It was padlocked shut, the Yale lock was shiny new. The light came from a small glassless window-hole at eye level. I stood on a dirt floor now. There was another door to the right, without a window-hole.

I looked through the peephole into the left-hand door. I blinked, and my eyes had to adjust to the increased light. An emergency light in a wire basket hung from an extension cord strung through a crack in the cement ceiling. Four people were slumped against a wall; in the dim light their chains glimmered like silver. The steel chain was connected to a support post in the middle of their room. I looked behind me—the hallway was newly dug, there might be tools. I found a dusty toolbox in a corner by the far door. The corner smelled strongly of urine. I bent and took a hammer and chisel from the box. As I straightened, I heard a rattle and a drawn-out scraping from the darkened door to the right. My throat constricted, I went to the door and pressed my ear against the wood. A raspy whisper from within. Someone spoke from the other side: *Now? Dry! Dry! Now!* A shriveled tongue had spoken, withered lips in a desiccated face. I couldn't see it, but I knew.

I turned away, feeling suddenly stifled, afraid the air would run out or the ceiling fall in. I was dizzy. Leaning against the wooden door, the one that leaked its comforting light, I steadied myself. I took a deep breath, and propped the chisel on the padlock. I brought down the hammer. The lock snapped, the door swung wide, someone inside exclaimed in Portuguese. I stepped inside, still holding the hammer and chisel. At the sight of me, or perhaps at the sight of my chisel, they cried out. One woman began to pray in her own language, a young man wept softly. I shook my head. "No, I'm going to free you," I said weakly. I bent to where the chain that ran through their cuffs was bracketed to the post. In three overly loud strokes it was parted. I drew the chain from their manacles and helped them to stand. They were gaunt and dirty, eyes wide and dreamy, fingers shaking. Two women, two men, all young, all dressed in dungarees and work-shirts.

"I'm sorry," I said.

In the corner of the room a trench brimmed with excrement. Several trays lay stacked beside the trench, mould growing on greasy plates. A grunting

163

moan came from behind. I turned, squinting against the light from the bulb that hung almost in my face.

At the far end of the twenty-by-thirty foot chamber a nude woman was impaled on a stake.

She was alive.

The stake was six feet high, impaling her through the anus, up into the bowels, the weight of her body forcing the stake in, slowly in. For how long? Perhaps for days. It looked as if the stake had passed through her intestines, up into her stomach. I didn't know if she was old or young. Her hair was white but it might have gone white during impalement. Her face was bloated, resembling a skin tumor with a hint of features; the slick purpled skin showed veins in pulsing red. One eye was crusted shut. The other, almost all whites, stared at me unblinking. Her mouth was caked with dried blood and phlegm. Her face had gone beyond agony. It had achieved an apotheosis of wretchedness. I heard myself say: "My father did this? My father? Yes, my father. *My* father. *Mine*." I choked, my tongue distended, my tears fell on its tip, I tasted salt—

Someone shook me violently. I shuddered and the panic passed from me. One of the Brazilians was shaking me. He murmured something, indicating the woman impaled. I nodded.

Together, moving mechanically, trying not to look at her, we lifted her off the stake and stretched her on the ground. She began to thrash, the huge rupture between her legs gouting blood. I turned away and, shaking, led the others up the stairs . . .

There was no one in the attic room. The light and clear air gave me strength. I went to the balcony and opened the French doors. It was three stories down from the balcony, but there was thick brush below it, and that exit was the prisoners' single hope for escape.

They didn't look at me, didn't thank me. Probably they thought I was one of the cultists suffering a temporary attack of remorse.

The sunlight made my eyes water; I shivered in the wind off the sea. There was no one, so far as I could see, in the backyard. One of the men had brought the twelve-foot length of chain with him. He attached it to the balustrade and let it hang over the side—that would shorten their fall. One after another, they climbed over the balcony, lowered themselves to the end of the chain and dropped into the backyard. I heard a muffled yell as the last man dropped to the ground—someone in the house had looked out a back window at the wrong time.

I turned to go down the stairs that led to the subbasement cell.

I stopped, stood swaying at the top. I very much did not want to go back down. I wished, then, that I had eaten something so that I could throw it up. I stared into the pit. To myself I said aloud: "He's *your* father."

And I descended, closing the trapdoor over my head.

As I reached the earthen floor, I heard footsteps from the attic. In the room where the political prisoners had been chained, the impaled woman lay inert in a pool of her own blood. She was dead. Relieved that I didn't have to take responsibility for her, I returned to the hallway. I heard shouts from above. And gunshots. Soon they'd come downstairs to see how their prisoners had escaped. They were in the attic: I couldn't go out that way. There was no way out from the chamber behind me. That left the right-hand door. I broke the lock with the chisel and swung wide the door. A blast of reeking air made me choke. I stepped back, took a deep breath, looked within. Darkness. A scraping, a moan of anticipation.

I backed up—afraid to turn my back on the door, and went into the room where the light hung from the extension cord. I pulled the cord from its staples, drawing the mesh-enclosed bulb out with me to the hall; it reached just halfway to the darkened doorway. But that was far enough—it threw a thin light within.

There was a pit instead of a floor. Four white faces blinked and covered their eyes in the light.

Revenants. Hollow, sunken faces, bleached and desolate. Gaping red mouths, each with just two long yellow teeth. Faces approaching me. I couldn't see their bodies, below floor level. The light showed only their heads below my knees, as if bodyless heads crawled toward me like monstrous snails. They groped to the edge of the pit, their faces a yard from my feet. I took a faltering step backwards. One of them came to the doorway's lower edge. He raised his bony hand and pointed at his mouth. *"Drink now? Dry!"*

Two things happened then. One, the trapdoor opened above, light poured down on me. Two, I recognized what was left of the face of the revenant in the pit, and a light went dark within me. Withered, mindless—but it was Carlton Caldwell.

I slammed the door in his face.

"So it's *you*," said Toltin, as if confirming a suspicion. He came down the steps with practiced haste. "You let them go."

I just stared at him.

Down the stairway after Toltin came two cultists,

a man and a woman, laughing, dragging one of the prisoners by the wrists. The man they carried between them was dead, his back ruptured by bullet-holes in three places. His feet banged the steps as they slung him downward.

Toltin opened the door to the revenant pit. The cultists, glaring accusingly at me, dragged the body around to the doorway and pitched it inward. I had a glimpse of Carlton's sunken face turning toward the body, mouth opening. I looked away.

"Why did you do it?" Toldin asked. "Your father'll be disappointed in you."

I stood very still. Then: "Are they all dead?"

"Yes. The Undine got one of them—a woman panicked and ran like a scared donkey into the surf." He smiled laconically. "A big worm—one of the pets in the yard—he got another. The kids are playing with what's left of the last."

"Playing with . . ." My voice trailed off. I could smell the revenant pit, I could hear them drinking. I moved, and mechanically climbed the steps.

.2.

Flanked by cultist guards, I waited in the anteroom, sitting on the bottom-most of the stairs on which I'd first seen Dracula. Toltin came up through a basement door. He stood looking at me with outright disapproval.

I shrugged and asked, "What did he say, Toltin?"

"He said there'd be no punishment this time, as long as you do your part at IBEX West, as long as you introduce the baffles. He is merciful."

"I am his *son*," I said, putting an edge on my voice. I stood. One of the guards put his hand on my shoulder. I shrugged it off. "Ditch your

167

Scientologically Dianetic Moonie HareKrishnic Eckankar pseudo-occultist goons here," I said, in as even a tone as I could manage," and we'll talk about IBEX, Toltin."

Toltin raised a thumb; the guards left us. He led me to a room that had once been my foster father's office. It was almost bare, except for two chairs and locked wooden cabinets. Toltin took a key from his pocket and unlocked a cabinet. He withdrew a metal box. This he unlocked with a second key. He motioned me toward a chair. I sat. He sat across from me, holding the box on his lap.

"What do you know of his project?" Toltin asked superciliously.

"I drank his memories last night. I know what it is. The baffles for the memory cells of the IBEX 790, the government contract. Foreign policy computer. He wants a positive slant for Brazil, so they can get the aid they're requesting and he can control a chunk of their land. Let me see the baffles."

Toltin hesitated, looking from me to the box. Then he took a pair of static-proof gloves from his pocket and handed them to me. I drew them on, and he handed me the box. I opened the box. Inside, set into foam rubber, were thin sheets of plastic that would fit snugly, longitudinally, in the memory-cell unit; they were minutely woven with silvery wires, which would deter the bubble-magnet impulses, distorting them so that the statistics would align in a trend opposite their present course. A very simple set up. Provided the baffles were inserted in exactly the right place—and right side up. But if they were inserted upside down? I repressed a smile. Upside down, the baffles would amplify the trend already implaced in the data banks, emphasizing the oppression of human rights in Brazil.

I could do it, probably even with Toltin watching me. Unless Toltin knew computers. "Yeah, uh, Toltin, who made this for you?"

"Lord Vladislav had them made. I've forgotten the man's name. But the man who designed them is, ah—"

"Dead. I see." I could do it. But Dracula would find out, sooner or later. Or I could cooperate, install the baffles as my father asked. I really *could*. He was my father, after all—

When I closed my eyes, I saw the woman impaled in the subcellar room. I made up my mind.

"Eh—So, *when*, Toltin?"

"As soon as possible. Today?"

"What time is it?" I asked.

He extracted a strapless watch from a shirt pocket, squinted at it. "Almost noon."

"Let's go, then. We can get there in forty-five minutes. I'll put it in while the others are out to lunch."

"Have you been involved with the 790 project?"

"Scarcely. I've taken a leave of absence, so I'm behind on developments. But they'll let me in. I've got security clearance anywhere in the plant."

Toltin stood, took the box, and led the way to the garage. I followed, thinking: *The only reason I escaped Dracula's punishment is that he needs my cooperation on the IBEX deal. But if I betray him this time . . .*

Forty-five minutes later, Toltin and I, accompanied by a burly young man with a blue-black beard and uneven blue eyes, drove to the IBEX Research lab in downtown San Francisco. It was a cylindrical white building in five stacked stories, with more glass than concrete. The afternoon sun splashed off the windows and onto the black hood of the car. It was too hot inside the car, and I was feeling ill again. But Toltin argued doggedly: "I've *got* to go in with you. Lord Vladislav commanded it."

"You wouldn't be *allowed* in."

"But I'm wearing a suit. And you've got authority. You could say I'm your personal secretary or something."

"No, you'll have to wait outside."

"How would we know it's inserted; The computer won't be used for two weeks—"

"I've given you my word."

"*He* gave me his *command*."

"Yeah. Okay, but your lug here waits outside."

"Very well," said Toltin, bowing slightly to me—bowing at an angle which permitted me to see the gun in its shoulder holster, momentarily exposed beneath his wrinkly suitcoat. He held that pose for a moment to be sure that I'd seen the gun, then he straightened. We went inside, into air conditioning and cool-colored furnishings, into the sterile, antiseptic building where the word "blood" was not mentioned unless secretaries whispered of menstrual difficulties.

I had once felt at home in this building. No longer. I felt like an invading virus, and the man in the white smock approaching me with questions in his wide face might have been a white blood cell about to absorb me. I bit my lip, the fantasy receded, the man became simply Roger Clemshaw, chief of projected designs. We shook hands; he glanced at Toltin, looked him up and down, raised an eyebrow—but merely shrugged. "Vlad, it's good to see you," said Clemshaw. "I'd heard you were on some kind of sabbatical or shore leave or something."

I managed a faint chuckle. "No, no, Roj, uh, I was—well, I took time off to write a book about computer marketing for Wall Street Publishing and, um, *this* gentleman is assisting me—he's something of a ghost writer."

"Oh." Clemshaw nodded, the inquiry in his jowly face drooping, as if in relief, to its characteristic bulldog repose. He scratched his pug nose, glancing at Toltin, and I wondered if I should tip him off about the whole thing and get out while I could.

But I said, "Don't worry, Roj, no design secrets going to the competitors. We're here to look at the International Relations Project. Nothing innovative there."

"Hey, if you want to sell secrets, fine with me, just give me *my* cut," said Clemshaw, winking, moving off.

The elevator was to the right of the receptionist's desk.

We went to the elevator. The receptionist looked up, started to protest, recognized me, and smiled. I did my best to smile back convincingly.

I pressed the button and waited apprehensively. The elevator doors slid aside and Toltin and I stepped into the tomblike chamber. I didn't like being in the elevator. Especially alone with Toltin. I could smell him. The elevator's closeness reminded me of that basement room, the woman impaled, her humanity burned away in agony as she collapsed like a slug writhing under salt, melting . . .

The doors hushed suddenly open; I jerked back, startled. But it was just an empty hall.

"What's the matter?" Toltin asked, looking at me sidelong.

171

"Nothing. I'm tired, feeling a little sick. Seeing things. I'll be all right."

But weariness, sickness, self-loathing—they came on me all at once in a wash of three dark colors. I closed my eyes, coughing, bile searing my throat. I wanted to fall on a bed and sleep. I wanted to fall right there on the rug. And sleep. A park bench, a sidewalk, anywhere.

A thud followed by a reverberating ache in my head made me open my eyes. I looked up. Toltin was bending over me, his face creased in suspicion. "Get up," he hissed, "if someone sees you like this you'll blow the whole fucking thing, stupid!"

I was lying on my back, on the rug. At my back the rug's softness, a promise of sleep. Seductively, it drew me down. But at my front Toltin's hand drawing his gun, imperiously ordering me *up*.

I was standing, then, and the transition had come as abruptly as my falling. I shook myself, and went to the water fountain, splashed my eyes; seeing my face distorted in the fountain's curved chrome, my features lost in the draining water . . .

Toltin saved me from another collapse: he kicked me in the shins. I grunted and straightened. The pain woke me, put things in perspective. Toltin put away his gun and we walked down the hall to the smoky-glassed door marked 716.

My impulse was to listen first at the pane, but I opened the door and boldly stepped inside. The data banks hummed in endless enigmatic arrays of lights and adjusting-nodes, the work tables were crowded with engram sections and microtools. The room was empty of people, except for those statistically laid to rest in the computer's memory.

"They've all gone to lunch?" asked Toltin softly.

"Looks that way," I said wearily. My head

throbbed, there was no room in it for his stupid questions. But looking at the workbenches, he asked another.

"The computer's not finished?"

"One branch of it is, one isn't. The branch we're concerned with is finished. I—"

"How will you know exactly where to put the baffle?"

"As I was *about* to say, I can ask the computer what subsection contains those programs. Sit down, shut up and wait." Taking the baffle from Toltin I went to the typefeed and typed out the inquiry. A reply appeared immediately, in electronic light-lettering, on the TV screen above the keyboard. My eyes blurred. But I repeated the coded answer over and over to myself as I went down the adjusting-nodes, subsection numbers, till I found the proper bank. I unlocked the subsection with a tool from the work-benches. Inside was styrofoam insulation, which would take several minutes to safely remove. I yawned, and swayed, struggling with dizziness, as I dug the insulation away from the plastic-facing over the magnetic-memory sheets. To keep myself awake and alert, I questioned Toltin as I worked.

"Do you mind telling me, Toltin, how it is you came to be my father's disciple?"

Toltin hesitated. "You're his son, and he has commanded me to respect you. So I suppose I will tell you. I was an initiate of the Order of the Golden Dawn. The *genuine* order. Like Lord Vlad, I am a believer in survival of the fittest, even in the psychic realms. So of course I attempted to enforce my superiority—"

"You tried to usurp the order and take over?" I asked, raising an eyebrow. "They are staunch

173

traditionalists. They don't believe in shortcuts."

"It was *not* a shortcut to power! Their endless rigors and tests and rituals were meaningless to a man whose Destiny makes them irrelevant."

My back was to Toltin. I wanted to laugh, but allowed myself only a mocking smile. I continued to work, removing the outer layer of insulation. He continued to talk, somewhat abstractedly.

"They expelled me from their worm-eaten order, yes. They are spiritual milksops, with no taste for power, no understanding of the exquisite realm of Siva. That's why they never *rise*. That's why they hate my master. And when I realized that they were cowards, I sought out the one who is their antithesis, whom they twice tried to destroy when I was with them. Lord Vlad is well known to them, you see. All the Orders of Illuminati fear him because he so effortlessly defeated the disciples of Christian Rosiecross, and because he destroyed Mathers and undermined Crowley's power. They blame him for Crowley's corruption, and the rise of Black Magic."

"And you went to Dracula partly as a, uh, a means to take vengeance on the order?"

Toltin smugly replied: "He has promised to destroy them for me. *With* me."

"But is it worth it? I mean, if you don't mind my saying so, you have to put up with a lot till then. The way I see it he treats you, frankly, like a dog."

I could hear Toltin's teeth gritting though I stood three yards distant. In an icily controlled voice he said: "It is an equivalent of karma yoga. We learn humility. It hurts him to debase us, but it is necessary as an adjunct to learning control of the great hunger."

174

"So that's how he's rationalized it. But how does he excuse the slaughter of innocents?"

My eyes were fixed on the shearing tool with which I cut through the transparent sheathing over the silver-inlaid memory sheets, but somehow I was aware that Toltin shrugged as he said, "Innocents? There aren't any. Anything that happens to anyone is the consequence of destiny. Furthermore, anyone consumed by the great hunger is not lost, but is absorbed into a greater glory. All things live on the flesh or substance of other things. The universe's living parts are predatory. This is the common denominator of existence. Hence it is the way of the intelligent man to harness this quality of depredation, which we call the great hunger, the electricity of exploitation and self-feeding. In religion it was called divine right, in politics it was, among other things, manifest destiny, in economics it is capitalism—"

"And for sadists it is vampirism," I said carelessly.

Toltin fell silent. I could feel him fuming. He began to pace, peering over my shoulder at intervals, biting his nails, glancing at his watch.

I removed the plastic sheathing and set to work installing the baffle.

There was a desk by the door. On the desk there was a phone. The phone rang. I turned and stared at it. The switchboard should have intercepted any calls for the programmers. So, since it was ringing, it had to be for me. Probably Clemshaw had told the switchboard I was in 716, should any calls come for me. But why should he do that, knowing I'd do it myself if I wanted to be available for calls?

And no one outside the building (excepting Dracula) knew I was at the lab.

The phone continued to ring, the light on its row of buttons blinking insistently. I felt myself drawn toward it. I walked to the desk.

"Don't answer the goddamn *phone*!" Toltin said. "Dammit, Horescu, they'll be back soon. Lunch hour's almost over—"

But I picked it up. "Hello?"

"Don't do it, Vlad." It was Lucifer's voice. Bill.

He didn't really need the phone to talk to me, but if I put it down, and continued to speak aloud, Toltin would know to whom I was speaking.

"Well, hello," I said vacantly. My mind was pirouetting in vast empty spaces.

"Vlad, you were about to install an engram baffle," said Lucifer-Bill. "And you don't really want to help that government step all over its people, now you do, Vlad? You don't want to give Dracula another Wallachia to terrorize, do you? The Brazilians are feeding people to revenants, Vlad."

"You misunderstand."

"You are trying to tell me you planned to reverse the baffle, yes? To make the Brazilians look really bad in the eyes of the State Department? But whether you know it or not, *you were installing it directly,* as Dracula intended. You *weren't* reversing it! Why? Because you're tired, and ill. And Dracula's will is with you, his suggestions of loyalty and fealty are still there, in your unconscious. You saw some things that made you loathe him, but you're still his son, and you were about to do as he asked—without thinking. You're drained by what you've seen, your resistance is low. *Think.*"

I hesitated. Toltin growled from behind me, "Who the hell is it?"

I waved him back. "I—understand. Certainly we can arrange that, sir."

"Oh, you're not alone? I see. I've been monitoring you but I can't pick up everything. This is very tiring for me."

"You weren't where you said you'd be."

"I take it you think I abandoned you because I promised to be there to advise you. But I'd have advised you if it were necessary. I decided not to chance warning Dracula by seeing you again before you contacted him. I was with you much of the time, anyway. Even as you slept. This has dispersed too much of me, though. I can't maintain the surveillance. Do you understand? You'll be on your own for a while. But *think* when you put in the baffle; don't do it automatically." He was gone.

I hung up and walked, rather woodenly, back to the computer. Toltin paced beside me, pulling on my arm.

"Now who the hell was it, Horescu?"

"Who? The old man." I smiled. "The IBEX boss. He wanted to talk to me about—oh, about when I was to come back to work." I picked up a tool and bent over the engram panel, trying to ignore Toltin's suspicious glare. "Clemshaw told him I was here." I set to work—thinking.

I examined the baffle. I swallowed. Lucifer was right. I'd been installing it as Dracula had expected. I extracted it, and reversed it, replaced the sheathing and insulation.

When the statistical read-out sheet on Brazilian Human Rights Status reached Washington, the Secretary of State would not be pleased by what he saw.

I finished, my hands shaking, and closed the section-drawer, just as the door opened and three surprised technicians entered. "Another inspection?" one of them asked with an ingratiating smile.

But I couldn't reply. The dark tide swallowed me again. In the distance I heard them arguing with Toltin.

"You wanna take him *home*? You kidding? He's collapsed! He's got to go to a hospital. Joe, call the—"

And then the sound went out, too.

.3.

"Blood poisoning," said the nurse, to my look of inquiry. "Must be quite a surprise for you, waking up here. You collapsed at work and you've been out ever since. It's good to see you came awake on your own. That shows you're recovering. We thought we'd have to use adrenalin. We're not sure where you got the infection, but the doctor said it might have been from blood in spoiled, undercooked meat. Have you had any rare meat lately? He found traces of blood on your teeth that—"

"Yes," I interrupted. "It was from rotten meat." I looked around. I was half afraid I'd see Toltin. But it was just an empty white room. "Uh, nurse." She had been about to go out; she turned to face me. She was a horse-faced woman, middle-aged, with a discerning glint of her gray eyes. "Nurse—"

"My name's Alicia."

"Alicia, is anyone waiting for me outside in the hall? Or in the waiting room?"

"Yes. A man. Would you like me to bring—"

"*No!* I— Is he a, uh, spindly sort of man, shaggy, and in a rumpled suit?"

"Yes."

"Christ! It's him! Listen, that man poisoned me. He slipped me that bad food—did it deliberately.

178

He—he's the one. I don't want him near me. Don't let him up here. *Don't let him near me.* And—hey, he'll try to sneak in. Really, I assure you he will."

"Calm down." The nurse chuckled. Just then I wanted to brain her. "We won't let him in, Mr. Horescu. Should I call the police?"

"No, no, my father would—oh, never mind, just tell the guy to go away. And did a Mr. Clemshaw give you the information on me when I was checked in?"

"That's right. IBEX accepted responsibility for your hospital bill."

"Good. Then on my forms he probably put my home phone number. Do me a favor, *please.* Call that number and have my servant sent out here. Jolson."

She shrugged. "All right. You *sure* you don't want the police?"

I cleared my throat. "I'm sure." I tried to sit up. "Better yet, I should go home."

Gently, she pressed me back on the bed. "No way. You workaholic executives are all half insane, if you ask me. You'd fall over if you tried to stand, Mr. Horescu. You're going to be weak as a kitten for a couple of days."

She was right. The effort at sitting had almost sucked all awareness from me. I sank back onto the pillows. I became aware for the first time of an intravenous tube clamped into my right arm, and an unconnected plasma bottle on a gallows-like stand on my right.

The nurse left, and I stared at the ceiling and hoped Toltin would go away peacefully. He had seen me install the baffle, and he wouldn't know that I had rigged it to do the opposite of what it was intended for. I hoped.

The ceiling was red.

A deep chocolate-red, like dried blood. I tried to

look away, wondering why the rest of the room was white. But looking away was difficult; the ceiling seemed to entrance me. I pulled my gaze from it, with considerable effort.

But now the walls were red, too.

"No," I said aloud. "Uh-uh. They're white. I remember. *White.*"

No, they're red, my sight replied.

They were liquid red, like sheets of blood falling as in a waterfall. A bloodfall shimmying and rippling. The walls of running blood closed in, enveloped me, and I choked, drowning. . .

Again, I heard distant voices. "I *told* you I heard a scream! He's on the damn floor. Oh, hell, he's throwing up blood—"

"Doctor Hannaly."

"Hey, get—"

"Turn him on his back—"

"He's trying to say something—help me to—Hey! Help me get him back on the damn bed. He's delirious. He was coherent a moment ago."

"Delirious?"

But it wasn't delirium. It was emphathic vision. The red falls had gone, replaced by a sea. Dracula stood there, looking out to sea. And then it was *I,* looking out to sea, from within him. His blood was still in me, connecting us, binding me to him, showing me what he saw, letting me experience, in a diluted fashion, what he experienced.

It was not delirium.

.4.

The sea churned in the rising storm. Dracula had called up the storm, for advice and the comfort of catharsis, purging himself in its raging. Temporary release. But as the waves steepened and crashed, as the wind honed its edge with icy rainwater and the beetling clouds clashed into lightning, Dracula paced the sands, growling to himself. The storm was little comfort. He wanted the woman and he wanted his son with him, and he was not used to having his yearnings thwarted.

The sea was steely gray pooled with indigo where shadows crawled and the sky was a charcoal billow edged with purple and shot with flickering tongues of lightning.

Margaret Holland, Dracula thought, *should be here with me, exulting in this. There's something in that one that is close kin to me.*

Wearing a purple cape and cowl over leather buckler and black-leather breeches, Dracula raised his arms and spoke a Name in an ancient language. Then he intoned: "I am He who was once ignorant and blindly hungry as a gray rat! I am He who is now wise as the ruins on the floor of the sea's deepest chasm! I am He whose feet are on the earth and whose eyes are in the icy voids of space! I am He who commands you!" And again he spoke the Name and made the sign.

A seawashed boulder twenty feet before him, lashed in surf, exploded into arching chunks, as a mighty bolt of lightning struck it.

Dracula did not flinch. He remained in the same position, arms upraised in the gutterally singing winds, steadfast in the furious rain-lash. Out of the steaming vortex where the boulder had been, a thing of phosphorescent fog took shape: man-shaped but vast, with small flickers of electricity where eyes would be. The elemental of airy electricities. It spoke.

Drakulya. . .

"I am troubled," said Prince Vladislav, his voice

181

carrying thinly over the hissing, crackling maelstrom about them. "And you have always advised me when I was troubled. I am thoroughly alone and my dreams are harried by visions of a woman, a woman I met only once. And my son Vlad—"

My advice is no longer yours, Vladislav Veovod Drakul. The Unwarming Light is my master and you have forsaken Him, said the hollow giant, the colossus of foggy glow.

The storm's howl rose to an ear-splitting paramount, as if the airs were shrieking their displeasure with Dracula.

"Lord of electrical airs, I am *your* priest, though I am no longer the tool of Lucifer The Light. I will sacrifice to you, and feed you—"

No, you are not my priest. You are interested only in your own advancement. You are smallsighted and not so wise as you think, though you have lived many man-lives. Advancement comes only in accordance with the intent of the invisible machinery.

"I don't believe that."

The existence of a law is not a consequence of your opinions. But I will tell you of your son. If you want his loyalty, keep him always near you. He is poisoned, alone in a sterile man-place, and there are other influences in his life than yours. He has betrayed you today.

"Betrayed me? *How?*"

But a curtain of blackness fell, a thick wall of rain tinted red by flashes of heat-lightning, and it was as though Dracula was drowning in a great wash of blood. But the dense downpour ended, a few final sprays spattered the sand, and the wind shattered the cloud-cover.

Wet to the skin, Dracula turned and strode angrily back to Chutney House.

When I awoke, Jolson was smiling down at me.

"I saw through his eyes," I murmured, not yet believing that Jolson was real.

"Through Dracula's eyes," he said. "I know."

I started, and looked around. The same room, windowless and chastely white, entirely white—not a drop of blood. I smiled. Then a queasy suspicion took me. I looked at Jolson. He stood beside the bed, his hands clasped behind him, looking slightly uncomfortable. There was a metal folding chair beside the bed. I gestured toward it and he sat. "*How* did you 'know,' Jolson?"

"I know what happened to you, where you've been and who your father is and much of what you've seen in the visions. Margaret Holland told me. And this—" He smiled. "This 'Bill' fellow told *her.*"

"I see. Lucifer knows-all-sees-all-tells-all but *does* little. He could have helped that woman. On the stake. Those people, trapped down there. They're dead, now." I glanced at Jolson. His eyes were moist. "So," I said, "they told you about *that,* too." He nodded. "Christ but I'm weak," I muttered, closing my eyes.

I felt Jolson's cool touch on my forehead. "Permit me. I have more energy than I need," he said, as carelessly as offering a glass of milk. But strength flowed from him, through his hand and into me. I shivered. I quivered in a short rush, and he withdrew his hand. I felt feverish, but stronger and more cheerful. I sat up and stared at him accusingly.

"Why didn't you tell me more about yourself?" I asked. "All this time you've been capable of more than astral projection—and until recently I didn't believe, privately, that you could do even that. And you've kept it all from me."

"The Unwarming Light is my master," said Jolson softly.

"All this time—?"

He nodded.

"Lucifer—?"

He nodded again.

Icy fury welled up in me. I had to look away from him.

"Don't be angry, Vlad. It was best that you knew nothing of me other than what I told you. Otherwise you would not have trusted me, and I'd not have been there when you needed me."

"Then you took the job with me—in preparation. You were a plant."

"Not entirely. Yes, Lucifer asked me to take the job, to be there to assist you and to report to him—he knew that Dracula was going to contact you. But I *wanted* to work for you. My karma—"

"But you *lied* to me. You told me you didn't recognize the man who came that night, the intruder, Lucifer. . ."

"I did not lie. I had never seen him in that form before, and he didn't bother to tell me that he was that very One whom I'd served since my apprenticeship to the sorceror Zo in Cheng. Always that One had been more a voice and a presence than a physical—"

"Oh, you *knew* all right. You'd have sensed it was he."

"Ah. I will regret it greatly if I lose your personal trust and regard—"

"You sound like a Hallmark card. How can I trust you? You've been part of his—*ugh*, it pisses me off!" I took a deep breath, "Part of his manipulation of me. All this time."

"Everything is manipulated by something else. Lucifer is as bound to you as you to him or me to him—we are all three interdependent interstices of one triangle—"

"Cut it out. Oriental mystics fall back on philosophical analogies as a defense mechanism. Just now it makes me sick . . . But, uh—I appreciate your strengthening me. The energy." I looked at my hands. I was a trifle embarrassed. His 'strengthening' of me had been almost a sexual act.

We were quiet for awhile. The anger drained from me, the strength remained. Minutes later I cleared my throat and asked, "Do you think I'm strong enough to leave here now?"

"No, not until tomorrow."

"Frankly—" I shrugged, feeling sheepish. "I don't feel safe here. I try not to think about it. But every so often I do. And then I'm terrified."

"I understand. I will remain and protect you. I have a special means. Something I can do that will help. Your father will come, probably. I'll have to meet him."

I said nothing. I was fascinated by the darkening red spreading over the walls. Jolson didn't seem to see it. But the walls were running with blood, falling sheets of crimson, carrying images to me like bizarre flotsam on a current. . .

.6.

Dracula waited impatiently in the limousine, glaring at the several 30-story cylinders comprising the hospital. Toltin fidgeted in the front seat.

The boy, Cooper, returned from the hospital reception room and opened the car's front door, sliding in beside Toltin. Cooper turned to Dracula.

"My Lord, they wouldn't let me in to see him either."

"But the Holland woman—is she there?"

"I believe so. I think it was her."

"Idiot! Was it or was it *not*?" Dracula snarled.

Cooper cringed. "I don't know, Lord. Forgive me. I have no picture, only your description. She fits that, but so could many women."

"Many women? Cretin! This woman—" Dracula realized then that he was shouting, and that it might seem a weakness since his fury was aroused on behalf of a woman. He lowered his voice to a steely monotone: "This *woman* . . . possesses an aura of Divinity. She is many women at once and she has eyes that take the light like new razors."

Swallowing, Cooper considered, his outsized head bobbing nervously in the dimly-lit interior of the car. It was eight p.m. The only light came from a corner streetlight, a mucous-yellow light spilling in through the back window. Cooper said: "Yes, Lord. There was a great kind of—a glow, I guess, about this woman."

"Oh. A 'kind of glow I guess', eh?" Dracula said, mimicking Cooper's tone superciliously. "But you weren't *sure.*" He leaned back, sighing, passing a hand over his eyes. "I'll have to go in myself. I can, perhaps, convince her to take me to Vlad."

Toltin demurred. "Respectfully, Lord, perhaps we should wait till tomorrow when they take your son home. They'll have to take him out of the hospital then. This servant, this Jolson, has hired guards to stand in the hospital lobby. He's convinced the hospital staff that Vlad's in danger—"

"Guards are human and I am not," Dracula said.

. . . Another, lesser entity—one who was still a man—might have uttered those words in a motion picture. But he could not have spoken them with the same conviction, in spite of, possibly, being a good actor. No one could speak so portentously and sound anything but laughable—except Dracula. Such declarations were the stanchions and girders upholding Dracula's character. When he spoke of his own lethality, his own grandeur, he spoke with the conviction of the utterly convinced. Certainly, no one in the limosine laughed at him. Vlad the Impaler didn't have to act. He was Dracula. . .

And he flung open the car's back door. He climbed out into the evening. He flinched; in the open air, the ten thousand sounds of a city night thrust in on him, the endless unfurling of urban scents assaulted him. He gritted his teeth and repressed a desire to find sensory-surcease in blood. *Not now. When I have them both safe with me,* he thought.

Dracula strode to the glass doors and, as casually as possible, pressed them aside and stepped into the hospital lobby. He looked around, frowning. He was uncomfortable there, feeling out of his element. The room was very much a thing of the 20th century. It was pastel and hard-edged and made of synthetics, set about with undistinguished furnishings and old magazines curling like wintery leaves. To either side of the broad plastic-sheathed reception desk two young, crewcut Burns Security guards stood staring at him with open suspicion. Dracula glanced down at himself, wondering what had evoked their mistrust. He wore a dark blue suit, a conservative cut, with matching vest and fedora. He caught a glimpse of himself in a pane of window glass—he was squat, a compact man-bristle of dark energy set off in relief (rather than concealed as he had hoped, camouflaged) by his mundane clothing and the bland surroundings. *It's the Hunger,* he thought. *It's growing in me. I can't hide it.*

The guards were walking toward him. If he killed them the police might show up before he found Vlad and Margaret. Perhaps he could frighten them off. Their shame at running might prevent them calling the authorities.

They halted a yard from him, hands on their guns. "I'm afraid we're going to have to ask you to leave unless you can give us evidence that you've got business here," said the blond young man in a practiced clip.

To Dracula's right a potted plant with broad green-blue fronds waved gently in the current from an air-conditioning vent. Dracula reached a livid, bristling hand to the plant's thick stem and closed his fingers on it. "This could be your neck," he said. "And I need not squeeze the plant to destroy it—I merely touch it. . ." At his touch the plant seemed to curl inward on itself like smoke sucked underground. The older man, with black hair and a walrus mustache, said, "Heyyy uhh—what—" and took a step backwards.

The plant crumbled, leaving only ashes where it had been.

"And if I merely touch *you*. . ." said Dracula softly. He reached out. One of them, the man with the mustache, bolted. The other bit his lip and snapped his gun up.

"That's a cute trick," he said, "and you're probably a helluva good chemist, but if you don't touch me you can't use whatever-it-was on me and I swear, man, if you try—"

Smiling cooly, Dracula took a step forward. The man's hand jerked as the gun went off; Dracula winced, then laughed, as the bullet kicked into his chest. The pain was only that of a pinch, no worse than a muscle cramp. The bullet would dissolve in a few hours. The guard stood there, gun wavering. His nicotine-stained upper lip beaded with sweat. His narrow nostrils dilated in a sudden intake of breath as Dracula stepped in and closed his fingers around the gun. Dracula locked his eyes on the watery blue eyes of the guard. After seeing the bullet fail, the man's determination failed, and with it his will. His mouth went slack. He stood stock-still, eyes moistly staring.

Hearing shouts from the hall as the receptionist ran for help and the mustached guard returned with three orderlies, Dracula reached for the face of the man before him. He vised his left hand around the gun, broke it in two, and let it fall. The guard didn't move. Dracula closed the fingers of his left hand around the man's neck; with the forefinger of his right he traced a dark, bloody line around the edge of the young man's face. The guard didn't move. Where Dracula's finger touched the guard's face, the skin shriveled, melted away till a rut of ruined flesh was dug along jawline and hairline and cheekedge. Dracula gripped the skin of the face at the lower right-hand jawline, and waited, timing it. Comprehension was leaking into the man's face as pain penetrated his trance. But he didn't move. His eyes widened; he looked down at Dracula's tightening hand at the corner of his face and opened his mouth to scream.

The oncoming men ran from the hall and into the lobby, one of them raising a gun. Dracula, still gripping the edge of the man's face, half-turned the captured guard to face the others, and spoke: "What becomes of this one will become of you all."

With a practiced twist of hand, snap of wrist, demonstrating a technique he had perfected long before in Wallachia, he neatly stripped the man's face from its skull. It came off whole, all in one piece like a mask, exposing rawness and spraying blood onto the orderlies. The faceless guard shrieked and staggered, blind. Dracula smiled, pleased with himself, and reached out; he casually broke the man's neck. The figure crumpled. The receptionist, a young woman wearing a battered Farah Fawcett-Majors T-shirt, threw up noisily. The mustached guard raised a gun and fired twice—his hand was trembling, his eyes were shut, his mouth was a grimace of terror—both shots went wild. Dracula struck him with the back of his hand; the guard bounced from a wall and fell unconscious onto his face. One of the orderlies, an older man with a long thin neck that invited breaking, Dracula thought, stepping toward him, was saved when he lost control of his bowels, his trouser legs (flapping as he staggered back from Dracula) dripping urine and watery feces. Revolted, not wanting to touch the man, Dracula let him run after the other two, who were fleeing down a hall to the right. The receptionist was hiding behind her desk.

Dracula yawned, felt his stomach contract with The Hunger, and putting a finger to a bloodspatter on his vest, touched the dampened finger to his lips. It tasted like the sea, it tasted like youth, it tasted like sex and the sweaty toil of a million generations of men. Dracula glanced at the corpse and considered . . . He shook his head. No time to drink—the police would arrive soon. He ran to the stairs, threw wide the door and took three flights in six bounds.

He flung himself into the upper hall and ran, glancing at door numbers. He scowled. It was demeaning that he should have to seek out his son this way, searching frantically for the room, and—there it was! Room 465. He stopped before the door and composed himself.

He reached for the doorknob. But before he could

touch it, the door opened, swung inward. There was a man without a face. But instead of the bloody mask Dracula half expected, the place where the face should have been was occupied by light. A shimmer-glow of white, cold white light and two points of black onyx for eyes. The light stabbed and burned. Dracula turned away, feeling sweat course his brow and tears swim his eyes. "Fucking hell!" he shouted, one hand shielding his eyes as he tentatively looked back. "Who are you?"

"Leave here, Vladislav, child. This one is no longer yours . . . As for myself I am the inhabitant of the final sphere of the Sephiroth, he who dwells in the body of the man Jolson as a king sits upon a throne. I am your Lord. Kneel before me. Or scurry away like a mewling revenant."

The light grew more intense, Dracula could feel it on the back of his neck. The light did not warm, and its burning was acidic, the burning of dry ice. . .

Three seconds passed, and that was time enough for Dracula to remember: Two hundred years before, traveling through Rumania, the women he had taken, the blood he had taken, and—straightening from her whitened sprawl—the bullet her husband had put in the back of his head, close range. It didn't kill him, of course, though it lodged in his brain for awhile, but it struck him down and he found he could not move. Could not move as they toted him away, kicking at his paralyzed body; still could not move an hour later when they lashed him to the stake and lit the brands at his feet. The flames were very hot, at first, and the pain was like some magnificent cathedral of hurt that rose to overshadow the world's largest mountains—until he felt himself near death. And then seeing death come like a white comet rushing for his eyes, recognizing the cold, cold white light therein, his strength had come back to him, the bullet in his brain dissolved, and with boil-covered flesh and third-degree burns, he burst his bonds and killed three of the villagemen in the crowd gloating at his pyre. And he ran into the cool, drippy forest and hid himself and lay for weeks, regenerating, trying to forget the sweet sanctity of that faceless face of white light, the purity of oncoming oblivion. . .

Now, Dracula turned and struck out, defiantly plunging his hand into the icy-burn of the stranger's face. His hand vanished into the brilliance, a fist reappeared there, coming from amidst that shining face—his own fist! Coming at him from where he had just thrust it—and he staggered back: Dracula's fist had struck Dracula in the face. He looked with horror at his hand. It sparkled, evenly coated with a bright crystalline powder. He shook it and the powder vaporized, leaving a bonedeep aching *cold.* The thing waited, implacably. Squinting against the entity's painful brilliance, Dracula struck out again, this time at the thing's chest. The figure's chest burst into light as he struck it and his hand and arm again seemed to sink through that glamor—and to return, curved impossibly back as if his mirror image were lashing out at him. Dracula staggered again. His own fist had struck him in the chest. And again his arm was crusted in snowstuff.

The venomous cold was spreading into his arms, and The Hunger was high in him. He felt weak. The thing took a step toward him.

Dracula had had enough. He ran, returned the way he had come, running as if his clothing were afire, sick with loathing and burgeoning self-doubt.

I am the inhabitant of the final sphere of the Sephiroth, He who dwells in the body of the man Jolson as a King sits upon a throne. I am your

Lord. Kneel before me...

"Not in ten thousand years will I kneel before you!" Dracula shouted, flinging himself through the glass doors fronting the lobby. The doors had been locked from the outside—they broke before him like thin ice. Glass flew outward from him in a jag-edged aurora, and tinkled on the concrete as he landed on his feet and straightened up.

Bright lights in his eyes.

"Not in ten thousand millenia!" he screamed at the lights. But this was a different sort of light, he realized—a warmer, manmade light. Searchlights, headlights, flashlights. He blinked, shielded his eyes with a hand. Men were coming toward him, out-lined against the lights mounted on police cars. The man-silhouettes were thorny with weapons, guns and clubs and unrecognizable things angling harshly from their belts. There just might be enough of them to take him.

"Do not move, if you want to stay alive!" boomed a bullhorn. The silhouettes, silver-edged like gathering winter stormclouds, were cautiously near-ing from several directions. He looked around. The limousine was gone. Apparently, Toltin had decided that discretion was the better part of valor.

It was too late to lie his way out of it—the orderlies would identify him.

Where was Margaret Holland?

Two of the policemen approached him from either side, one unslinging handcuffs.

Dracula stepped left; faster than a finger could squeeze a trigger he seized the nearest cop, spun him so he faced the others, and bellowed, "I can tear his head off with my hands and I'll do it if you—" But the policeman to the right drew his gun and fired. Dracula took the slug in his side, grunting—and he squeezed the uniformed man in his arms; in an instant the heavyset policeman split, spilled (screaming) his insides redly onto his (quivering) outsides, and Dracula lifted his remains overhead and threw the corpse at the lights ... As he had expected, the policeman's friends were momentarily stunned by what he'd done to their companion. Dracula had time to sprint and leap over the hood of the nearest patrol car, on the left, dodging into the hedges bordering the hospital grounds, running in a crouch.

He was nearly a block ahead of them when another shot stung him in the back of the neck—it snapped the vertebrae and his head lolled. His legs seemed to vanish beneath him. He stumbled, fell, cursing, flat on his belly in the damp grass. It would take hours for a broken spine to heal. His lower half was numb. Shouts, sirens, lightflashes, the thud of boot-tread.

He crawled over the sidewalk, smelling crushed grass, blood, feeling the coarseness of the concrete on his fingers—but now the cruel sharpness of his sensations was absent, and for once this absence was unwelcome. It meant his arms, his upper parts, were numbing.

A flashlight's beam spilled over him; a high-pitched yell: "The bastard's over here!"

A car pulled up in front of him. A small yellow car. A door swung open and instinctively Dracula pulled himself, with the failing strength of his arms alone, along the curb, up the doorframe and onto the front seat.

Dragging Dracula's feet, the car U-turned and sped down the street, turning the corner. It stopped and someone he couldn't see helped him inside. The door slammed, sirens whooped behind them. The

194

car plunged ahead, turned almost immediately, swept into an alley, and, lying half crumpled on the floor, his cheek against the vinyl front seat, he saw a garage door roll up, as if by electronic command. And the car rolled inside.

The police cars sirened by, unseeing, their whines becoming distant, like angry wasps.

Someone helped him to climb from the car and lifted him in thin but strong arms. The muscles of his face would not respond properly, he could not open his eyes to see who it was.

SEVEN

.1.

I woke up writhing, slapping at the air, sobbing.

Ghostly policemen came at me; they faded like smoke in the wind. I blinked, I clawed at my eyes, shaking my head to clear the red waterfall from it, trying to drive the vision out.

"Out," I said, biting my tongue till I tasted my own blood.

And it was the taste of blood that woke me. The hallucinations faded. But I felt awful. I felt terrible. Awful and terrible are odd words, their meanings are self-contradictory in various contexts. Awful can mean *very unpleasant*, and that's how I felt; and it can mean *forbiddingly powerful*, as in *awful majesty*, and that's how I felt. I felt terrible; I felt the terrible ecstasy, the terrible dark glory. Awful and terrible, rotting and exalted—that's how I felt just then.

And very cold. I sat up, shivering, wrapping the blankets of the hospital bed around me. The bedclothes were soaked in sweat.

"Oh, *shit*!" I said, between gulps of air. I felt like Lazarus, arisen from the dead.

Jolson sat beside me. He smiled. "You missed all the excitement, Vlad."

"You mean—Dracula's attempt to crash the hospital? The police?"

Jolson arched an eyebrow. "Your connection with your father is stronger than I'd have guessed. Your blood is poisoned with his in more ways than one. You followed the whole thing from his viewpoint, then?"

"Yes. He's been hurt by a bullet to the spine. At the neck. Someone helped him escape from the cops. She did it a little too easily. I suspect she used some sort of occult screen. Or perhaps it was simply good planning. She—"

"She? It's a woman?"

"I—I think so, yeah. Her arms about me—about *him*, I mean—felt like those of a woman. But I'm not sure, because my body was going numb—damn it! I mean *his* body." I grimaced.

"Do you know where she took him?"

"Uhh, no. No, I was—*he* was on the floor of the car at the time. Leaning on the seat, sort of. And—couldn't see." That was a lie, all right, yes. I knew where they were, yes. But I didn't want to tell Jolson, not yet anyway. I was afraid that he would inform Bill. And I didn't know what Lucifer might do. But Lucifer might know already, if he'd been monitoring my mind.

"Jolson, how did you keep him out of here? Where did that—the glowing face—"

"I can't take credit," said Jolson with an odd, shy smile. "I was a vehicle for another. It was my meditation, though, my mantric invocations which bridged the gap between It and I, permitted It to enter me and to confront Dracula."

"And if Lucifer taught you how to—"

"Vlad," Jolson interrupted, raising a hand palm outward, "I think it would be best for Lucifer to—"

"*No*! You! I want *you* to tell me. What exactly is Lucifer *doing*?"

Jolson sighed. "I'm sorry. I can't. My ability to connect to those higher forces depends on my mental orientation, Vlad. I have vowed to obey Lucifer in this, a sacred vow. If I were to break it I would be uneasy, you see. Of a divided mind. Disoriented. And no longer, then, able to protect you."

I sighed, and shrugged. "That's a pretty good excuse but I don't believe it for a minute. You just *reek* sincerity, you know that?"

I was feeling profoundly irritable. The blood poisoning was again beginning to tax me. Blobs of darkness slithered at the edge of my vision. When I turned to look at them, nothing was there. "There's always something unclean slinking about just out of sight," I said in disgust. I frowned at the sheets, they seemed yellowed. "These sheets need laundering. And the walls," I said, glancing around, could use a scrubbing." I looked at Jolson. "In fact, Jolson, *you* look a little rumpled yourself. Do I hire you to—" I cut it off with a bitter chuckle. "I forgot. You work for Lucifer, not me."

"My clothes *are* a bit tawdry. I've been sitting here all night, I'm afraid I haven't had time to change."

It occurred to me that Jolson had been sitting there, in that chair, beside me, since yesterday afternoon. Now it should be about dawn. Probably he hadn't slept. Or eaten or excreted. "God, Jeez, I'm sorry Jolson. I'm really sorry, man. I slide into idiotic moods where just everything seems like a vector of the plague."

The door opened and a nurse rustled in, a young woman in a short white dress, her nurse's cap pinned at a jaunty angle on piled brown hair. She pushed a cart before her and on the cart was a covered tray. "You're going to have a little soup this morning, Mr. Horescu," she said.

"Okay." I turned to Jolson. "Go on, go home. It's daylight, he's unlikely to come. Light gives him a headache. And his boys won't come with the place swarming with cops."

Jolson stood shakily, bowed, and left.

"Yes, I wonder what it was all about," said the young nurse, speaking to the tray she was arranging on the swingshelf over my belly. "All *sorts* of sordid goings-on. I wish I'd been here." She laughed briefly.

"I wish I'd been somewhere else," I said, reaching for a spoon.

.2.

Dracula was awakened by the roar of the city.

He sat up, hissing in pain, hands over his ears. He took deep breaths, pressed his thumbs into his ears, trying to stopper up the cacophony. It diminished slightly; he was able to think. Experimentally, he turned his head. The gun-wound had healed. He was still Dracula. He examined the room. Curtains and shades drawn over windows that leaked too much light. A walnut dresser and mirror, rustling sheets of the bed on which he sat. A rather barren room, furnished for residency, but without a feeling of having been lived in. The sounds the sheets made pained him, the texture of his clothing, sticky with sweat, prickled him, the unfamiliarity of the room oppressed him. Hearing the door open, he looked up.

Wearing a white nightgown, holding back a yawn; brown hair tousled about her ears looking velvety as smoke, her dark eyes pools of comfort: Margaret Holland.

"You?" Dracula asked, his dry throat rasping.

She nodded.

"The noise—the sights—senses—I am attacked, in pain, weak—" Dracula managed. He looked at the pulsing vein at Margaret's throat. He fought himself. "Get out of here, run. Or get me blood. I need it or I'll go—I'll lose control—the world intrudes—"

"I know. Vlad told me. Blood like morphine." She smiled. "I rather enjoy seeing you so vulnerable. Wait. Lay back, I'll see what I can do. Ah, does the blood have to be human?"

He shook his head.

"Good. There's a pet shop a few blocks away." She made a face, a parody of disgust. "I don't like to, but I'll bring you—"

"Rabbits. Very close to—human blood. Or white mice."

She nodded, and left. He heard the phone dial turning in the next room; the sound grated on him. Clickaclickaclickaclickaclack.

Was she calling the police?

Perhaps she'd changed her mind about protecting him from—

But he heard her say, "Hello . . . You have rabbits? And white mice? . . . Listen, this'll sound silly but if you agree to deliver all you have, I'll pay you three times what they're worth . . . Yes, all of them . . . Not far. 675 Trinity, Apartment B—it's in the basement, part of it—go 'round the back, through the alley . . . Yes. I'll pay in cash, right there . . . Okay, thank you."

Dracula lay back and waited. He closed his eyes against the sunlight that stole through the corners of the shades.

Small white rabbits. As a boy, in Wallachia, he'd set little stakes about and . . . his mind drifted, he dreamed, and smiled to himself . . .

He heard them squeaking as she brought them in the door.

He sat up. There were forty white mice in a cage, a second metal cage of eight white rabbits. Margaret set the cages on the floor and hastily left. Dracula rose and went to the cages.

He bent, wincing at the rich animal scents blossoming from the cages. The rabbits cried in panic, scenting impending death. Dracula pulled the cages to the edge of the bed. He sat, reached in and, as casually as a tired husband opening a twist-top beer bottle, he twisted the head off a rabbit and raised its spasming body to his lips.

Again and again and again.

Eight dead rabbits, drained, and a puddle of blood sticky between his legs on the floor. Tension drained out of him, the cityscreams subsided. He looked at the cage of mice, fascinated by their terrified movements as they felt his gaze on them.

Margaret came into the room with a sponge and a towel. She handed him the towel and he dabbed at his lips and his shirtfront. Once more, his smallest movements defined strength and confidence. He watched as Margaret, still wearing the nightgown, got down on her hands and knees and sponged the blood. She went to the bathroom, squeezed out the sponge, returned, and bent to the task again. He watched her breasts bob like running white rabbits as she worked, her long smooth neck like an arc of foam.

Dracula, Lord of Vampires, exiled King of Wallachia, immortal demon, trembled as he attempted to control his need to surrender to a strange woman.

Cleansing completed, Margaret carried away the

cage of torn fur and the reddened sponge.

She was a long time washing her hands.

When she returned for the cage of mice Dracula raised his hand. "No, leave it. I'll want more, shortly. And I like to watch them move . . . these little packets of life . . . small concentrations of life, running on legs of instinct and craving, tiny hearts beating fast . . . I love to watch them, Margaret." He motioned, his eyes still on the cage. "Sit down beside me on the bed. There will be words between us."

She sat a yard from him, the cage between them on the floor. She gazed at him impassively, and he was pleased that there was no fear in her face.

"People have said, Margaret, that I have no regard for life. No love of life. They believe me to be antilife, abusive of it." He slowly shook his head, indicated the cage with his hand. "But it's not true. I adore these creatures. I love all life. It's more than just a desire to satisfy my craving for it. It's *devotion*, Margaret. I worship at life's wellsprings when I drink. Look at the mice! Balls of fur with hearts of fire. Living blood like wine that struggles against the drinker. That's a quintessential beauty, Margaret. Do you understand that?"

"I do," she said softly, a husky undertone in her voice.

"Lovemaking and murder have been collaborators, in me, only because," he paused to smile at her, making his eyes cheerful and his voice mild, "because those I sought to *explore* were unwilling, were terrified of me. They could not accept me. But a woman who loved me, a woman *I* loved—" He hesitated, cleared his throat to remove the catch in it. "There need be no killing if she opens her heart to me. I can take her love instead of her blood, if she accepts me as I am." He reached out and lifted the cage of mice, set it behind him. He stood, and bent over her. She stiffened and drew back. Her eyes hardened. That flicker of sternness in her eyes was like a needle through his chest. He turned away; he paced. She sat, waiting. He returned to her abruptly and fell to his knees.

He laid his head in her lap. She made no move to reject him. He encircled her waist with his arms, inhaled the exhalation of her musk, her sweat, some coma-inducing perfume under it all. "I'm not going to ask you who you really are, Margaret." He said it as gently, as evenly as possible so as not to upset the delicate balance between them. "I'm sure you'll reveal that to me when it is appropriate, if ever." Dracula looked up into her face as a child looks at his mother; he tried to remember what his mother had looked like. She'd died young. All the Dracula women died young. He looked into her face and remembered other women, women he'd married or mistressed, women he'd taken or murdered, their faces as alike as labels on one brand of wine, but this woman's face stood out like a stroke of lightning against clouds. Margaret. What was her real name? Her hand rested on his shoulder, casually as a bird on a twig. Why was she unafraid of him? She was wary of him, but fearless. She had seen what he could do, she knew his life had gone on for centuries, an endless replay of variations on a horror theme, a life like a psychotic's compulsive reliving of a trauma. She knew, but her fingers kneaded the back of his neck.

He considered the past. Since Lucifer had taken him, raised him—transformed—from the dead, made him into the undying Dracula, life was a hall of mirrors. On and on, cycling reflections. And here was the first significant landmark in that endless slalom of time: a woman's face that stuck with him, that spoke itself and was unfogged, that would not be consumed in the acids of his ego. A face unobscured by fear. Was fear their masking? Was it their fear of him that had made them all, all the stolen women, seem like china dolls in pastel variations? Equations of confrontation: Sufficient heat applied to contained water produces steam. Dracula applied to human intimacy produces terror, terror like a steamy cloud rising to obscure individualism in his victims.

But this woman would not be obscured. The equation was not contradicted: Margaret Holland was obviously not human. He would not ask her what she *was*. Dracula had his own—well-concealed—capacity for fear, too.

Admitting to himself that he was afraid of her made him frown and sit up. He defied his own fear and looked into her face. Her eyes were sharp with intellect. He glanced at her neck. He smiled. Moving slowly so as not to alarm her, he reached up and slid his little finger under a fine silver chain. On the chain, just beneath the cloth of her bosom, something argent hung. He drew it out, his smile broadening. It was a crucifix. He held it in his hand. "Protection against *me*?" he asked.

"No. I'm not naive. I wear it for my own pleasure."

He regarded the cross fondly. "It's odd how the Christians have assumed that their church is terrifying to me. While I was Lord over Wallachia the only thing I honored beyond myself was the Church. I built churches for them, and gave them money and all was well. My enemies hated me but the Church—our Church—revered me. As a boy I

204

was a hostage of the heathen Turks and I yearned for the sanctity of a cathedral. The only peace I knew as a boy was in a cathedral. Now the religion means little to me—just another pattern on the perfect chaos—but sometimes I go to the cathedrals in the evening and sit in the hush, the shadows, the orderly spaces, and I can forget the hunger, for a while."

"Lord of Wallachia," Margaret murmured. "Prince Dracula, you are a pitiful and majestic gentleman." There was a flavor of mockery in her tone. But she slid her hand up his shoulder, to his thick corded neck and pressed gently, as a jockey pats a horse to relax it, and Dracula sighed, shuddered, and felt a delicious limpness go through him. He again laid his head on her lap.

"I didn't know . . . those muscles were so taut," he whispered. "I had no idea."

"You're always more tense than you know."

The mice scurried and scuttled, but the noise did not annoy him; the distant cough of an engine revving hardly penetrated. He felt that he might go to sleep there, with his head on her lap. Moving without guile, like a kitten seeking a warm hollow, his right hand slid along Marg's calf, past her knee, smooth and round as polished agate, beneath the labialike fringe of nightgown. His fingers slid between two silks, the silk of her skin and the silk of her slip, relishing the full and equine curve of her thigh, attracted by the heat of her groin.

There was no assult or demand in his approach to her, there was only reverent exploration.

She sighed, and a ripple went through her. He felt her arm drawing him closer. His fingers found a damp place of division and he thought of the spring at Lourdes issuing from a vertical crevice. Here was a spring of heat and feminine energy and a fluid meeting of two halves of her body, a soothing opposition of her right and left halves elaborated in the labial rose-bloom; clitoris, velvet embossment of mons pressing out through musked flesh. He thought of the rose intaglioed on the silver perfume bottle he had given his first wife, centuries before.

His fingers found her clitoris. With great care, he caressed it, downward as one would seduce juices from a grape.

She shivered and opened wider her legs. Her inner scent drew him, like a bat, to the earthy dampness of a cave, the skirt above his head. Between two silks: his head, his face, pressing deeply but without urgency, the lips of his face meeting the furred lips of her genitals, his tongue burnishing a pearl, his fingers invoking sensations from her thighs as a sorcerer calls forth airy entities with intricate and subtle gesticulations.

He invoked her pleasure. For a long time this entity possessed her with rippling into wriggling then wriggling into writhing and writhing into a graceful sort of spasming and then she lay back and he rested, listening to the promise of the mice chirruping.

He stood and lifted her onto the bed, all in one sweeping motion.

He moved to lie beside her.

"No," she said. "You have been good and generous and shown that your heart is more than take. But not yet. The time will come when I'll take you inside me, all of you ... inside me." She smiled enigmatically.

Margaret rolled off the bed and went to the door.

Still suffused with a cottony-cloud of flesh-hunger, he stood watching her, confused, piqued.

She opened the door and turned to him a look of promise. "I'm going to leave. Use the mice. And begone, Vladislav. There will be another time."

She opened the door and ghosted—moving as if not touching the floor—out into the hall.

Dracula stood looking after her, thinking. He could go after her, force her. Like the others. The weapon that was a part of his flesh squirmed at his crotch.

He could force her.

Not her.

If he could have wept, he would have.

.3.

The vision receded like the light of a train's caboose sucked down a tunnel. But it took more than ten minutes for the sickness to pass.

I sat up, winced. My stomach was still upset.

Jolson smiled at me, sat down beside me. I wondered how long he'd been there.

Again, I was soaked in sweat. My head throbbed. The room swam with dark blobs. I forced myself to speak. "Jolson, Dracula has just made love to Margaret Holland."

Jolson feigned surprise. "Ah? Yes? And then?"

"She left him. He took no blood from her. I don't know where she went. I wish Lucifer would—damn!—would get in touch with me." I sighed. "I need my puppet-master, my strings are slack."

Jolson smiled. "You're cynical. Really, Vlad, you direct your own life. But of course there is the question, 'What is that which is actually *you*?' "

"Whenever I get close to the truth you start getting inscrutable on me. Screw you. I don't care, just now. The look of this room is making me *ill*, man. I want the hell out. I want to go home and have a drink and a cigarette. You understand? *Out.* I don't care *what* the doctor says. If I need a nurse we'll hire one. Get me out. Spread bribes, hire ruffians, anything—anything."

Jolson nodded. "Your wish is my command."

I snorted. "That's sickening, coming from you, closest thing to a djinn I'll ever—"

"We're going home," Jolson interrupted gently. "It's already taken care of. They were reluctant to agree to release you, but I—influenced them. A nurse is coming with your clothes."

I grunted and stretched, cursing the pang in my stomach. "Blood poisoning, a properly ambiguous term, in this case. Jolson, how long will it last? The visions, the rapport with him? I don't like it. I'm beginning to lose myself in him."

"Actually, you're experiencing what he experiences only as one lives through the events occurring to the protagonist of a movie—a sort of two-dimensional, vicarious experience. You would not survive, I suspect, were you to experience Dracula's sensations directly. He is not—well, it's stating the obvious but it's best to remember: he's not a human being. You have tasted one-tenth of the hunger, perhaps."

"That was more than enough."

A nurse, looking tired and ill-tempered, shuttled in and began laying out my clothes. She left, with a suspicious glance at Jolson that made me wonder what he had done to insure my release. I took a deep breath and swung my legs over the edge of the bed, stood, stretched, growling at nausea and dizziness. The qualms subsided, and I drew on the clothing, annoyed that it hadn't been washed. I frowned at a particularly repulsive splotch of coffee on a shirt collar.

"You are, I think—experiencing the compulsive fastidiousness?" Jolson asked.

"I—" I sputtered a moment. He had caught me by surprise. "Yes." I had always a respect for his perspicacity, but I'd no idea he was so *shrewd*. But then, till the day before, I'd had no idea he could permit himself to be possessed by beings with shining visages capable of cowing the Lord of Vampires.

Jolson said, "It's the result of your self-image in conflict with the influence of Dracula. The conflict probably produces—"

"Make up your mind, are you a mystic or a behaviorist?"

"Produces the fastidiousness complex, a guilt-compensation."

"Clinically, you may be right. But subjectively, to me, it happens that everything is beginning to look despicable and ugly and I can't live with it. So," I said, zipping up my pants and sitting to put on my shoes, "what am I to do about it, huh?"

"Defeat Dracula's influence. Shake it off. Completely. I think you're giving in to it too easily. You're enjoying his viewpoint, to a degree—"

"Bullshit! It makes me sick!"

"Morphine makes your wife sick, but she enjoys it, craves it. Exert willpower. I'll help if I can . . ."

And where *was* Lollie? I decided not to ask, not yet.

"Yes. Well, I'm not ready for the struggle just yet," I said. But it was not that. It was that I didn't *really* want to remove from Dracula. Not deep inside. I hated what came between visions—the disorientation, the revulsion—but I was seduced by living a part of my father, Dracula the demiurge, the dark power, the nighted glory.

There is no glory here, Vlad, Carlton had said.

Silently we rose and left the room. I walked as if sleepwalking, aware only of a desire to be gone from this place. In the hall, I had to look away from a bitter-eyed amputee stumping along on crutch and lone leg, waving the scarred stump of an arm.

I noted, however involuntarily, every finger smudge on the walls, the dust between the cracks in the floor tile, the muck collected in the crevices of overhead light casings. We rode an elevator, I closed my eyes all the way down. I waited impatiently as we were checked out, scrawled my signature on a release form.

Leaning on Jolson's arm, I was walking gratefully toward the brilliant squares of sunlight dancing on the glass doors, when someone delayed me with a hand on my arm. I turned to look, and groaned.

The policeman smiled. He was a black man with yellow instead of white eyes, and relish stains on his collar. Sweat stains made Rorschach blots of screaming faces under his arms. *Look away*. And dust on his shoes. *Look away*! I had to get home before the world transformed into an endless sea of sludge. "What the hell d'you *want*?" I asked.

He shrugged expansively, as if to call attention to the authoritarian blue cut of his uniform, and slowly removed his helmet. "A few questions. At the station. It seems there is some connection between you and the maniac who killed—"

"Forget it," I said too quickly. I turned away and started obstinately for the door. Two cops— large fellows with beer bellies and brickish complexions—came from the sides to block my way. I stared at them, noting their every blemish and, even at ten paces, the dirt under their fingernails. "It seems every year the cops get a little bigger. Are they breeding them for that, in some secret place?" I asked Jolson.

He sighed. "Perhaps we should accede—"

I turned to the black cop. "What's your name?"

"Sergeant Caldwell."

"Do you have a warrant for my arrest?"

"Just for questioning we don't need—"

"Look, I'll go with you *if* you force me, but I won't speak. Won't answer a single question, not even 'What's your full name?' or 'How long have you lived in San Francisco?' You understand that, Caldwell? I mean it. Nothing. I'll just shake my head to whatever is asked. Because if I'm going to the station with you, then I have to have proper representation, and the only man who will suit me, a certain lawyer, is out of town." (I lied glibly.) "I mean it. You can lock me up for a month and I won't say yes to 'Do you want a glass of water?' On the other hand if you—"

"Oh, hey, come off it man, there's no reason for you to be—" Caldwell began, attempting to win me over with a hey-we're-bro's tone and a fatuous wink.

"I said for*get* it," I interrupted, closing my eyes to keep from staring at the oil on the man's skin and the crusts of dirt I saw—or imagined I saw—on the ceiling. "But listen, Caldwell, if you guys wait till tomorrow, I'll answer *all* your questions frankly—in my home. *Not* at the station. You come to my house and you can record the whole damn thing. Is it a deal?"

Caldwell let out a long breath and murmured, "Just a minute, have a seat please." He whispered something to the two flanking cops—probably *Don't*

211

let him leave—and went outside to radio the station for instructions.

Jolson and I sat on hard plastic seats beside a plastic potted palm, staring at the far wall. I glanced out the window, stiffened. "Jolson."

He turned to me. "Yes?"

"It's getting dark outside, near sunset, but only minutes ago it was morning and Dracula was with Marg and the light—"

"No. The visions took you this morning. Then you slept. But they were still fresh in your mind when you woke. Actually, it was hours ago. It's almost six."

"It's going to be *dark* soon, idiot!" I whispered urgently.

Jolson smiled indulgently. "I can protect you."

"I don't know. Out in the open like that. One of his boys could shoot you from behind. Maybe we should hire some security or a police escort."

"All that would take too much time, I'm afraid, Vlad."

"Then summon Lucifer."

"Lucifer is not mine to summon."

"You're not a whole hell of a lot of use to me, are you Jolson?" I said irritably. Irrationally. I leaned back against the wall, then remembered the fingermarks on it and sat up. I glanced at the doors. I could see Caldwell standing by a patrol car, speaking into a hand microphone.

Beyond the patrol car, between two tomb-like office buildings rearing porcelain white against the skyline, I could see the dying glow of sunset, tinging the sky the flesh-red of a first-degree burn. "The sky is sunburnt," I muttered, "and *I* feel like I've got a bad sunburn and I'm standing in a goddam sandstorm nude. Get me out of here,

212

Jolson."

"Close your eyes," he said.

I shook my head. "I'm afraid to. I feel—oh, awfully tired alluvasudden. Like I might drop off if I close my eyes . . . and I don't want to be—to see as Dracula . . . I'm too damned weak." But I closed my eyes. They were too heavy to keep open just then. Ghostly silhouettes contested behind my eyelids. I seemed to see a gray-black image of a cage of white mice, a hand reaching in. I heard someone say . . . strange syllables . . . "Ahura T'gth Reg'Na," I whispered to myself.

"Vlad!" Jolson's tone made me snap my eyes open.

He looked alarmed. "Vlad, what did you just say? Where did you get those words?"

I frowned. The words slipped from my mental grasp. "I dunno. I thought someone else said them."

Jolson's voice betrayed a tremor. "Your father's influence . . . is strong in you."

I glanced at the glass doors. Beyond, the night was pooling in doorways and alleys, welling like some ethereal petroleum to drown us in the effluvium of a dead age.

A cool hand on my forehead tingled with electricity and seemed to flash a new, clean light into my brain. Strength filled the gnawing pit of unease in my chest, and the blotches on the walls diminished. The shadows seemed less palpable now.

Jolson removed his hand from me and smiled weakly.

"Thank you," I said. I felt a little embarrassed. "That's twice you've channeled strength into me. You look wan."

He inclined his head slightly, his eyes misting dreamily. "I'm fine. It takes strength to give

213

strength. I lose a little, for a while. I'll be all right in a few minutes."

I sighed. "I am my father's son. I'm draining strength from you," I said sadly. "Like a vam—"

"No!" Jolson interrupted vehemently, turning cold features on me. "Don't think of yourself that way or you'll give in to *him*."

I nodded, taken aback. Jolson had never before spoken sternly to me. But he was right.

"Mr. Horescu?"

I looked up. Caldwell stood over me, his badge gleaming dully. He went on, "The captain says that we're to escort you home. A man will be sent to talk to you. Tomorrow night."

"Excellent," I said, getting to my feet with a grunt. I felt a little dizzy, but better overall.

I had to assist Jolson as we walked toward the door; his steps were unsteady.

We rode in a police car; the sirens occasionally yelping, for a few seconds at a time, to help us through busy intersections.

At the corner of Polk and Sherman, our way was blocked.

Carrying flashlights and placards, at least three hundred blue-jeaned short-haired young women marched, chanting: "No more rapists, no more cops. No more rapists, no more cops. No more rapists, . . ."

Endlessly. They were marching in a parade to City Hall. When they sighted the three police cars in our caravan, they shouted and cheered, pointing their flashlight beams at us in parody of police spotlights, yelling challenges.

I was in the back seat of the second patrolcar. A young patrolman in the first car got out and went to inspect the protesters' demonstration permit.

214

"He's wasting time," Caldwell muttered, "they've got a permit."

The signs read:

COPS—WOULD YOU STAND BY
IF IT WERE YOUR WIFE?

and

RAPE: A WEAPON OF
THE POWER STRUCTURE

and

RAPE RAPISTS

"Can't we go around?" I asked wearily.

"Nope. Traffic's backed up behind us. There should have been someone back there with detour directions. Traffic Control is going to catch hell."

"So what's it all about?" (But I knew: Dracula's emanations. His strategy.)

"I guess you haven't seen the papers in the hospital, huh? Oh, there's a rape epidemic. It's really nasty. It's *weird*, man. It's like, like a disease going around, y'know? Guys people would swear would never harm a kitten suddenly jumping on the nearest chick—or, Christ, old ladies, for that matter—and in broad daylight inna middle of busy streets and trying to slip it to 'em *right there*." He shook his head. "And little girls. It's weird. I think maybe it's something in the drinking water, 'cause it's happening in certain areas more than others, and some places have different water sources than others . . . North Beach . . . Chinatown . . . Oakland, San Jose, and—" He glanced at me over his shoulder. "And in the vicinity of *your* hospital"

He stared at me.

I shrugged. I couldn't believably explain Dracula's

long-range psychic influence. It suited his strategy to evoke the rapist in us all.

The cop looked at the protesters and went on, "I mean, *dozens* an' *dozens* of rapes every night. And they think we're condoning it because we just can't handle all that. Fuck, we had our hands full *before* this happened. We can't give rape more priority than armed robbery."

"No, no I, uh, I see your point," I said. But I thought: When have the cops *ever* done even half of what they could about rape? It was always too low on their priority list, even before the surfeit of it. Ask Inez Garcia.

Two cops were walking on either side of the lead patrolcar, waving their nightsticks, clearing a way. We rolled slowly forward, into the melee. The faces of angry women filled the windows on all sides. I stared straight ahead, feeling irrationally guilty, as if it were I, personally, they accused.

We'd just crossed the street when Caldwell yelled and pulled the car to the right-hand curb. He pointed east, along Polk Street. "That fucking limo! That was there, at the hospital the night that killer got away. It was just leaving when we got there. They left *real quick* when we got there." He turned to me, "Who is it, Horescu?"

I shook my head. The long black car was pressing slowly through the protesters, honking. I couldn't see through the glare of flashlights off its window. But my chest felt icy: It was *him*.

Should I tell Caldwell?

I stared at the limo, indecisive.

To the right, a crowd of men, most of them drunks, had gathered in the protective cone of a streetlight's glow. They jeered, and one of them tossed a bottle at the demonstrators. Dracula's limo was blocked by the crowd. A policeman walked stolidly toward the long black car, signaling it to back into an alley and turn around.

But my father knew I was near.

The limousine lurched forward, the cop dodged, the car rolled like a glacial avalance past him, cold and inexorable, into the cluster of women. The crowd scattered, one woman, heavy and closer than the others, was struck on the hip. She spun and fell onto a curb, knocked senseless. Dracula's vehicle turned, pulled up next to ours, facing the opposite direction. The driver got out; it was Toltin. He opened the limo's back door, Dracula put a foot on the ground, prepared to step out, his eyes meeting mine.

Caldwell leapt from the car and unholstered his gun. A cop ran up from behind the limousine.

The crowd of women, those not bending over the injured woman, ran toward us, faces contorted with righteous rage.

Dracula stood and turned around, his silent command issuing to the suggestible drunks standing beneath the streetlight. The men surged forward, impelled by Dracula's will; moving as one, they intersected the charging women. Fists and broken glass wheeled over the mass of bodies. Women shouted encouragement to one another; men leapt onto the three protest leaders and, pupils shrunken to pinpoints, pinpointing mindless purpose, began to rend their victims' clothing, fumbling with their own zippers. Other men flailed, satisfied with violence. One of the policemen, an oddly intro-verted look on his face—as if he were fighting himself—drew his gun with one hand, unzipping his pants with the other.

More policemen moved toward the riot, swinging nightsticks.

Caldwell was running toward Dracula, gun in hand, shouting, "Freeze or die, motherfucker!"

Dracula reached for my locked door, yanked the handle—and it came off in his hand. He bellowed, his squat figure seeming to swell with fury.

He drove his right hand, fingers straight out, at the window. The window glass creaked, cracks spread out from his hand as it penetrated the glass, like webbing around a spider. The window, held together between layers by a plastic film, failed to shatter, but his hand broke through and came at me like a monstrous fleshy arachnid leaping from a hole in glassy webwork. "Shit!" I shouted, recoiling, crawling backwards along the seat.

Through the window glass I could barely make out Caldwell closing with Dracula, bouncing off him like a balloon from a concrete wall.

The car surged ahead, though I'd thought the driver had left. I looked. Jolson had climbed over the front seat and taken the wheel. The rioters screamed, sirens howled, the car growled as it jerked forward, Dracula roared, his wildly grasping fingers closing on the doorframe. He held on. The car's wheels turned but lost friction, squealing in place; we were going nowhere. Jolson floored the accelerator, the car leaped again, and the entire right back door snapped off in Dracula's hand.

I looked back as we raced away, the wind through the door-gap whipping my hair. I glimpsed:

Caldwell, dangling, choking, from Dracula's outstretched arm.

Toltin, firing a pistol at a cop who was firing back; Toltin catching a bullet in the throat and buckling.

The rioters dispersing beneath a cloud of tear gas; two women beating the inert body of a rapist.

And then Jolson turned a corner, and the city swallowed the scene all in a gulp.

.3.

The doorbell rang. I answered. "Hello, Marg." I said, opening the door for her. She came in and we sat warily across from one another.

I wondered how much she would tell me of her tryst with Dracula.

"I've got some odd things to tell you," she said after a moment. "At least, I'm going to feel odd telling you about it."

"And I have some—odd things . . . things to, uh, tell you. Who's first?"

"You."

"Okay." I considered. I watched clouds float past the skylight, the morning sun burning a corner of the window frame. "My wife's gone, for one thing. After I got back from the hospital, she was gone. How much do you know about what happened at the hospital and the riot and—"

"Jolson told me about it when I called to see if you were home. By the way, aren't you afraid to stay here? Dracula knows where you are."

"It's what Lucifer wants. Ah, anyway, anyway, Lollie hasn't been home for days, according to her nosy landlady. And she hasn't been *here*, because the place is neat and she's not. If she'd been here it'd be a mess. She's gone. Maybe in search of morphine, if she's run out of it already. Jolson can't find her, even with his—his, oh, call them extra-abilities, I guess. Hey, did you say Jolson told you *on the phone*?"

"Yes. You're worried about the police listening in? And connecting you with Dracula? Yes, that's possible." She smiled and glanced around. "For that matter, this place could be bugged. I think it's too soon in the game for all that, though. But maybe not. Poor Jolson is not very American at heart. Too honest. It wouldn't occur to him that they would tap the line. The trustworthy are too trusting."

"You know him well, for one who has spoken to him very little," I remarked evenly, no longer troubling to conceal my suspicion.

She shrugged, and adjusted her vest and the cuffs of her filmy white blouse. Even with her absurd glasses, Marg looked lovely in this light—but perhaps it wasn't the light. Perhaps it was a less perceptible radiance. Her air of complacency, possibly, her confidence, poise, even a quality of triumph.

Triumph over Dracula? Or over all of us?

"Tell Lucifer," I said slowly, curious as to what her response would be, "that I want to contact him in person. I want to see him. Soon as poss—"

"Bill? You have as much access to him as—"

"Don't give me that bullshit!" I snapped, tensing. "You and Jolson can contact him whenever you like. You're his. I'm not stupid, you know."

Her mouth quirked. "He will come when the time is appropriate."

"Yeah?" I quelled angry words, and with an effort put aside bitterness.

"Something more than the press of events and Lucifer's absence is bothering you."

I shot her a glare. "Am I to have no private life at all?"

"I'm not reading your thoughts . . ."

I leaned forward, smirking. "Then you *can* read my thoughts, right?"

"Only—" She hesitated. "Only at certain times. When Lucifer ordains or when I'm taken by the white light of the upper spheres."

Questions formed on my lips, trembled there. I swallowed them. Asking questions of Jolson and Marg and Lucifer produced replies which raised more questions than they put to rest.

"What are you thinking about? Mind telling me of your own free will?" Marg persisted.

Absently she removed her glasses and hung them from her fingers, let them swing by the ear-piece. The lenses swung there, catching the light of the sun now a quarter exposed over the rim of the window frame.

"I—shit, okay: It's Lollie. Lolita. My wife. She's sort of—well, she's particularly vulnerable to *him*. Psychically."

"Oh." Marg frowned.

There was silence. I twitched nervously when the refrigerator clicked and began to hum. "Well?" I asked finally.

"Well, what?"

"What do we do, Marg? About Lollie?"

"What makes you think *I* know what to do?"

"Still playing games with me, huh? That doesn't keep me from knowing that you're not anything like what you pretend to be. Right? Come on." She gazed at her fingers and didn't reply. Pointedly didn't reply. I went on. "You can help, Marg. I know that because I don't have to listen to your story about Dracula, your meeting with him in your apartment. I was there. With him mentally, in rapport." I searched her expression. No surprise there. "I was going to keep that under my hat, Marg. To see if the version you told of what happened was accurate. To check your honesty. But I've already verified your *dis*honesty. I saw—"

"What do you expect of me?" She said savagely.

221

The irritation in her tone gave me some satisfaction. "Do you expect me to be embarrassed, Vlad? Yes, there was intimacy, up to a certain point. And I fed him, I saved him. Bill wants to get Dracula but only in one particular way. He didn't want the police to get him. Dracula would simply have mended, then killed more cops escaping. Pointless to let that happen."

"I don't understand why Dracula isn't suspicious of you. You—you told him little of your motives, they're still a question mark to him. And he's by nature suspicious of everything and everyone."

"That's our advantage: he trusts *me*, and me alone. He has to. He's in love with me. That's the way he is. I'm the first woman he's met in centuries that was *real* to him, beyond a source of blood and amusement. He can be human, with me. And that's what he really wants, though he'd never admit it. He wants to let go, and be human. He's nearly invulnerable, as long as he's the dark demiurge, Devil's Son, the Immortal Impaler. When he becomes a man, though, he's just a man. And that's when he can be lured and trapped and—taken. That's why I'm involved in this. Lucifer *knew*. It was a predictable sequencing of psychic chemistries. Inevitable result: your father *had* to fall for me."

I was only half listening: I was thinking of Lollie. I blurted out, this talk of love triggering the remark, "I've fallen in love with my wife."

Marg laughed. "There's a note of distress in your voice, pal. A very male reaction, that. 'Good heavens, I've fallen in love with my wife!'" She began to laugh again until she saw my expression, and her own became serious. "Sorry. I forgot for a moment. You must be in pain. I'll see what I can find out about Lollie."

"Miss Holland," Jolson had come into the room. "A phone call for you."

I looked back and forth between Marg and Jolson. Their eyes met and lingered and I sensed some sort of silent exchange between them. Marg nodded faintly.

"Tell him I'll call him later," she said flatly.

Jolson turned to go to the next room. To hang up the phone?

I stood up and hurried past him; he glanced up at me in surprise. I went to the bedroom, picked up the phone, listened. A dial tone. I slammed the phone back down, went to the living room. Jolson stood beside Marg's chair. He looked sheepish.

"You should have made the phone ring, at least," I said. " 'There's a call for you,' " I mimicked. "I wonder what that means, really, between you—and why the hell you couldn't say whatever it means, in front of me."

"I'm sorry, Vlad—" Jolson began.

"Leave us," Marg said sharply.

Without hesitation, Jolson did as he was bid. As if he were used to taking orders from her.

She glared at me, looked as if she might burst out angrily. But then she shrugged, and relaxed, smiling thinly.

"You've certainly changed," I said, mostly to myself. "You used to be—I don't know uneasy. Self-conscious. Now you look like you're in charge, all the time."

I was hoping this would catch her off guard, but she seemed to accept it equably. "Don't worry about it," she said mildly. "As for the phone thing—what can I say? It was corny, perhaps. But, ah, there are some things I didn't want you to know yet. You'd get panicky. The call was an agreed-on code between him and me, yes. It means that your father is stirring early, making preparations. Jolson found out. I'll have to attend to some things. And he informed me through another method of something else entirely: The police are outside."

"Yeah? They were here earlier this morning to reclaim their car. They asked some questions, that was all. I guess they decided they had nothing solid on me. I lied beautifully. All it said in the paper was, uh, something like, 'Two police officers died in the riot, but no charges have been pressed for homicide as yet.' I thought I was clear, but if they're outside maybe they're going to—"

"No," she interrupted impatiently. "I don't think they have a warrant for you. From what I've been able to find out. Tell you what—you send Jolson to answer the door, to tell them you're not home. He's a good white-liar, he'll convince them. They can't search without a warrant, and we'll be free of them for tonight, anyway. Which is just long enough."

She stood and said, "Never mind, I'll tell Jolson myself." She went to the dining room where the whine of a vacuum cleaner had just begun. The vacuum cleaner's song was cut short and faded with a reluctant sigh. Jolson came into the living room, and the doorbell rang.

My stomach jumped.

Marg signaled me to follow her. We descended to the study. Jolson had, apparently, anticipated us: a fire crackled on the hearth. Pine logs. Pine doesn't burn long, but I prefer it because it spits and crackles, making for a merry fire, with sap popping, the room fragrant with the scent of fir.

The fireplace gave the small, cozy room its only light. The ranked bookbindings danced their titles through oscillating shadows.

We sat across from one another, each in a leather easy chair. I listened; I made out, faintly, the officious voices of policemen and Jolson's suave assurances.

After a minute, through which for every one of the sixty seconds, I worried that the police would not take no for an answer, I heard a car door slam, and the car driving away. Jolson came downstairs, looked in on us, said complacently, "They're gone." And left. But probably someone would remain to watch the house. And it occurred to me: *Vlad, you could be the fall guy here.* Someone would have to be blamed for the killings. I could become the scapegoat. After I had fulfilled my part in Lucifer's plans for Dracula, my only other use would be as a scapegoat. After all, Lucifer had stated that his interests were in expediency, not sentimentality.

In the wavering half-light Marg's features were hermetic, unfamiliar. Her shadow was ominously large on the wall to my right.

I caught myself muttering: "Lollie . . ." I wanted to hold Lollie near the fire, to rub life into her cadaverous flesh. To awaken her by the hearth.

I glanced at Marg, and then away—quickly away. She sat so still, so self-contained, wearing the shadows well. I was afraid of her, I realized. I felt like shrinking into my chair, hiding in the leathery crevices. And Jolson, too, was a part of Lucifer's cabal. Perhaps he and Marg were not evil, but they were not loyal to me, certainly. At times, Jolson seemed to have a real affection for me. Still, only Lollie was mine. As if she represented the scared, obsessed part of myself, the living dead man inside me, awaiting redemption.

"Jesus," I murmured.

"Are you aware," Marg said suddenly, startling me, "that the city has declared a state of emergency?"

"Yeah." My throat felt dry, talking was uncomfortable. It was strangely hard to breathe. "I saw it"—I coughed— "in the morning paper. Ten o'clock curfew for *everyone*. They trust no one. National Guard called in. Which may be a big mistake—no reason the Guard should be immune to the rape fever. And *they* are dangerously armed. Orders to shoot rapists, yeah . . . ACLU trying to get that overturned on the grounds it violates the right to surrender peaceably."

"Nothing will work as a deterrent," Marg said, yawning. "Tonight will be the worse night of all. Dracula will see to that. He'll poison everyone with ravening selfishness. Because he has to get to you, Vlad." She seemed to be enjoying my growing discomfort. "And with the police watching, it might be hard for him. So the police have to be decoyed—"

"Tonight?" I coughed. Tried to keep the sudden inrush of terror from cracking my voice. "Tonight? What—hey, what about *Lollie?* And—"

"Take it easy, Vlad." Marg had a handkerchief over her nose. Her voice was muffled. "We're going to look for Lollie, Vlad. In a few hours. At dusk. Till then—just breathe in deeply, and relax. Take a—a little nap."

"*What?*" I scowled, sat up straight, blinking. My eyes burned. I loosened my collar, wiping sweat from my cheeks. "How do you mean?"

She didn't reply. Tears leaked from my eyes. The room seemed unnaturally dark, the air acrid. I glanced around. Smoke was gathering near the ceiling. "The fireplace," I said, conscious that my

226

voice was slurred. I stood, shakily. "Damn, the flue must be stuck. I feel weird. I thought I was over it but maybe it's the blood poisoning." I coughed. "Why the hell did Jolson start this fire in the middle of the day? It's too hot in here."

"I asked him to," Marg said, standing. She placed her hands on my shoulders, pressed me back into my chair. "Have a seat, old boy." She remained standing close in front of me, the fire behind her giving her a nimbus. She became a penumbral figure as the room congealed with smoke. I leaned to look past her, at the fireplace. The two top logs had half burned through, revealing something else behind. It looked like a thatch of weeds of some kind, wired together and smoldering. I looked at Marg. She had her handkerchief tied around her face. There was a stain on the handkerchief and I guessed that it had been treated with something preventing her from succumbing.

As I did.

When I woke, the room was darker, the swirls and whorls of smoke, hard to see in the vague light from the embers in the fireplace, seemed to slide into recognizable patterns, faces, tenuous outlines of bodies dancing wildly.

My lungs burned, my eyes were caked with salt from constant tearing. I choked, the smoke was strangling me. I tried to get up, to leave the room. No go—nothing worked. I was paralyzed. A voice from someone on my right—it might have been Marg's voice, but it sounded as if it were a little too deep for her—said, "Relax, Vlad. The discomfort will pass. You've been asleep for hours. It's dusk or past. I had to make certain preparations, and you had to be prepared with your nap so you could be freed for our little journey. Morpheus has strict requirements; he guards his gates jealously, you see."

I tried to move again, and failed. But it was as if the effort of moving severed a psychic umbilicus, something that had tied my mind to my body. Because there came, then, a *click*—and I was standing over my body, looking down at myself. My body was sitting, staring into space.

I looked at myself, the self constituting my new, detached, viewpoint.

I had no body. No hands. Nothing. The pain was gone. Now it was a dreamlike *being there* without a physical *being* to define the *there*.

So this is astral projection, I thought.

Yes, thought someone beside me. That's what it is.

I turned to look. By "turned to look" I mean I shifted my viewpoint; I had no body to turn.

The thing that had spoken beside me had a body, and it wasn't Marg's. Her body was standing, stiff with trance and staring.

The thing beside me had many bodies, and it flowed from one form to another. I wasn't ready for the totality of it, of the thing beside me, and I think if I'd had a throat with which to scream, I'd have screamed.

The thing made an exertion of some kind—its formlessness formulated and became: Lucifer, as a whitebearded man with golden hooves.

Things around us were recognizable, but enhanced. Each object—book or mantel or chair or brick—seemed to extend itself infinitely in strobed images of diminishing size; if I looked at the chair from the left, it extended itself infinitely to the right; looking at the chair from the right gave a vista of an endless array of chairs stretching along a

228

corridor to the left. Things rayed themselves. And between any two objects, between chair and wall or between mantel and corner, windows of faceted crystal flickered, split-second glimpses into other worlds.

Don't look, said Lucifer beside me. Don't look long into an astral window, or you'll be drawn through.

Everything, I said (though we didn't speak in audible voices, our words were clear as shouts on a still morning), is leaping out at me.

Objects are revealed as infinite, each having its own continuum of self-articulation, Lucifer said. They intersect somewhere.

Where's Marg? I asked.

Marg? The Lucifer image beside me said. Marg is here. She's bodiless, unseen, like you.

He smiled. His teeth flashed infinite ivory, rays of sharp-edged denticulation.

I asked, Now what?

We tread the corridor paved with ideas, it ("he" is somehow an inappropriate pronoun for the sexually flexible Lucifer) said.

And then there was travel: we stood still and the universe rotated past us, walls and other obstructions drifting by us like transient shapes in mist.

Faster, on a manic carrousel in an ever-changing carnival.

Then there was a house by the sea. Slowing, we drifted through its walls (I glimpsed wires and crawling things). A room full of revelers, and an ugly sort of energy—red-edged and bristling like the hair on a tarantula's back—radiating about them from Dracula, the energy arrayed like iron filings over a magnet . . .

There was a butchered girl lying unmoving on the floor.

Two people knelt by the sundered corpse. One was Dracula, the other—

Dracula sensed us, and looked up, seeing through the fabric of space, into the astral plane; and (two people knelt, the other was—) he looked straight into my eyes. The revelers danced and yowled, their voices coming to us like distant bells chiming. (The other was—) They could not see us.

The other, the woman kneeling beside the riven corpse, the woman lapping blood and weeping: Lolita Horescu.

Oh, God! Lollie! I cried (with my mind). Lollie couldn't hear me. Dracula looked at me and laughed. Then, for the first time, he seemed to see Lucifer. He snarled.

He raised his hand, made a sign, and spoke words in an arcane sign.

A great wind bore us away, and shapes dissolved into shimmer.

"Lollie!" I screamed, sitting up in my chair.

The room was empty. Marg was gone. The smoke was almost gone. My paralysis was gone.

But *God*, did I have a headache!

EIGHT
.1.

The phone rang. I picked it up. "Hello?" There was a pause. I was sitting uncomfortably on a vinyl-topped stool, by the kitchen counter. The receiver stretched from a wallphone. I sipped a Tequila Sunrise and asked again, "Yes?"

"Vlad?" It was the Old Man. My boss.

"Yes, sir?" I took a longer drink.

"The first thing I ask you, Vlad, is—Who leaked it?"

"Leaked what?"

"I suppose it's *possible*. Possible you don't know. It's just possible you didn't see the afternoon papers. *ESPIONAGE AT IBEX*, it says, in big black letters. It's possible you haven't seen that, but it's not possible that you don't know anything about it. Because it had to be you."

"Uhhh . . ."

"Come off it, Vlad. Everyone knew you were there that day. You collapsed from blood poisoning right there in the lab. And it was only two days after you were in the lab that we found the baffles you installed. Ingeniously devised—I've never seen anything like them. I'd like to know where you got them. I don't suppose you'll reveal the source.

"Well, uh—"

"That's all right, I didn't think you would. I suppose you're wondering how we knew?"

"Actually, um—"

"An anonymous phone call. We thought it was bull, but that was a classified operation, so we had to look."

Anonymous phone call? *Toltin*, I thought. *Jealous of Dracula's attentions to me. He wanted to discredit me in my father's eyes. He wanted Dracula's approval more than he wanted him to succeed. No concept of loyalty.*

"But what I want to know is, how did the newspapers find out?"

"Well, maybe, er—"

"Yes, I suppose it was someone on my staff, someone with resentment toward *you*."

That would be *what's-his-name*, the dapper young eager beaver always looking for a chance to replace me. What *was* his name? My old life was fading. It came as no unpleasant shock when the Old Man said, "Needless to say, Vlad, your employment here is terminated. I suppose it was antifascist sympathies on your part that led you to sabotage the Brazilian statistic bank. The Brazilian authorities are a dictatorial bunch, I'll agree, but there's a more legitimate way of dealing with that. Let the CIA undermine governments, Vlad, that's what it's for. At any rate, we've managed to keep *your* name out of this. So far. The FBI's getting pretty pushy, though. You may be hearing from them. Well, good-bye, Vlad. And good luck."

"Uh, well, sir, I—"

He hung up. And I realized that Dracula's deal for a haven in Brazil had just fallen through. And it was my fault. He wasn't going to be pleased with me. I wondered if he'd let me live. Maybe—life of a sort.

With all the shades pulled, with all the lights blazing, I thought perhaps we could ignore the coming of night. But though I couldn't see the encroaching darkness, I felt it. And I felt, at the same time, a quiver of excitement: My connection with my father warning me that he had awakened.

I paced the livingroom—I was afraid to go down to the study—glancing periodically at Marg, who sat at the bar, calmly sipping a drink and glancing through *Time* magazine. Jolson was downstairs. "Jolson!" I called.

I heard his gentle tread on the steps. In a moment he stood beside me, his posture one of polite inquiry. His dark eyes were restful; I looked into them and relaxed. He glanced at my drink and shook his head chidingly, smiling. "You weren't to drink till your blood is entirely purified. Doctor's orders."

"Jolson, either I drink tonight or I climb the walls. *She*"—without looking at her I crooked a thumb toward Marg—"sits there like a sphinx refusing to get me in touch with Lucifer, and just seems *not to give a damn*"—I emphasized those five words for Marg's benefit—"that my wife is with Dracula. So what I want to know is, uh, what can *you* do, Jolson? You've done—*things*. Like—*you* know. You could get in touch with that—that faceless thing of light. Request that it influence her to return to me."

Jolson looked sincerely sad, and opened his mouth to reply, but Marg interrupted: "What the hell you think this is, Vlad? The Wizard of Oz? Do you think Jolson's the Good Witch of the East? He's going to give you a magic formula like clicking

your heels and saying there's-no-place-like-home?"
She set her drink down with a decisive clack, and
stood, stretching.

"The quality of your sarcasm is like that of
Lucifer," I observed.

"More innuendoes," she said, a trifle defensively.
"I won't deny that he's my mentor. One is influenced by one's mentor. But look, Vlad, lay off.
Lay off me *and* Jolson. He is fully aware of the
situation. But he's a Taoist at heart. He knows that
all things come to one who waits and that water
flows downhill—"

I groaned. "Don't ever write haiku, all right? You
do it poorly. Of all the corny bullshit—"

But she went on implacably, "And events will
flow toward a resolution, and soon. No sooner than
appropriate. Nature abhors a vacuum. By which I
mean: Lolita Horescu is coming to fill a gap here.
She's coming here all on her own, without our
having to do anything."

"On her own?" I asked suspiciously.

Marg cocked her head and scratched beneath an
ear. "Well, it was her idea, as I understand it. She is
coming with your father, but it *was* her idea to
come. She hopes to convince you—"

The doorbell rang.

I groaned, and it rang again. I groaned again, and
as if in planned counterpoint, it rang. I swore. I ran
to the stairs, preparing to descend.

"Wait, Vlad!" Marg hissed.

I waited, my back to her.

"Going to run and hide in the basement? When
you were so eager to find Lollie?" Marg whispered
mockingly.

I quelled panic, and slowly turned. Marg came to
me and whispered, "Go to the door. Jolson will be

right behind you. He will protect you if Dracula is there. If it's Lollie, talk to her, try to seize her, if there is an opportunity. Don't forget, the cops may be watching us."

"They're no longer there," Jolson put in. "I've been keeping an eye on them. They drove away. Another mass rape outbreak, emergency status."

I went to the door and had to make an effort to control the shaking of my hand as I turned the knob. The brass knob squeaked as it turned in the collar, and the noise set my teeth on edge. I hesitated, considering locking the doorchain. But if it were Dracula, the chain wouldn't hold him anymore than a length of twine would stop a mad dog. I took a deep breath, squared my legs, and opened the door.

Lollie was crying. But though her tears were causing her makeup to run, she did not sob; she was neatly dressed in a blue and white suit trimmed in beadwork. Her hair had just been permed, and it fell in jouncy pin curls immaculately arranged but designed to look prettily haphazard. "They dressed you and did your hair to make it look as if you're free and well," I remarked, my voice quavering only faintly. The prominent bones of her face glistened in the slanting beam of streetlight, her tears like raindrops on a timeworn tomb's marble figurine.

She ignored my remark, and recited: "Vlad, darling, it's so peaceful there, in the daytime; at night he gives us all we want of whatever we want." She rattled it off like a Girl Scout reciting her oath. I don't need morphine, Vlad." This last was hard for her to say: It was patently a lie.

"You've replaced it with blood?"

"The—" She cleared her throat, her eyes went to the side as if she were trying to look behind her without turning her head. I gazed over her shoulder. A blue sedan, dark blue like the horizon at dusk, waited, engine running, at the curb. There were four still figures inked within it. "The blood," she cleared her throat again, "it's communion wine. A sacrament. It washes out desire in—" She hesitated.

"Yes?" I chuckled. "Did you forget what they asked you to memorize?"

She stamped a foot angrily, her lips curled back as she whispered urgently, "Vlad, come back to us . . . You're one of us. I'm scared without you. I don't think I—Oh, I don't know anyone there and after the—" She stopped, stammering.

"One of 'us'?" I sneered. "Perhaps I am. Certainly I belong with *him* more than you do. You're not one of 'us,' Lollie. You're merely exchanging one escape into numbness for another. And you're magnetized by his mystique. He's had centuries to practice *that*. Yeah, hell, I could be one of them—because I *have* been, in a way. But I reject it."

At the curb, the door to the car opened. Hearing the door click and creak, Lollie uttered a small half-sigh, half-moan of frustration and turned to go. I grabbed her right elbow and in one convulsive movement hauled her in through the door. Both of us went sprawling on the rug. There were rapid footsteps coming up the walk. Jolson stepped over me and opened the door. I looked up, seeing him from behind.

His head was missing.

His head was replaced by a bowl of shimmer. I heard a ravening howl of frustration—something profoundly animal (and at the same time super-human) in that howl—and then receding footsteps, running.

The light, white and cold, flashed more brightly

and then vanished. Jolson looked normal, though his expression was more beatific, more Buddhalike, as he turned to us after closing the door.

Lollie stood up and went to the door, breathing heavily. Marg went to her, and I stood, taking Lollie's left arm. Together we dragged her back. She gave up resisting and slumped on the couch.

I felt weak, and it was hard to breathe. "Vlad?" Jolson said, looking at me with concern. I sank to my knees. *It was hard to breathe*—why? Because of the red swell, the onrush of blood, filling the room.

"Father," I said, before sinking.

.3.

Dracula paced back and forth, his eyes locked on the front door of the house, his head turning to accommodate that fixed gaze. He was not aware that he was pacing. He was scarcely aware of it when he impulsively leapt to the hood of their rented car and stepped from there onto its roof, to try and see into a second-story window.

There was the skylight, Vlad's pretentious stained-glass skylight. Dracula hoped the skylight had a crucifix of stained glass, so that he could dive through it. He frowned, and looked around. He had a sense, an intuition, that someone was looking over his shoulder. His acolytes were with him. Three of them, in the car. But at times he felt there was someone unseen . . . But then, of course, there always was someone unseen, no matter where one went. The invisibles would naturally be observing him. Still, it seemed disturbingly *near*.

He shrugged, his need to find Margaret Holland superseding all other considerations. "Margaret," he breathed.

Dracula leapt from the car's roof to the earth, took three long bounds, like a cheetah preparing to strike, each leap taking him higher than the preceding one, and launched himself to the roof of the house. He landed squarely, his feet sinking a quarter inch into the tarpaper. He smiled, hearing a noise of consternation from within the house, as they deduced the meaning of the thump from their ceiling. The roof was split-level, and he was at the first-story level that slanted sharply to a wall supporting the second roof. He approached the skylight, which lay in the shadow of the second roof. He was able to get within only three feet of it before drawing back with a snarl of disappointment.

The damned radiance.

It made him cold and weary, the oriental, the unwarming light.

He prowled the roof, looking for an unprotected entrance. He approached each window. Even the upper-story windows exuded Jolson's meditation on god-principle.

"Why didn't they stick to wolfbane and crucifixes, damn them," he muttered.

He stepped off the roof, as casually as a commuter stepping out of a bus, and landed in the soft earth of the back yard. He circled the house, sniffing. Margaret was there, he was sure of it.

He circled the house twice, pausing for a moment beneath each window, sniffing. No entrance. It was entirely protected.

He returned to the car, glaring at the acolytes. What now?

Set the house afire and drive them out? No, that would attract the fire department, too much potential for interference. Something to drive them out that would be less likely to alert the neighbors.

He glanced at the car, remembering the two revenants hunched unmoving in its trunk. Probably he could compel them to enter the house, despite Jolson's radiance. They were too stupid to feel the radiance keenly. "Fuck them *all*," he said emphatically. He resolved to kill the woman, Lollie Horescu. She'd hardly attempted to entice Vlad.

Vlad. *My son.* He snorted. Son no longer.

Margaret . . . Dracula closed his eyes tight, clenched his teeth to hold back a shout of despair. The great hunger rose up in him then, and all the thin, piping sounds of night came to him as shrilly as a butcher's sharpening of knives sounded in the ears of the soon-to-be-slaughtered. Through the walls of the house, he could hear Vlad and Marg talking, could hear them breathing, even through the hum of the air conditioner and the whine of cars on the highway below them. The air conditioner. The lights. He nodded to himself, spoke to an acolyte. "Frederick." The young man came and knelt. "Frederick, find an unobtrusive means with which to cut their electrical power."

Frederick went to comply.

Dracula glanced over his shoulder. The houses on the suburban street were dark, except for the ghostly blue light cast by television screens.

The wind changed, and the scents of the sea came richly to him: he choked on its myriad rots. Since they were near the sea, perhaps he could call the Undine, if he needed her—but no, she would be terrified of Jolson's radiance. Justifiably. *And perhaps I should take warning, and flee it,* Dracula thought. *It implies great hidden power. But Marg.*

Dracula waited. Frederick acted: sparks bled blue from a cable at the house's seaward side. The lights went out. The murmur of the air conditioner ceased. The sounds of the house's occupants—breathing, fingers rasping on one another, heart-beats—became more audible; Dracula heard it all. He felt them within the house, sensed their life-heats moving about. The blood-song calling him.

Like the Sirens calling ships to the rocks, Dracula warned himself. *Run! You haven't survived these centuries by ignoring portents, by mocking the power of the invisibles. That One is near . . .*

But . . . Lucifer had somehow found out about the Brazilian deputation, the submarine. Probably by reading young Vlad's mind. And Lucifer had destroyed the sub. He, too, had oceanic allies. Too much power! *But . . . Marg.*

But it was no use. Because: Margaret.

Dracula's mouth was very dry.

"Frederick," Dracula said, not taking his eyes from the darkened house.

Frederick came to stand at Dracula's right, passively awaiting a command.

"Frederick, go and see if you can find me—something. I need surcease. The world impinges. Get me something human, but don't break into any houses. Someone who won't be missed for a few hours. A child at play, perhaps . . ."

The man hesitated. His speeding heartbeat was heard by Dracula. He was indecisive. He found it difficult to bring himself to kidnap children for Dracula's feeding.

Dracula longed for Old World Wallachia, and the mid-European inquisition, places and times where people were more sensible.

He determined to feed Frederick to the revenants when the night's work was done. He turned the acolyte a hard look. "Never mind. I can see you haven't the stomach for it," said the Impaler in

240

insouciant contempt. Frederick relaxed slightly. "But go and steal a dog for the revenants, and watch for police." Frederick bowed and moved off into the night.

Dracula looked at the house and at the woods behind it. He listened to the woods. Small life-heats rustled there. Small feral things. Some of those things would obey him.

He went to the car and opened the trunk. He gestured peremptorily. The sunken figures lying fetally in the trunk climbed laboriously out, tumbling onto the street. They stood, and stumbled toward the house.

Dracula closed his eyes. He exerted his will over things crawling in the woods, as a man would will his muscles to tense—and as a man exhales a sigh, the woods expelled a stream of humping, running shapes. Small things and many of them. Surrounding the house.

The revenants circled the house, one to either side. One of them began to crawl, slowly and as if in great pain, up a drain pipe to the roof.

.4.

And I woke clawing at myself, trying to rid my skin of the thousands of crawling horrors swarming over me, the four-legged gnawers borne to me on currents of blood.

And I woke, really awakened this time, on my bed in my room, Marg musing silently beside me in a chair, her legs crossed, foot tapping empty air as if she were in a doctor's waiting room.

I was sick. Cold chills rode waves of nausea. It passed in minutes, and Marg handed me a towel. I wiped away the sweat bathing my face and chest.

"We're going to be attacked," I said, thinking that every time I woke, the disorientation was a little worse.

"Don't worry about it. We'll handle it," said Marg with what seemed to be ridiculous over-confidence. "Go on, go to the living room. Talk to your wife." The room was dark, her features lost in shadow.

There was a scraping sound from the ceiling. "But listen! There! Did you hear? They're on the roof, Marg!"

"I know," she said with maddening calm. "Go on."

Weakly, I went down the hall to the living room. Long dark corridor, candlelight at the end of it. Two candles in each room, and a kerosene lamp in one corner. Just an ornament, but it gave out a weak light and thin aromatic smoke.

I went to sit beside Lollie, who was still hunched over on the living room sofa.

I put my hand on her arm. She clasped it between hers, bent over it, rocking; where before she had been weeping without sobbing, now there was sobbing without tears.

She had hold of my right hand and clung to it so desperately I was afraid to withdraw it, though I wanted to put my right arm around her and pull her close. I tried to ignore the scratching sounds at the door, and wondered if she held my hand only to keep me from touching her further. No, she felt differently about me, then—as I had learned to feel differently.

I was distracted by an ugly squeal of nails on glass from the opposite window. I looked up. The shape staring at me from the window wasn't immediately identifiable as a face. It resembled the

242

torn and rotted stump of a tree branch, with knot-hole whorls where eyes should have been and a saw-gouge for lips. In the gray light it was inhuman and vague-edged as a lump of putty. But it had once been a man with whom I'd spent part of my childhood, a man who had sat with me poring over hundreds of books, who had accompanied me on seemingly endless treks through the mountains of Europe, a traveling companion, an advisor, a comrade in faith, become a psychotic, a blood-fiend, a living corpse, a walking hunger, clawing at the windowpane.

Marg, at the head of the stairs, was gazing unmoved at the remnant of Carlton Caldwell, who scraped ineptly at my window. Without looking at me, she asked, "Do you have any weapons?"

"Uh—" I was breathing heavily, it interfered with my ability to speak. "No—not much. A ceremonial sword in the cabinet to the right of the door in the study, and a twelve-gauge shotgun and maybe four shells in a closet to the right, uh, down the hall."

"I'll get them," she said, pounding down the stairs.

Jolson sat in lotus position in the center of the living room rug. His face was composed, his eyes seeing something in some farther place. "Jolson, hey!" I cried, the panic breaking loose in my chest.

Jolson stared ahead, didn't flicker an eyelash. He was entirely occupied with preventing my father from nearing the house. He couldn't do that and also stop Dracula's children, as it were. The revenant, what was left of Carlton, braced and shoved—revenants are slow but strong—and the window frame splintered, popped inward. Carlton hunched over the frame, clutched, climbing awkwardly, his mouth hanging open, the two greenish teeth digging into the shredded remains of his lower lip. One of his shoulders, it seemed, was crawling up onto his head, and it had two red eyes of its own. I looked more closely: It was a rat, a black wood-rat, and two of its fellows followed it onto the floor. Unhesitating, squeaking in tiny extensions of Dracula's pent-fury, they ran towards us. I glanced at Lollie—she sat still as iron, her face in her hands. Four fat rats now, and then three more. There were seven squirming there, and the revenant succeeded in climbing over the sill. He fell on his face, tumbling into the room, began slowly to get to his feet, leaving large scales of oily gray skin sticking to the rug, his stench preceding him. He kicked list-lessly at the broken glass around the raped window.

I snatched up a lamp to smash the rats. "Marg," I called, too shrilly. The rats came on, I swung at them, they retreated, then began to advance more slowly. They came with deliberation.

A shadow draped me. I looked up. Something blocked out the half-moon that had dimly shown through the stained-glass skylight. Another vampire, a crumbling revenant. *Damn it, that's an expensive piece of glass*, I thought inanely as the once-man stepped forward and came crashing down in a cloud of jagged glass, bright shards. He hit me slantwise, knocking me back onto the sofa, his shin against my ribs; yes, and the metal lamp I still held caught his ribs and the rats scattered, fragments of colored glass like frightened hummingbirds rebounded from walls, cutting my cheeks.

And Lollie sat unmoving a yard to my right, her knees drawn up.

Every damn thing in sight looked as ugly as vivisection.

But Marg came to the head of the stairs. She

leaned the shotgun to one side, and hacked at the increasing numbers of rats with my old brass-and-silver saber. They fled before her, though she hit few of them, as if her touch were more a terror to them than her blade.

What is she? I wondered again.

Carlton—so to speak—had got to his feet, was shambling toward us.

The revenant who'd jumped through the skylight had broken his leg in the fall and the rod atop the shade-support of the lamp was jammed into his ribs. It fell away, clunked on the floor, and rusty fluid flecked with gray followed it, thinly spattering the rug. The vampire made childlike faces denoting hurt as it stumbled, trying to control its broken leg. Marg chased the last of the rats out the window, though I suspected a few were lurking under furniture or in adjacent rooms. Marg returned, swinging the saber. She struck Carlton with a short *shunk* across his spine. He bent unnaturally backwards, flopped like a beetle on his back, waving his skeletal arms. I dodged the swiping hands of the nearer revenant and ran for the shotgun. I picked it up, swung about, cocked it, all in one motion: It felt good. But Lollie was in firing range, too close to the thing. Hitting him, I'd hit her.

So I stood there, paralyzed by uncertainty.

The revenant rolled its white-marble eyes and seemed to notice Jolson, who sat rock-steady on the floor a few feet from us. It hobbled toward him, balancing on its good leg, the broken bone-ends of the other limb glistening slick-green and jagged through bare skin. It nearly fell, waved its arms for balance, yellow foam flecking its paper-dry lips. Small shiny things crawled in its matted white hair and out of its ears. It raised a fist over Jolson—it had moved from Lollie—I tilted the gun barrel up, well over Jolson's head, to be sure he caught none of the buckshot, and yanked the trigger. The gun seemed almost to explode in my hands and I bounced from the wall behind (I'd bought the shotgun to use it hunting, had never actually fired it). The revenant had gone in the opposite direction, portions of him reaching the farther wall before his main bulk, what was left of his brains running down the wallpaper. The corpse crawled, as if searching for its head, a few shreds of which clung to the uneven stump of its neck. Small white slitherers and shiny many-legged crawlers issued from that stump, in place of blood. Finally, its dinosaurian nervous-system realized that the eternal ordeal was *really over* and that it could die and be really dead; it collapsed with a final quiver of what might have been the ecstasy of abandonment.

Jolson sat unmoved, unchanged.

Marg was shaking Lollie, trying to force her to stand and leave the room. "Go lock yourself in the bathroom for now," Marg urged her. "There's no window there." Lollie didn't move.

The Carlton-thing, even with its back broken, crawled toward me, its mouth opening and closing with a noise like a rusty hinge swiveling. One of its eyes was missing, but something looked out at us from the socket. The stench from the revenants was beginning to overwhelm me. I gagged and pulled my shirttail up to cover my nose.

The Carlton-thing paused over one of the dead rats, and sank its suction teeth into the furry hump.

I wanted to kill it. The revenant. Or re-kill it. To kill it for Carlton; and so I could get it the hell out of there and air out the room. But I couldn't bring myself to get nearer. Marg looked up from Lollie,

246

glanced at the skylight—itself a jag-edged socket with the half-moon for a cat's eye—and down at Carlton. "I brought up two more shotgun shells, Vlad," she said. "They're on the table by the sofa. By the kerosene lamp." It was her way of saying: *He was your friend. You kill him.*

So I did. Mechanically I loaded the gun, walked over to him, braced myself more carefully this time and, as he looked up, the rat he'd drained still in his mouth, I pulled the trigger. His face was gone in blue flame and smoke. What remained . . .

I would have vomited then, if the rats hadn't returned to distract me.

They came from the window and dripped from the skylight and scuttled in from the next room, all seeming intent on reaching Jolson. Dracula had sent them to kill Jolson and drop the barrier round the house. Breathing hard, Marg and I stationed ourselves to the right and left of Jolson—his face calm and peace-washed, undisturbed by the turmoil like a mountaintop over a thunderstorm—she with the saber clenched in both hands, I swinging the shotgun in mine. A sort of camera-eye aloofness fell over my viewpoint, then I killed rats. I killed rats, that's all. And yanked them from my pants' legs and felt them sink their teeth into my ankles and smelled their sour pelts, saw the ticks that shared their fur; insects drinking from pools of rat blood collecting about the dead rodents. But all this (and the green-gray husks of revenants, the shards of stained glass mixed with tiny furred corpses, Lollie's sobbing from the corner, ignored) I saw as if it were on a television screen, removed from me. I saw it, thought about it, acted on it, but my heart was unmoved. I killed rats, and killed rats, and thought about it as if I were considering a strategic situation during a chess game.

I thought, too. Scientists use rats for experimentation because they are in so many ways like human beings: their metabolic system is almost a scaled-down replica of Homo sapiens, their blood types are very like ours, and they react to reflex-stimuli much as do people. They're clever with their small, thumbed hands. They're like little furred toothy caricatures of us. They'd come because Dracula had sent them, as an extension of himself, his ill will, his malevolence, encapsulated in each rat. They'd overcome their natural fear of us, attacked us uncharacteristically, senselessly, because they were moved by a wave of Dracula's hate (I killed rats, and my arms ached) and compelled by his will. I looked into a hundred pairs of rapacious red eyes (my fingers clutching the gun barrel throbbed with weariness) and yellowed teeth and angry hisses and thought: red eyes, angry hisses, snapping fangs—each one is a miniature of Dracula's hatred, furry embodiment of his hunger. Come for me, come for us, come to—

I recognized these things, but just then there was no horror in me. I felt them claw my legs (my arms ached and swung and ached) and mount my sides and snap at my face but I shrugged them off and they fell away like grisly snowballs. No horror just then. But it would come.

It came, when they were all dead.

The last few made desperate running approaches to Jolson, but none had quite touched him. My father's control over them was not absolute. They feared what Jolson radiated.

And they were all dead, then, more than a hundred rodent corpses.

Vaguely, without nearly enough of the appropriate concern, I hoped that none of those which had bitten me had been rabid.

Jolson had remained cross-legged, robed and complacent, as we'd killed two vampires and scores of large rats, as we'd fired shotguns over his head, swung the saber and shrieked. Through it all he remained implacable . . . but vulnerable in body.

After the rats were dead, I began to feel—ah, something of what one feels after being bitten by a single mosquito, and imagines feeling hundreds more biting, though there are no more. Or seeing a spider crawling a wall and killing it: the spider is dead, there are no more, but from somewhere, from suggestion probably, there is the clear sensation of many small spiderfeet treading the legs, crawling up the spine . . . just out of sight.

I began to itch all over, to see—so I thought—rats boring into me. I remembered that during the Middle Ages one punishment for adultery was to entrap a rat under a bell jar on the adulteress's belly. After a while, with no food and no place to go, the rat begins to chew its way downward.

They were all dead, but I felt every one of them chewing its way into me.

And I was very unclean.

I retched, gagging, picked up a lamp, ran to the stairs (trying not to notice what I had to step over) and down, to the darkened downstairs bathroom.

I set the lamp on the cover of the toilet seat and, wishing I had more light than the kerosene flicker, filled the tub, thinking: Go back upstairs. Dracula could come now, Jolson and Lollie have only Marg to protect them, he could send his acolytes to snipe at Jolson from a window.

But I ignored self-reproaches and stripped, settling into the tub (thinking, to hell with Lucifer's advice, call the cops, Lucifer's deserted us anyway, we need protection, call the—), immersing myself to the neck in hot water, letting it sting me. I inhaled steam and wept.

.5.

Reeking of disinfectant, carrying the smoking lamp, I went upstairs. Marg cleaned out the rats. One of the revenants, Carlton, was gone; the other remained, rotting where it had fallen. Jolson sat on the floor, unmoved; Lollie lay full-length on the couch, staring at the ceiling and shivering. Marg sat beside her, wetting her forehead with a cloth. "What did you do with the little bastards?" I asked, leaning against the wall and looking around. In the half-light of the kerosene lamp and the candles, the room's shadows were impudent, overactive, wavering mockingly.

"Dumped 'em into that trash burner out back," she said absently.

The lamp was becoming hot in my hand; I set it on the kitchen counter. I poured myself a drink, straight Scotch. And another, and one more. And one for the road. And one in salutation of—

"That's enough booze," Marg said sharply, glancing up from Lollie. "If you're drunk you can't stay alert."

I was beginning to nurture a comfortable numbness in my chest, and I sighed as I put down the glass.

"You burned the rats on the patio? *He* might've caught you unprotected out there," I said.

She shrugged. "*You* can clean up the last one."

"The—" I looked at the corpse of the revenant. "Uh-*uh*. No. Not me," I said slowly. "It's time we

250

stopped coddling Lollie. She wants to be *part* of Dracula-Vlad-the-Impaler-Lord-of-Vampires. His walking dead are *part* of him," I said, rather histrionically. "They're his goddam *pets*. She should get *used* to them." I raised my voice, walking towards her, "She should get *cozy* with 'em. If she wants to be *near* Dracula." I couldn't keep the sarcasm from my voice. "So let Lollie dispose of the thing. Let her *get into* Dracula's world—at least up to the elbows."

Lollie sat up abruptly and looked at me with open accusation.

"So you're not as catatonic as you've been pretending," I remarked. She ignored that. Her skullish face was even more drawn than usual, her eyes red-rimmed, her hair in disarray. She swiped at her nose with a shaking hand, pouted at a broken fingernail. She was verging on morphine withdrawal.

Marg nodded to me, her expression coldly ruminative. "I think Vlad's right," she said softly.

"I'm not going to touch that fucking *thing*," Lollie croaked out.

"I don't have morphine, but I have some Valium," I said, looking at Lollie. "If you take enough Valium, ten or twelve hits, say, it should get you through for a while. I'll give it to you if you do it. If you clean the thing up. With your bare hands. I want you to know Dracula *intimately*."

Lollie stood up, then sat down. She wore but one shoe. She searched about the couch for the other, found it beneath a dislodged cushion, and pulled it onto her petite foot with a petulant yank. Her lips trembled, her hands shook so much they were a blur. She stood, and shuffled slowly toward the headless remains, gingerly stepping around the blotches of rat blood. She stood over the corpse, wrinkling her nose, swallowed. "I *can't*—things are crawling on it," she said in a hoarse whisper.

"That's all a part of *him*," Marg said emphatically. "Go on. Take its wrist and drag it out back."

Slowly she bent, and looking at the wall, holding her breath, she closed thumb and forefinger around the outstretched wrist of the corpse. She backed off toward the patio's French doors, towing.

But as if its fingers were those of a glove, the hand slid neatly, like well-cooked meat, off the bone, liquifying into purulence in her grasp. She coughed, gagged, ran to the bathroom, shaking yellow-green *stuff* from her fingers.

Marg nodded, satisfied. She went to the magazine rack, took up a newspaper, wrapped it around her hands, and went to tow the thing, by its bone. The path on which she dragged it was littered with stinking shreds.

We cleaned the floor with insect-killer, disinfectant, and a wire-brushed broom. Both of us glanced repeatedly at the broken window, expecting attack. *Nothing more, not yet, please,* I thought fervently. *Not for a while.*

Jolson sat, implacable. It occurred to me that Lollie could go out through a window. But no, she'd want to claim her Valium.

Walking more steadily, her eyes brighter, Lollie came back into the living room. "You found the Valium?" I asked, picking slivers of broken glass out of the rug beneath the dashed skylight. A cool wind licked through, now and again. She nodded. "How many hits you take?" I asked.

"What was left."

"Sixteen! Jeez." I wondered what sixteen Valiums would do to her. Normally, they'd probably just put her to sleep. But she was strung out—and she had seen what we had seen.

Lollie picked up one of the candles by its brass holder. She walked—or, rather, she drifted—to the bedroom. I trailed after, grateful to be away from the scene of the carnage. I found her lying on the bed, her arms over her eyes. She'd picked the guest bedroom—it had no windows. The only light haloed from the candle on the seat of a chair beside the bed. I closed the door and sat beside her, on the edge of the bed. I wasn't sure if I was welcome. Haltingly, "I'm—I'm just plain *sorry*, Lol'. About making you touch that thing."

She shrugged. "Maybe it was a good idea. Maybe it did me good." But she didn't sound as if she meant it.

"How did you end up with *him*?"

She didn't reply for several minutes. Finally, "He came for me. I was strung out. He put something to my lips. The ugliness and pain left and I was numbed again. I looked to see what he'd given me—it was blood." She shrugged. "I went with him."

The line of her jaw, the only part of her face visible beneath her arm showed white skin drawn drum-tight over bone.

She's essence, and nothing more. Exquisitely attenuated, I thought.

"And are you done with him?" I asked.

"I might ask the same of you. But as for me, I think so. At least for now."

"Look, at-least-for-now is far from being good enough. *I know*. You've got to be utterly determined or—"

"Hey, Vlad, come on, man. Don't. Just—" She fluttered one of her fey hands over her head as if waving away a fly. "Don't pressure me just now.

Can't handle that shit."

I let the anger die out in me, like a coal growing cold. And it sat there, inside me, cold and gray and bitter. "Sure, okay," I said at length. "God, hey—don't you think the fucking pressure's on *me*? Can you feel it out there? In the living room? It's in here some, too, but not as much. It's a tension in the air, a kind of charged *coldness*. And then, uh, there's a contrasting sort of pressure. Coming from Jolson. Like they're both exerting to overcome each other. Dracula's will and Jolson's. You can feel—"

"That's *enough*," she said, half-pleading. "Gimme a break, Shakespeare," which is what she always said when I indulged in rambling.

She removed her arms from her face and turned to look at me. "You're a part of *him*, too." She said it as an assertion and not an accusation.

I sighed. "Not really."

"Yup. You fell down, just before the lights went out, man. You were mumbling and your eyes were open, but you weren't conscious of us. Marg says you were in rapport with your father. Because he made you drink some of his memories and because you're his son."

Why did she tell her? Aloud I said, "That doesn't mean I'm *part* of him. Or that I—that I condone him." My hands clenched defensively. But she had me: I'd been feeling it for an hour. A yearning for Dracula's gift of numbness, surrender of responsibilities, release of all those things my behavioral therapist had worked nearly a decade to control in me. Like a man yearning for deep sleep after insomniac wakefulness, like a junkie yearning for heroin antibeing. Through the door of sleep, and out into the garden of dreaming.

What the hell. Lucifer could be wrong.

But I saw, then, in my mind's eye, as clearly as if it were a photograph: Carlton Caldwell's ruined face. And then, another image: another Caldwell, Officer Caldwell, strangled by Dracula. "Two Caldwells," I murmured. "I hate coincidences like that. It bugs the—"

"You're avoiding the truth, Vlad," Lollie said with what passed for passion in her. "You need your father."

"What do you want me to do?" I asked, nearly shouting. "Give in to him?"

"No, the contrary. I just wanted to point out that you're not purity personified, you jerk." She moved her arm and smiled at me, resembling an ectoplasmic nymph in a Waterhouse painting.

I was afraid to move. The darkness outside the room called to me, and I felt that I was very, very close to surrendering. I was afraid that if I moved it would distract me, set off a ripple that would break down my defenses. "Lollie," I said, whispering, "I'm afraid to move. No kidding. I'm afraid he'll reach in and take me. The walls are turning—" I closed my eyes, but the falling sheets of red were there, behind my eyelids. "Lollie, he's closing in. I think he's realized that I can share his viewpoint and he's using it to get *at* me."

"*You're* afraid?" said Lollie. There was overt pleasure in her tone. "Thank God for that. Yeah. That's the first time you've admitted fear to me, Vlad."

And that was the first time I knew, clearly and consciously, what it was that had held Lollie and me apart.

I felt her move on the bed, sinuously unbuttoning, unzipping, shedding skins. But still I was afraid to open my eyes. I tottered on the brink of rapport with Dracula. But cool arms enfolded me, attenuated fingers coaxed the knots from my back and enticed the clothing from my limbs. Red walls faded, and I sank into Lollie's embrace.

The necrophiliac fantasy didn't make an appearance. I was making love to a stranger, and that was the excellence of it. I'd never previously admitted to myself that I didn't know Lollie. It's one thing to echo the cliched platitudes to the effect that people who live together are usually strangers—we all give a nod to such wisdom. Few of us have the guts to act on it. Sometimes one is lucky, and is forced to face the pretense, to break through, to surrender to utter comprehension of one's own ignorance. And this stranger was unfolding in my arms, roiling her thighs about the stiffened extension of my electrical being, sensations of her satin enclosure, the life pulsing in her coming out of its damp hiding to embrace mine, feeling like—this the picture in my mind's eye replacing the bloody falling—electrical arcs furling and unfurling about an electrode.

I walked in her body, approaching a distant light that was orgasm, as I might walk through a nighted landscape in the half-light just prior to dawn; getting closer, emotionally closer to her, as the dawn light brings into sight more and more of the landscape about me, and I realize I've been walking through my homeland, amazing grace, I was lost but now—

I kissed her because I felt like it, not because it was expected of me. I kissed her as a greeting, not because I was trying to excite her. And, unthinking, my fingers searched out her nipples and her clitoris and evoked the unseen flares, so that (and I know it's damn unusual but I swear to you it's true) our climaxes were simultaneous, a dual flash-flash of electrical lights, recognition in the light given off by lovemaking.

We recognized each other, were closer, and then it was over. And Lollie was *still* a morphine addict.

The Valiums were not enough. The fear, the estrangement from feeling, both came back to her on a wave of post-coital ennui, and she began to tremble. "The phone's out, isn't it," she said, and it was not a question.

"Yes. I doubt if we could call anyone for a fix this late. Nothing pharmaceutical, anyway."

"Maybe *he*—maybe he's gone now. Maybe he gave up."

"He's not gone."

Silence reclaimed us. The candle guttered, two inches left to it. Its flame wavered in currents created by our muted breathing.

The musks of sex steamed invisibly upward, and I inhaled her quintessence, essence of essence.

Then, sadly, she got up and, mechanically, dressed. I watched her, and I felt raw and tender. "Hey, don't leave, Lollie."

"I'm just going out for a glass of water," she said.

"Hey—" But she had left the room. I heard her walking hurriedly down the hall.

I was afraid.

Lollie was in need. And she had been frightened by our closeness. She might—"Oh, *shit*," I spat, hearing her pass the bathroom, and the kitchen. She wasn't after water. I got up, pulled on my pants, picked up the candle. An ague in my hands, the shivering, caused hot wax to drop on my wrist. I cursed, tilted the candle, extended it ahead of me to light the dark course of the hall. Anything could be out there, I realized when I was ten steps outside the bedroom door. "Lollie?" I called, trying to make my voice carry without making it loud.

I heard Marg's voice, but couldn't understand what she was saying.

I hurried. When I heard a thump, a crash, a shout, the front door swinging open, I began to run. Preceded by a pool of milky candlelight, I ran into the living room.

Jolson was lying on his side, his head staved in from the back, the shotgun lying behind him, blood on the stock, Marg was standing in the open doorway, shouting at Lollie, who was running toward the car parked out front.

I glimpsed Dracula, and a bearded, bald-headed man running toward us.

I picked up the shotgun, acting in a fever, borne on impulse, and ran toward the door. "Lollie," I shouted, "God *damn* it!" And I raised the shotgun to my shouder. Marg stepped aside.

Lollie ran to Dracula, threw her arms about his thick neck.

He slapped her aside. She spun through the air for a couple of yards, fell on her back, and lay twitching.

Dracula and the bearded man came toward us. Dracula's acolyte was cocking a pistol.

I aimed the shotgun and pulled the trigger.

NINE
.1.

Sirens. The neighbors had heard the earlier gun blasts; the police arrived in time to see the flame and hear the noise from this one, as Dracula's bearded acolyte fell back, streaming fingers covering the ruins of his face.

Throwing whirligig beams of light, two California Highway Patrol cars pulled up behind Dracula's rented limousine.

Dracula took the shotgun from my limp fingers and broke it over his knee.

The right side of his face was peppered red from shotgun pellets, but he seemed otherwise unhurt. His face came at me like a livid, two-lamp, locomotive.

I jumped aside, the blow he'd intended to kill me with catching me glancingly on the shoulder, and the lawn rushed up at me. I fell across Lollie. I sobbed, "What the hell am I supposed to *do*?"

I rolled till I could grasp Lollie by the shoulders. Her eyes were closed. She lay still. I shook her, wondering if she was dead.

A warning shot, an angry shout from the police cars. I looked up.

Dracula was standing beside the porch. Marg stood slightly back from the doorframe, looking impossibly unconcerned.

Another warning shot ricocheting from a metal drainpipe over Dracula's head caused him to turn in annoyance, facing the police.

His face was one large snarl.

In two bounds he'd crossed thirty feet of yard and was alighting, *clang*, on the hood of one of the cars. His boots dented the hood. The cop nearest him was frozen in astonishment. There was a dark blur as Dracula struck, and then the cop was missing his throat. He crumpled. But four more approached, two of them leveling guns.

I looked away, down at Lollie. She was still breathing, half her face purpled with a massive bruise. She made love to me, and it frightened her, I thought. Her terror of real feelings drove her to Dracula. Morphine or blood. She had bludgeoned poor Jolson just to please Dracula, permitting the Impaler to enter. (She was temporarily mad, strung-out, didn't know what she was doing, I told myself.) And now the left side of her face was swollen purple as a rotted fruit.

Marg stood at the doorway, leaning against the frame, seemingly bored.

She's provoking him on purpose, I thought.

I lifted Lollie in my arms, staggered toward the house.

"Hold it, you!" someone boomed through a bullhorn. A bullet kicked dirt from the grass by my feet. I turned to face the spotlight. One uniformed figure was looking toward me, the other three were firing at my father, who was in midair, just then, coming down on them from on high, his eyes soul-less sockets of black, bared teeth gleaming. Even then, with Lollie limp in my arms and Jolson dead in the house, I thought: *In his way, Dracula is magnificent.*

Dracula connected, and two highway patrolmen went down beneath him. The other two turned and,

260

fraid to hit their companions, who were pinioned
eneath Dracula's knees, holstered their guns and
umped him, leaping on his back. That was a
mistake. They might have stopped him with a bullet
o the spine or the brain, at least temporarily. But
n four swift movements—two elbows down-crushing
he chests of the men beneath him, then arms
ut-swinging scythes, catching the other two in the
ead, crack-splash—four more dead.

Dracula stood, glared at the people watching
ervously from the windows down the street. He
linked as the whirling lights atop the police
ehicles struck his eyes. He went to the cars, and I
hought he'd smash the lights. But with absent-
minded methodicalness, he opened the car doors,
eached in, found the switch, and cut the lights. His
omposure, concealing mounting propensity for
iolence, terrified me.

He closed the car door and turned to face me.

.2.

And ignored me. He strode past, a few feet away,
vent directly for the front door, and Marg. I
vondered how long it would be until more police
howed up. A while, I decided, with the rape
pidemic paralyzing the city. Lollie stirred in my
rms.

In the gleam from streetlight I glimpsed blood
eaking from Dracula's back and side. They'd hit
im several times. If he felt it, it didn't show. For
he first time, I noticed what he was wearing—Army
atigues.

Lollie shifted and opened her eyes. She winced.
One eye was swollen nearly shut. I put her on her
eet, helped her to stand as she gained her orienta-

tion. "Let's get out of here," I said. "Marg can get Lucifer to help her, she's up to something."

But Lollie had seen Dracula, who now stood on the front porch talking to Marg. Lollie slapped away my restraining hand, and ran toward him.

She went a few steps—and slowed to a walk, biting her lips in self-doubt. But she slowly approached my father, her arms outstretched, half-stumbling.

"Goddammit, Lollie!" I yelled, my voice shrill.

She was a stride away from him. Lollie was taller than the Impaler, but he was full of stolen life, throbbing with stolen heat, and she was a feather beside him, a wisp. I loved her.

She was fragile, feverishly fragile, and I wanted to speak of those few minutes in which she'd stopped fearing and stopped avoiding and let her need well up, that furious abreaction, a feeling becoming an edifice of being, a furnace consuming us. Inside her contrived aloofness, within her cold and fragile shell, was love enough to explode a sun.

But I'll be damned if, even had I time, I could have told her that.

I could not have made her believe it. In this age, one finds it hard to convince one's wife that love in marriage is possible.

But her hand was on Dracula's shoulder. She was caressing Vlad the Impaler. She was moving to embrace my father, declaring herself the property of the son of the devil.

"Ugh," I said. "Oh, God, oh, Christ," I muttered. "That's ugly."

Dracula was talking quietly to Marg. I couldn't hear his words from where I stood (why did I stand there, as if rooted?). But I could *feel* the substance of his words, subsonically, because—though he whispered—he uttered them with such passion, such purposeful vibrancy, that the house hunching over s reverberated slightly in response.

Lollie attached herself to Dracula, winding her mbs about him, the torn lips in her battered face egging him for blankness and living death; and now er feet had left the ground and she was *climbing* im, sobbing, though he stood unwavering as a tonehenge monument.

Just then she was all conditioned, submissive vomen; she was the end result of millenia of xploited women, taught to rely on men, given hildlike surrender, daughterly archetype as urrogate identity.

My father's time is done; Lucifer is right to claim him, I thought.

But Lollie put her hand to Dracula's lips, bscuring the words he fixedly directed at Marg cool-eyed Marg who stood with arms crossed, one eg cocked to cross the other at the ankles, gazing ver his head at the stars, employing a time-honored echnique: attracting his attention via her own etachment), and forced him to notice her.

Oh, yes, Dracula took notice of Lollie. Without aking his eyes from Marg he made his right arm amrod straight, to the side, so that she was flung •ff. And when, instantly, she was up, rushing ysterically to him, he stopped her with his hand, ingers opening to take her by the throat (though ll this time his head had not turned to regard her, is eyes were locked on Marg's), closing, mechancally compressing. He stood, legs planted, talking to Marg, with his arm extended fully to the right, traight *up* from the shoulder, garroting Lollie with is fingers. She dangled, her feet thrashing ten nches off the ground, at the end of his arm,

turning pink then red then blue, her soft pin[k]
tongue extruding, her eyes exposed more than wa[s]
natural, clawing at his hand—but there was no ange[r]
in her expression.

And all the while, Dracula had not looked at he[r]
he stared at Marg.

It was the lack of anger, anger in her for wha[t]
Dracula was doing to her, it was Lollie's grotesqu[e]
submission that made me uproot myself, tha[t]
moved me to turn and run to the corpses of th[e]
police whose blood mixed with asphalt (which wa[s]
only right for highway patrolmen); searching th[e]
red-wet uniforms till I found the .38 Special.

I was jealous, too, I suppose, of Lollie's utte[r]
devotion to him.

So I took the gun, went for Dracula. It took [a]
long time to get there, or so it seemed. He g[ot]
bigger and bigger before me, she writhed in his gri[p]
in slow-motion, the house loomed over me like [a]
cresting wave of lava.

But then I was directly behind him, raising th[e]
gun, pressing it to the back of his head, trying t[o]
control the shaking of my hands, both hand[s]
wrapped around the handle of the gun as I clumsil[y]
pulled the trigger, and just before the gun made it[s]
gutteral shout, I heard Dracula say: "... if
compulsion is made by destiny—the inevitabilit[y]
cooked up by the Gods, if you will—then it i[s]
divine. I can bear no guilt for divine purpose, th[e]
hand of Siva is—"

And then the gun went off: "Goddamn you!"
the gun shouted, in place of a bang. Or so [I]
thought.

He took notice: his head snapped forward, an[d]
back. His fingers relaxed, letting Lollie drop to th[e]
ground, foam at her lips.

At the back of Dracula's head was a red vertical crack like a post-birth vagina, gouting red. He turned the awful lips of the head wound away from me, he turned his face toward me, he coughed, he spat something at me. The bullet, gory and warped, bounced from my chest. He snarled, his face was as contorted as that of a man who's just had a noseful of Mace—but there was a childlike hurt in his eyes.

And he raised his hand to break me in half.

Then the blood-sewn bond between us made me feel what *he* was feeling, the hurt of bullet and betrayal; I melted before his white-hot pain, and shock was kind enough to take me and numb me more thoroughly than morphine.

.3.

When I woke, I was sure there was a hole in the back of my head. My head throbbed with hurt. And I felt weak, as if from loss of blood. I raised a hand. The hand refused to go where I wanted it to; it missed my head and swayed like a drunken cobra, until the feeling came back into it. Finally, I got the recalcitrant hand up to my head and felt the back of my cranium. No bullet hole. It had been an illusion of the rapport. And as I recognized that, the throbbing diminished. My head felt oddly clear.

I sat up, looked around. Marg and Lucifer were not apparent. I had the distinct impression that only a few minutes had passed. The cool night soughed in the telephone lines. A dual-pitched muttering came from behind me. I turned, saw two men, middle-aged fellows with paunches and white short-sleeved shirts. One of them had a doberman on a long chrome chain. The dog was sniffing at the corpse of a patrolman. The men looked at me uncertainly, wondering whether to help me or set their dog on me.

I wanted them to go away.

I stood, and almost fell flat. My right leg had gone to sleep. I'd been lying half on the front steps, the concrete corner cutting off the flow of blood.

I shook blood back into the leg, growled in the rush of cold and pain, stamped feeling into it. Then, thinking *To hell with them,* I went to the bushes beside the house and urinated. I felt better after that.

Beginning to shake, as the images returned (Dracula's split skull, Lollie's choking, Marg's cool eyes), I turned to go into the house.

But I stopped on the front porch. Just inside, in the doorway's shadow, my wife sprawled on her back. She was breathing shallowly, blood bubbling at the corners of her lips.

I felt sick.

Inside the house was darkness, and something warned me not to go in just yet, not to give in to the temptation to descend to see what was going on downstairs, in the den, my study. I suppose I knew that's where they were, Dracula and Marg. And perhaps Lucifer, too. I don't know how I knew.

I turned and peered at the street. The two men were standing there yet, looking stark as photo-negatives in the blue-white light thrown by the streetlight.

I started toward them. "Hey—" I cleared my throat. "Hey! Call an ambulance!" I shouted. "For Lollie—it's my wife, you see—go on, call a doctor!"

They backed away from me. One of them turned to bolt. The other, holding the dog which strained at its leash to get at me, said, "Wuh—waitaminnut, mister, don't come closer—"

I was running up to him, hurdling the bodies and ignoring the snarling Doberman, shouting, "Idiot! Call the—"

Then the man let go the dog. As if the leash were a fuse that had just burned down to ignition, the dog exploded at me.

The red-black hound knocked me onto my back with its first leap, its paws like trowels digging my chest, jaws angling to close on my throat, its slaver—smelling like Purina *Dog* Chow for God's sake!—dripping onto my cheeks. Black eyes ringed in red eyes not so different from Dracula's

But I'd just looked into the pain and rage of the Lord of Vampires. And next to *that*, the dog's attack was trivial.

Much frustration boiled out of me then: I trapped its snout in my hands (saw the veins stand out on the back of my hands, the fingers livid with strain—hardly aware that *I* was doing this thing), pushed the animal's jaws away from my throat, began to pull them apart, the dog raking me, rolling violently as it tried to escape, a high-pitched howl sirening from its throat, then the crackle as its jaw-bone broke and splinters found its brain. It shook, yelped briefly, once. I threw aside a sack of cooling fur and dead meat.

Breathing hard, confused by a mixture of triumph and revulsion, I sat up. I put my damp hands to my temples; the throbbing had returned.

My shirt was torn, the frayed cloth-edges clumped with blood. Mine. The dog's saliva stickied my fingers. I stood, grimacing with pain, wanting to whimper, holding it in. I tottered, wiping my hands on my trousers.

The dog's owner returned. He was carrying a pistol, half upraised. I ignored the gun. He looked at the dog's body, shook his head sadly, lowered the gun. "I thought I'd have to shoot him," he said.

After a moment I decided that he meant the dog. I asked, "Did you call the goddamn ambulance?"

He nodded. "But it'll be a while." His eyes were on the dog as he spoke. "These riots in the city. Hell breakin' loose. All ambulances busy. Red Cross, 'n' National Guard. . . . The San Rafael ambulance's gonna come after they deliver the one they got now."

He looked up, over my shoulder, at the house. I advised him, "Go away and lock your doors and be kind to your children if you have any and don't read books about dead things that walk, unless they're fiction." I probably wasn't intelligible, for there was blood in my mouth, slurring my words.

I spat blood onto the walk, turned, started for the house.

I was at the door of the den, standing in the dark hall. Getting there had been like sleepwalking. I was tired, wanted to sleep. Knew I'd be unable to sleep, though, if I were to try. Lollie was sleeping, or dying, upstairs where, moving like a zombie, I had laid her out beside Jolson, on the couch.

I wanted rest, but first I had to learn something.

I gazed blankly at the floor. I stood there by the half-open door for a full minute before I gathered my wits and focused my eyes.

There was blood on the rug by my feet.

I looked up, pushing wide the study door. There was my father, and there was a thing that we'd been calling Margaret Holland. The room was lit by a single candle, its unsteady flame throwing shadows that shook like dirty laughter. The rug had been ripped from the floor; it was nowhere about. On the concrete, someone had chalked a complex geometric figure, a series of interlocking triangles which, when one looked at the center of the design, seemed to stretch into an infinite tunnel walled by teethlike angles. The triangles were surrounded by runes, and the runes were enclosed in a red chalk circle. Incense smoked from a brass cup.

Marg, nude, stood in the heart of the sacred circle. The candle was by her left foot, the incense by her right. On the floor, Dracula . . . was crawling toward her. The back of his head was matted with blood. He was weak and deranged from the wound, the wound that would have killed a man. But he was alive. He crawled on his hands and knees, supplicant. Or like an infant.

Marg's eyes were fixed on Dracula's. Her eyes were cool; but now, too, they were bright. Her eyes were small orbs of cold white light, the light that never warms. She was bigger than I remembered. I blinked, and revised my estimate: She was *far* bigger than I remembered. Larger than anything human had a right to be. More than eight feet tall and thick as a weightlifter. Her breasts were uptilted and pointed; she wasn't overly muscular, nor fat—but *solid*. Between her legs, just above her huge vagina, was a complete set of male genitals. Somehow, it all looked proportionate. Marg's—the hermaphrodite's—features were hardening, sprouting beard, hair receding atop, transforming—

Lucifer. The head of Lucifer. The hermaphrodite. Bill. Lucifer. Margaret Holland. One person.

Smiling to myself, I realized that I wasn't surprised.

Dracula crawled, slowly advancing on the hermaphrodite, and Marg/Lucifer spread his/her legs. She? He? I'll call the hermaphrodite manifestation

269

it, for convenience, though *it* wasn't neuter. It was all sex. Dracula crept weakly, determinedly, toward All-Sex.

Reaching the hermaphrodite, Dracula got to his knees, straightening between its legs, pulling himself up by grasping its knees.

I watched unblinking, unbreathing. As the hermaphrodite's great vagina began to gape, to blossom like a monstrous flowerbud seen in fast-action film, efflorescent flesh widening, opening impossibly wide, the hips outspreading to compensate. Marg-Lucifer-It growing, evenly swelling, filling up the room, crowding out the books with its bulk, and Dracula trembling, entranced, mewling, pressing his head into that gaping, moist maw, the womb that opened to engorge. . .

There was was a sickening sucking sound.

I had to look away.

When I looked back, Dracula was head and shoulders into the ingesting vertical mouth, his clothing peeling off him and falling to the floor as he went. The male genitals dangled over Dracula's shoulder blades.

Marg-Lucifer-It stared—now!—at me. It looked at me from where its head, big as a big man's chest, pressed against the ceiling, its silvery beard framing the feminine mouth, eyes viewing me impassively, pure-white emptiness glowing from behind the pupils.

I tore my eyes from that murderously beautiful visage, the face of a demon goddess, and looked down. Dracula's hips and legs were drawn into the immense vagina, the furred labial lips conforming to his cross-section shape purpled with blood, stretching like elastic—very much the skin of something *human*.

I took two steps back, and tried to grasp it and file it in my mind. I couldn't find a place for it. I was number two man in the West Coast Branch of IBEX computers, so I suppose it's excusable if I say: It did not compute.

Because there was a man-woman big as an elephant filling the room with its flesh, while between its tree-trunk legs a candle and an incense vial glowed like the luminous eyes of a ghoul; my father, Lord of Unliving Hosts, was *gone*, swallowed head and foot like a mosquito into a Venus's flytrap, and yes, I can safely say that it did not compute.

The room wavered—but only because I was shaking so much.

And all that was left for me was to throw up. But my stomach was empty and I was left dry-heaving.

Vlad, child, said the palpitating woman-man straddling the infinity of triangles, *Vlad, babe, don't be afraid.*

Maybe it meant for me to be next.

I backed up, sputtering, bumped against the wall behind me. "No."

I won't swallow you, honey-son. And your Ol' Man is safe within me, it said, without moving its lips. A voice like the whine of a knife honing on a fast-spinning stone.

Vlad, Vlad . . . Vlad, the younger. I have Dracula in here. Your father. The one you called your father. It patted its protuberant gut, which bulged like that of a pregnant giantess. *Vlad, look away, for a moment. Move away from the door. I'm too full, I'm too gorged, and he's restless, he struggles within me, and I've got to put him to sleep for a while, take away his strength and his hunger and his material substance. And there is the second law of thermodynamics to consider; so, Vlad. . .*

No argument from me. I moved down the hall, turned my back, put my face in a corner, covered my head with my arms, and closed my eyes.

But even there, with my back to the door, my eyes closed, and ten feet down the hall—even there, the flash startled me. And I blinked, my eyes burning, filling with tears, I looked hastily at my back. My coat was smoking, smouldering. I took it off and slapped it against the wall, till a violent crackling sound called my attention back to the den. I went to look, because I had no other place to go—the only way out was past that hell's-mouth doorway.

It was hell's mouth because it shone with the light of flames—large flames. An urgent, feeding sort of glow. I looked in, squinting against the brilliance, and saw Bill, Lucifer, as I had first seen him. Hooves and beard and canary-yellow suit, walking toward me across the coals. . .

The floor was streaming flames that arose from burning books. Over these he strode, through fires that licked up burned walls.

"You've set my house on fire!" I said, with more astonishment than resentment.

He shrugged, and—unburnt but oozing smoke—he stepped out into the hall, to stand beside me. The flame-light turned his left side to glowing copper. "Sorry about the house. It caught when I discharged all that extra energy. Spontaneous combustion. Old moldy books. Didn't *mean* to. But I'm not going to put it out. Hell, it'll simplify things." The flames crackled an agreeable counterpoint to his words. Smoke gathered in thickening wreathes over my head, sending seeking tendrils down the

272

hall. Lucifer continued, "It'll help leave you in the clear for the inevitable police inquiry . . . possibly." He yawned. "Anyway, it's *traditional* for the house to burn down. Right? Or fall into the tarn, like the Ushers'. There's a reason for that cliché reappearing, beyond lack of imagination. There's a solid root to all myths. And clichés. Just ask Jung." He scratched his beard, sniffed, glanced up at the burgeoning smoke. "Archetypes are insights of the collective—"

"Oh, *Christ!*" I shouted, getting angry to avoid hysteria. I turned and bounded up the stairs, swearing as flames unfolding from the den singed the back of my head. Slapping at my hair to keep it from catching, I turned the corner at the top of the stairs and, slowing—not eager for the spectacle of Lollie bloodied and Jolson's corpse—I walked hesitantly into the living room. Clattering up behind me on his almost delicate hooves, Lucifer followed.

We stood in the half-light, listening to the growing roar from downstairs answered by the nearing yowl of sirens.

Lollie was lying very still.

"Bill—can't you—?"

"Yes, seeing that she's not dead." He bent and put his hand on her forehead. "Hm. She's *almost* dead, though." He closed his eyes, shuddered as he conducted life-energy into Lollie—and she shuddered, receiving it. But some of the rigidity went out of her, and her breathing became strong and regular.

I sagged with relief. "What about Jolson?" I asked, feeling tears course my cheeks as I gazed at him. He removed his hand from Lollie.

Lucifer shook his head. "No. He's gone to the godhead, absorbed; I wouldn't—and maybe

273

couldn't—bring him back now. That'd be an awful thing to do to him. He's where he's striven for. He was a fine giver of love, the best. Wish I could join him, hang up my ego and merge. I will, at the end of this cycle. It's not wise to bring dead things alive—your old friend Carlton is an example. Besides, it's hard work. My manifestations have avoided it, since Lazarus." Straightening, he said: "Let Jolson's shell burn with this house."

I didn't mind losing the house. It was tainted. The rats, the revenants, Dracula, had violated it.

From out front came a commotion of high sounds and bright lights.

Lucifer bent, gathered Lollie in his arms, and led the way through the kitchen door to the back yard.

Quickly, we went into the woods back of the house, following a sparse path through pines and sage.

The air was crisp and fragrant.

The shouts of firemen and policemen dwindled behind. It would be but a few minutes before some of them searched the woods.

Lucifer, effortlessly carrying Lollie, led me up a hill. Occasionally I slipped on the pine needles and moss. We reached level ground, and in a small clearing floored with mulch and nodding ferns, he stretched Lollie out on her back. He straightened up, looking at me with—perhaps for the first time—an unshielded gaze.

Light came from him, a light without warmth or glare.

"What now?" I asked, my voice breaking.

"That's what I was going to ask you. Did you expect me to vanish in a puff of smoke or something? Everything has consequences, and if a package isn't tied, it comes open in transit."

"Is—" I pointed at his belly, then dropped my hand, feeling presumptuous for making so crude a gesture regarding him. "Is my father in there now?"

"No." He laughed. "I drank the drinker. I swallowed the swallower. But he's not in there now—it was a transitory phase. When I radiated the energy, starting the fire, he was expelled from this plane. He's locked dematerially in another—oh, an Elsewhere. My womb was a door into another world. As wombs are."

"But— Well, what will become of my father?" My voice broke with agitation. I was fighting a sense of loss over Dracula.

"He wasn't your father."

"What?"

"He can't have children of his own. No vampire can. That's one part of the legend that's true. He took the seed of a dead man—not even *I* know which one—and drank it into his empty glands through the parasitic demon he used as a sexual organ. He reinjected that seed into your mother, as he raped her. The semen of the dead survives its maker, for a few hours."

"Some unknown dead man." The night seemed abruptly colder.

"Yes. But you *do* have some sort of spiritual affinity with him. Such is the nature of conception, even when the seed is stolen."

I sat down on the damp leaf-rot, crossed my legs, and put my head in my hands. I wanted to slide into imaginings . . . and things around me seemed to blank out for a moment, as dream-quality decided the form of the world. Trees flexed like arms and ferns rained music.

"No!" Lucifer's voice, harshly bringing me back. "It's *not* a dream," Lucifer said, his voice harsh. He

275

was speaking from his lips now. "It's childish of you to pretend that—" his voice became mocking "—'it was all a dream.'"

"But—"

"Too much to assimilate?"

I nodded.

"Tough!" He chuckled. "You have to do it."

I reached out and touched Lollie. She smiled in her sleep. And her flesh was warm. Realizing both these things, I felt better. "Can't you cure her of her addiction?"

"Could. Won't. Don't believe in toying with the karmic scales. It's for her—the cure. And those who love her."

"She—she doesn't love me. I don't think . . ."

"Maybe not yet."

"I want her to—" I felt like a child, confessing to him. Which made me feel a little better. "But she seemed to love Dracula."

"*Seemed* is the right word, laddie-buck. He symbolized numbness and escape and surcease, for her."

I had an idea. It was a very bad, very stupid idea, but I didn't know that at the time. "Listen. My father . . . I mean Dracula . . . Is he gone for good?"

"From this plane. I have use for him elsewhere. He's going back to work for me. Till he dissolves his karmic burden. A thousand lifetimes, perhaps."

"So—won't you need someone to replace him, on this plane? Some apotheosis of the unknown to provoke people to learn?"

He smiled. Probably he'd been waiting for the suggestion. "Yes, well . . . I was thinking that maybe a vampire is old-fashioned. Perhaps a hydrogen bomb will do . . . or maybe I could invest Anton LaVey with the hunger. Or Johnny Rotten—he's just *begging* for it . . ."

"Why not *me*?" I spoke rapidly, trying to overcome the terror I felt at the prospect of receiving what I was asking for. "You said I had a spiritual affinity with Dracula. I've always secretly identified with the role. Hell, you know that. That's how I got into this thing—"

"No, it's not. But—you don't want the hunger, Vlad."

"Why not? Someone has to do it. I know what it's like—I had the blood-empathy with him, I saw through his eyes, felt what—"

"You did not feel a fourth of what there was! You experienced only a suggestion of it. A dilution." His voice was like an iceberg's cracking. His eyes shone white. His beard sparkled blue electricity. Against the sky's sidereal glamor, his aura was like the glow of Earth seen from space.

"I *want it*," I said, not at all sure I wanted it.

"When I gave the hunger to Vlad the Impaler he was freshly killed—I had altered him. He was no longer human. In fact, he'd been inhuman in life, possessed from childhood. But you—"

"I can . . . I can take it."

Lucifer seemed to hesitate, considering. I sensed he was playing some obscure game with me, one whose outcome he knew full well.

The night let go a wind and I shivered. The chill of the earth seeped into my buttocks and thighs. I stretched out my legs, got to my feet. The wind resurged, the trees creaked a warning.

"You think she'll love you," Lucifer suggested softly, "if you become as *he*?"

"Yes." I hesitated. "Maybe."

"Or is it another, uglier need in you?" There was no accusation in his voice. A cold statement, more than a question.

"Yes, I—Maybe. No, uh, I don't know."

"Well, we'll see, if you survive it. So you want to take Dracula's *place*." No accusation—but his tone was all mockery. Suddenly he laughed and my head rang with it, and behind me a pine less sturdy than the rest crackled and fell away from us, crashing into the undergrowth, struck down by Lucifer's laughter.

I trembled and could not look away from him.

A light as abrupt as arrow-flight stabbed from the right. Flashlights. Someone was coming up the hill. "The police . . ." I murmured.

He nodded, almost imperceptibly. "Do you really *want it?*"

His voice was very loud, so loud my ears rang when he'd finished the question.

I swallowed. "Yes."

"Do you really want it?"

His voice was louder. I put my hands to my head. Lollie stirred restively in her sleep. Shouts from below. "What the hell was that?" said someone.

"Do you really WANT IT, Vlad?" louder than a sonic boom beside my head. I yelped in pain. Behind me, three small trees fell.

"Yes!" I shouted, inwardly wailing: No!

Lucifer bent forward and put his hand on my shoulder. "All right, little Vlad, I'll give you a portion of it. A quarter of it."

His voice was dangerously soft.

That's when I knew it was a bad idea.

He put his hand on my forehead. Something was coming out of his hand and into me. I opened my mouth to tell him not to give the hunger to me. Too late. I couldn't speak. But I could *howl* . . .

278

Lucifer removed his hand. I screamed: the thing took control of me.

You experienced only a suggestion of it. A dilution.

I was achingly hollow. I was a man of skin filled with nothing—nothing except a red, churning mist. Hot, skirling, *hungry* smoke.

And then all sense of my body vanished. I was just a moving force, a vector of something. Vicious energy on the move.

Lucifer was gone.

Lollie was to one side, moaning.

Two men were coming up the path. A flashlight beam shone in my eyes. "Shit! Look at his *face*!" one of them said. He's the one I went for.

I hurtled at him. Smelling his blood, screaming (he and I both), driven by dolorous waves of sheer need.

The pain of saturation, too much sensation, of *knowing* the world physically a thousand times over. Nerve ends split down the middle and quartered and penetrated by stimuli. Colors coming at me like spears, textural impressings of air and ground and weeds like bludgeons. Gradations of temperature and the tastes in my mouth, the cacophony in my ears—all of it vastly amplified, exploding impression whose shock waves carried me along, made me feel minute in comparison to the immensity of the world pressing in on me; and the only escape from insignificance was *attack*, and the only surcease from the pain was *blood*. And all of it carrying me along, throwing me, forcing me at the throat of the white-faced man who flayed at me with a billy club. All because the hungry fog within me told me that there was peace in stolen blood . . .

Listen. Once, at the beach, knocked down by a

particularly large wave, I'd panicked. I'd floundered reaching wildly, looking for something, anything solid in the battering seas, the proverbial straw—and when a log drifted into reach, saving my life, made for it single-mindedly as if it were all there was to desire in all of life . . .

That's something of how I felt, just then, trying to prise blood from the living receptacle struggling with me (he was not a man, he was just a *thing* to be torn and drunk from). But it was much worse than the episode at the beach.

And it hurt indescribably.

I was on fire with need. But I hadn't Dracula's strength. The two cops wrestled me down. couldn't bear it, knowing I wouldn't get what needed to extinguish the inner rapacity. I felt i turning against me, sucking the life from my brain

So I ran from it, inwardly. I retreated, to some where within me.

And I didn't come out again for six months.

.4.

The hunger is gone, now. I suspect that Lucifer came, and took it from me, while I was in shock Still, it was months and months before I felt safe enough to come out into the world.

It was a dog that brought me out. That sounds peculiar, I know, but it's true. Dogs are used as psychiatric aides, now.

The others tried in vain—all the pink, biped things with the inquisitive orbs in their upper parts these were "doctors" and "nurses" as it turned out They probed me, tried to get through to me with wheedling, massage, shock treatment, films, drugs. Nothing worked because I trusted no one. I *refused* to come out. I lay on my back and tolerated the intravenous feeding, the manipulations of my limp limbs. I kept my eyes closed whenever they'd let me, and I watched—like an infant fascinated and uncomprehending at a TV set—the wheeling orbs of light and shade, ragged-edged colors welling and breaking behind my eyelids; and I was safe, in there, untroubled . . . aside from an occasional nightmare, a vision of a woman bloated and impaled still-living on a stake in a subcellar dungeon . . .

But then something warm and unquestioningly friendly leapt on my lap, and licked my face, and breathed warmth on my cheeks. It was a black wire-haired terrier named Bobby. Bobby didn't have any ulterior motive for wanting to bring me back. He didn't have to write a paper on catatonia, he wasn't trying to get a promotion to the hospital supervisory staff, and he wasn't blinded by alleged diagnoses.

He simply wanted to play.

So I sat up and said, "Hey, can I take care of him?" I tousled the dog's fur behind his neck, and wrangled with him a bit. "Could I keep him a while?" My first words in six months.

The astonished nurse said, "If, uh, well, *sure*, I'm sure that'd be—you, um, promise to attend the group's sessions." Then she added with half-serious sternness, "*And* participate, speak to the doctors."

"Yeah, okay," I said grudgingly. "Just as long as I can keep—what's his name?"

"Bobby."

That was two months ago. I've learned to trust a few people. My lawyer's been by frequently, and he's a help. He's a broad-minded young man, newly graduated, and he's got long hair, smokes pot on weekends; so he's no stickler for legal trifles. He didn't mind helping me bribe the assignment nurse to get Lollie moved in next to me.

Lollie's in the next room. Right next door. She's going through a murderous withdrawal. But she's going to make it. Both of us have rooms with padded walls, and we have to sleep in leather restraints at night; me, because of the man I nearly killed when they brought me in, and Lollie because she claws herself otherwise. But not for much longer. My lawyer says I can move to the open ward next week (and it was he who brought me the pens and a ream of paper). Lollie, too. It's a coed ward. And we can take Bobby. And we can work outside together, do some gardening. And take walks. I'm looking forward to it.

Sure, the police have been by to ask questions. But the neighbors who saw Dracula kill the policemen verified that it wasn't I. They're blaming it all on the Los Angeles bloodfiend—Carlton Caldwell, if they knew. And they claim that the charred skeleton of one of the revenants belongs to the man who killed so many policemen in San Francisco, and who's probably the L.A. killer. They're half-right. Essentially, it's a can of worms to them, and they were relieved, I suspect, when my attorney got the judge to drop the case against me for insufficient evidence. Made it easier to close the case altogether.

I remember too much. I've written this as a sort of catharsis, to take the memories from my mind and press them safely onto paper. I'm beginning to forget—this text is nepenthe.

They haven't let me see Lollie yet. Not in person.

But she's in the very next padded cell over, and at night, when she's hurting, she cries out. Sometimes she screams. I scream along with her, to keep her company. We communicate that way. I'm sure she knows I love her.

We have our own sort of harmony. We scream together.

END

A CAVALCADE OF TERROR
FROM RUBY JEAN JENSEN!

SMOKE   (2255, $3.95)
Seven-year-old Ellen was sure it was Aladdin's lamp that
she had found at the local garage sale. And no power on
earth would be able to stop the hideous terror unleashed
when she rubbed the magic lamp to make the genie appear!

CHAIN LETTER   (2162, $3.95)
Abby and Brian knew that the chain letter they had found
was evil. They would send the letter to all their special
friends. And they would know who had broken the
chain—by who had died!

ANNABELLE   (2011, $3.95)
The dolls had lived so long by themselves up in the attic.
But now Annabelle had returned to them, and everything
would be just like it was before. Only this time they'd never
let anyone hurt Annabelle. And anyone who tried would
be very, very sorry!

HOME SWEET HOME   (1571, $3.50)
Two weeks in the mountains should have been the perfect
vacation for a little boy. But Timmy didn't think so. Not
when he saw the terror in the other children's eyes. Not
when he heard them screaming in the night. Not when
Timmy realized there was no escaping the deadly welcome
of HOME SWEET HOME!

MAMA   (2950, $3.95)
Once upon a time there lived a sweet little dolly—but her
one beaded glass eye gleamed with mischief and evil. If
Dorrie could have read her dolly's thoughts, she would
have run for her life. For Dorrie's dear little dolly only had
murder on her mind!

*Available wherever paperbacks are sold, or order direct from the
Publisher. Send cover price plus 50¢ per copy for mailing and
handling to Zebra Books, Dept. 3001, 475 Park Avenue South,
New York, N.Y. 10016. Residents of New York, New Jersey and
Pennsylvania must include sales tax. DO NOT SEND CASH.*

TERROR LIVES!

THE SHADOW MAN   (1946, $3.95)
by Stephen Gresham
The Shadow Man could hide anywhere — under the bed, in
the closet, behind the mirror . . . even in the sophisticated
circuitry of little Joey's computer. And the Shadow Man
could make Joey do things that no little boy should ever
do!

SIGHT UNSEEN   (2038, $3.95)
by Andrew Neiderman
David was always right. Always. But now that he was
growing up, his gift was turning into a power. The power to
know things — terrible things — that he didn't want to know.
Like who would live . . . and who would die!

MIDNIGHT BOY   (2065, $3.95)
by Stephen Gresham
Something horrible is stalking the town's children. For one
of its most trusted citizens possesses the twisted need and
cunning of a psychopathic killer. Now Town Creek's only
hope lies in the horrific, blood-soaked visions of the MID-
NIGHT BOY!

TEACHER'S PET   (1927, $3.95)
by Andrew Neiderman
All the children loved their teacher Mr. Lucy. It was astonishing to see how they all seemed to begin to resemble Mr.
Lucy. And act like Mr. Lucy. And kill like Mr. Lucy!

*Available wherever paperbacks are sold, or order direct from the
Publisher. Send cover price plus 50¢ per copy for mailing and
handling to Zebra Books, Dept. 3001, 475 Park Avenue South,
New York, N.Y. 10016. Residents of New York, New Jersey and
Pennsylvania must include sales tax. DO NOT SEND CASH.*

MASTERWORKS OF MYSTERY
BY MARY ROBERTS RINEHART!

THE YELLOW ROOM   (2262, $3.50)
The somewhat charred corpse unceremoniously stored in
the linen closet of Carol Spencer's Maine summer home set
the plucky amateur sleuth on the trail of a killer. But each
step closer to a solution led Carol closer to her own imminent demise!

THE CASE OF JENNIE BRICE   (2193, $2.95)
The bloodstained rope, the broken knife—plus the disappearance of lovely Jennie Brice—were enough to convince
Mrs. Pittman that murder had been committed in her
boarding house. And if the police couldn't see what was in
front of their noses, then the inquisitive landlady would
just have to take matters into her own hands!

THE GREAT MISTAKE   (2122, $3.50)
Patricia Abbott never planned to fall in love with wealthy
Tony Wainwright, especially after she found out about the
wife he'd never bothered to mention. But suddenly she was
trapped in an extra-marital affair that was shadowed by
unspoken fear and shrouded in cold, calculating murder!

THE RED LAMP   (2017, $3.50)
The ghost of Uncle Horace was getting frisky—turning on
lamps, putting in shadowy appearances in photographs.
But the mysterious nightly slaughter of local sheep seemed
to indicate that either Uncle Horace had developed a bizarre taste for lamb chops . . . or someone was manipulat-
ing appearances with a deadly sinister purpose!

A LIGHT IN THE WINDOW   (1952, $3.50)
Ricky Wayne felt uncomfortable about moving in with her
new husband's well-heeled family while he was overseas
fighting the Germans. But she never imagined the depths
of her in-laws' hatred—or the murderous lengths to which
they would go to break up her marriage!

*Available wherever paperbacks are sold, or order direct from the
Publisher. Send cover price plus 50¢ per copy for mailing and
handling to Zebra Books, Dept. 3001, 475 Park Avenue South,
New York, N.Y. 10016. Residents of New York, New Jersey and
Pennsylvania must include sales tax. DO NOT SEND CASH.*

J.J. MARRIC MYSTERIES

time passes quickly . . . As *DAY* blends with *NIGHT* and *WEEK* flies into *MONTH*, Gideon must fit together the pieces of death and destruction before time runs out!

GIDEON'S DAY   (2721, $3.95)
They mysterious death of a young police detective is only the beginning of a bizarre series of events which end in the fatal knifing of a seven-year-old girl. But for commander George gideon of New Scotland Yard, it is all in a day's work!

GIDEON'S MONTH   (2766, $3.95)
A smudged page on his calendar, Gideon's month is blackened by brazen and bizarre offenses ranging from mischief to murder. Gideon must put a halt to the sinister events which involve the corruption of children and a homicidal housekeeper, before the city drowns in blood!

GIDEON'S NIGHT   (2734, $3.50)
When an unusually virulent pair of psychopaths leaves behind a trail of pain, grief, and blood, Gideon once again is on the move. This time the terror all at once comes to a head and he must stop the deadly duel that is victimizing young women and children — in only one night!

GIDEON'S WEEK   (2722, $3.95)
When battered wife Ruby Benson set up her killer husband for capture by the cops, she never considered the possibility of his escape. Now Commander George Gideon of Scotland Yard must save Ruby from the vengeance of her sadistic spouse . . . or die trying!

Available wherever paperbacks are sold, or order direct from the Publisher. Send cover price plus 50¢ per copy for mailing and handling to Zebra Books, Dept. 3001, 475 Park Avenue South, New York, N.Y. 10016. Residents of New York, New Jersey and Pennsylvania must include sales tax. DO NOT SEND CASH.

MYSTERIES TO KEEP YOU GUESSING
by John Dickson Carr

CASTLE SKULL   (1974, $3.50)

The hand may be quicker than the eye, but ghost stories didn't hoodwink Henri Bencolin. A very real murderer was afoot in Castle Skull—a murderer who must be found before he strikes again.

IT WALKS BY NIGHT   (1931, $3.50)

The police burst in and found the Duc's severed head staring at them from the center of the room. Both the doors had been guarded, yet the murderer had gone in and out *without having been seen*!

THE EIGHT OF SWORDS   (1881, $3.50)

The evidence showed that while waiting to kill Mr. Depping, the murderer had calmly eaten his victim's dinner. But before famed crime-solver Dr. Gideon Fell could serve up the killer to Scotland Yard, there would be another course of murder.

THE MAN WHO COULD NOT SHUDDER (1703, $3.50)

Three guests at Martin Clarke's weekend party swore they saw the pistol lifted from the wall, levelled, and shot. *Yet no hand held it*. It couldn't have happened—but there was a dead body on the floor to prove that it had.

THE PROBLEM OF THE WIRE CAGE   (1702, $3.50)

There was only one set of footsteps in the soft clay surface—and those footsteps belonged to the victim. It seemed impossible to prove that anyone had killed Frank Dorrance.

Available wherever paperbacks are sold, or order direct from the Publisher. Send cover price plus 50¢ per copy for mailing and handling to Zebra Books, Dept. 3001, 475 Park Avenue South, New York, N.Y. 10016. Residents of New York, New Jersey and Pennsylvania must include sales tax. DO NOT SEND CASH.